Love & Chocolate

Holidays in Hallbrook

Elsie Davis

Sweet Romance Publishing

Sweet Romance Publishing

POB 778

Liberty, NC 27298

This story is dedicated to my husband

~You light my heart and my life with love~

1 Corinthians 16:14
Do everything in love.

Chapter One

♥

AMANDA FLIPPED THE SIGN on the front door of the bakery to show she was closed. She used to keep the Sweeter Side of Life open later, giving every romantic at heart a chance to pick up a last-minute sweet treat for their special someone. But not anymore.

If she wasn't the only bakery in Hallbrook, she'd close the entire day. And not because it was a day to celebrate, but because it was a day *not* to celebrate. Valentine's Day. *Yuk!* More like February Fool's Day.

The cold blast of air chilled her through and through as she stepped outside. She set down the box of desserts she'd created for tonight's silent auction fundraiser and turned to lock the door. After tightening her wool scarf and yanking her hat lower over her ears, she picked up the box. She headed down the street, preferring to walk the short distance to the Masonic Lodge where the annual Heart to Heart festival was being held.

Charity work as a single person on Valentine's Day was one of the best and most rewarding outlets on a day that traditionally honored couples. At least it was according to an article she'd read in a magazine not long after her ex-boyfriend dumped her. The write-up had listed volunteering to help others as one of the top ten things to do as a single person on Valentine's day. The idea was to *not* focus on being alone.

She'd volunteered for last year's festival, knowing it was mostly older people and young kids with their families who attended. People either too young or too busy for romance, or past all the silly romantic trappings of Valentine's Day. Not that romance was entirely missing. There were some who, no matter how old they got, always managed to find themselves on the dance floor.

Her continued single status had kept her at the top of the list for volunteers this year again. Everyone knew everything in Hallbrook, and there was no way to hide the truth. At times, it made her want to run and hide, but the small town was home, and she loved it. Not even the busybodies in town could change that.

The volunteer work had renewed her spirits and helped her not to dwell on being alone as she helped the Masons raise money for local families in need. Unfortunately, if things kept going the way they were, Amanda might be one of those standing in line for help from the organization. After a bakery in Glen Haven opened six months ago, business had fallen off at the Sweeter Side of Life. It would take a miracle to keep it open.

The idea of closing up shop broke her heart. Her mother had opened the bakery twenty-three years ago, and most of the memories Amanda had were from making pastries and desserts together. Most of her childhood outside of school had been spent there, and it was when her mother taught Amanda almost everything she knew about baking.

Her mother's passing two years ago had left a hole in Amanda's heart the size of the Rio Grande. Dealing with Greg Miller's betrayal at the same time had widened the chasm to the size of the Grand Canyon. Not a day went by that she didn't miss her mother or face the guilt of not being at the hospital when she died. As for Greg, not a day went by that she didn't remind herself what a jerk he'd been, and that he and his new wife were welcome to each other.

She picked up the pace, the cold permeating her jacket. Her outfit underneath was not her usual down-home warm and cozy attire. Instead, she wore a thin blouse and a pair of wool slacks to dress for the occasion.

"Good afternoon, Mr. Hanson," she greeted the older man who worked in the post office and always had a ready smile for everyone in town.

"Good afternoon, Amanda." He smiled and held the door open for her. The old house had been remodeled and was warm and welcoming to lodge members and guests alike.

"Thank you." She appreciated the help, not wanting anything to happen to the contents of the box.

"My pleasure, young lady. What's in the box? Some of your excellent cooking?" He followed her inside.

"Just some pastries for the party." It was more than pastries, but Amanda was sworn to secrecy. "Looks as though a lot of people are already showing up. That's a good sign."

"Question is, why are you here? Again. That's not a good sign. You're too young to be hanging out with a bunch of old folks. Don't you have a special man in your life taking you somewhere tonight?" With age, comes the ability to let loose one's tongue apparently. He knew darn right well she wasn't dating. The whole town made it their business to know. Mr. Hanson was on a fishing expedition.

"I have enough to worry about without adding a man to the mix. Someone's got to be able to keep up with all of you old people." She winked, managing to shock the older man, his broad smile proof he wasn't offended by her bold teasing.

"I've got to drop these off." Amanda nodded toward the box and walked away, headed for the kitchen. She scanned the room, noting the festive appeal the decorations added. The Masons wasn't a decorative group of guys, but Gemma, the event coordinator, certainly knew what she was doing. The place had red, pink, and white decorations everywhere. Hearts, hearts, and more hearts. Pink carnations at every table. Red napkins. The room draped in white tea lights. It was beautiful, if you were into that kind of thing.

She used her hip to push open the swinging door that led into the kitchen.

"Am I ever glad to see you, Amanda." Jack Johnson smiled as he took the box from her and set it on the counter.

"Thanks. I got here as soon as I could." She removed her hat and scarf, the heat in the room quickly suffocating her. Jack pulled the tape from the carton as she hung up her coat.

"These look fantastic. I wish I could bid on them. Thank you so much for helping out. I know you're busy with the bakery and all, but I prefer to use different secret chefs to keep people guessing. You didn't tell anyone, did you?"

"Not a word." She slid her fingers across her lips like a zipper.

"Perfect. Is there any way I can get you to take out some of the snacks and make sure all the bowls are filled? I've got someone else working on the beverages." He pointed at the table overflowing with bags of chips, pretzels, cookies, and candy.

"Of course. Just don't blame me if I snack at each stop," she joked. "You know I enjoy food."

"Snack away. It's not as if there isn't plenty, and it's not as though you have to worry about it."

"Ha! Too many extra taste tests at the bakery and I've got the curves to prove it." She grinned, grabbed a few bags of chips, and headed back through the door into the main hall. For the past few months, she'd tried to lose the extra fifteen pounds she'd put on after she tried to eat her way through her grief. However, nothing seemed to work, and honestly, she didn't have the time to do much in the way of working out. The shop was time-consuming, and her downtime, well, that was better spent at home preparing for another day. At least she did get multiple daily walks with Cupcake, her chocolate Lab. Those counted for something.

Amanda spotted Jennifer coming her way. She hadn't expected to see her best friend here because she was hot and heavy in a relationship with a guy she'd met in Lancaster. At the bowling alley of all places. Two mixed-up food orders, and ever since then, the couple were almost inseparable. Jennifer was in love with being in love, and it was the one area Amanda and her friend agreed to disagree.

"What are you doing here? I thought you'd be at some fancy restaurant being wooed and schmoozed by Will?" Amanda couldn't help but tease her friend since Jennifer never missed a chance to try and hook her up with a blind date.

"Well, hello to you, too. And for your information, I'll be at a fancy restaurant later. And I'll take all the wooing and schmoozing I can get from my fiancé. We're not all anti-Valentine's Day. But I love you anyway." Jennifer hugged her and then stepped back, her gaze traveling from Amanda's head to her toes. "You look nice, but your outfit doesn't exactly shout *look at me*." She frowned.

"Haha. It's cold outside, in case you haven't noticed. Not about to get all gussied up and freeze. It's bad enough I felt the urge to put on a silk blouse to dress up and at least look the part of a volunteer here."

"Red is a great color on you. It'll work." Jennifer nodded as if coming to a decision.

"Work for what?" She knew better than to ask, but with Jennifer, sometimes it was better to find out what she was up to before it bit you in the backside.

"Get you noticed." Jennifer smirked. "I was telling people all week this is the great new hot spot for singles on Valentine's Day." She looked around the room as if searching for some of those people.

"You're bad. I don't want to get noticed. I just want to go home." Jennifer meant well, but she didn't understand. Once upon a time, they'd both believed in love, but life had changed all that for Amanda. There was no looking back now.

"Will's friend was disappointed you wouldn't double date with us. You could still change your mind. I'm sure they have more than enough people to help out here if you don't want to play meet-and-greet with the guys I specifically told that you'd be here."

"Thanks, but no thanks. I'm needed here, and other than filling snack bowls, I'm not interested in anything else." She held up the bag of chips in her hand as proof. "Especially not meeting people. You've got to stop trying to set me up, Jennifer. What are you doing here if you have a hot date?"

"I'm here to check on you and lend my support, and of course, warn you about...well, the others who might drop in. Our dinner reservation isn't for another hour."

Amanda wanted to be upset with her friend, but she did have the best of intentions. Warding off suitors was something she was quite experienced at by now, and tonight would be no different.

"May I have your attention, please?" A man spoke over the microphone from the front of the room, catching their attention. A hush fell over the place as everyone turned to listen. The man was dressed in a three-piece suit, which was a tad overdressed for the affair.

"Thank you all. I won't take much of your time, but I have an announcement to make that I'm hoping will be of great interest to you all. My name is Zach Billings, and I'm with the Mega Online Marketing Corporation. Our company has decided to run a statewide recipe contest, and we're announcing it at various events across the state today. My good friend, Jack Johnson, invited me here to share the exciting news. We chose today, Valentine's Day, to kick off the event because it's quite appropriate based on the theme. The contest is called Anything Chocolate. To enter, simply submit your best recipe for any food category, as long it includes, well, chocolate." The man grinned, his gaze scanning the crowd as the buzz of excitement filtered across the room and everyone started discussing the news.

Mr. Billings held up his hand to continue. "The deadline is in two weeks at midnight. The last day of February. A select panel of judges will create and test the top recipes selected based on the initial appeal. The winning recipe will receive twenty-five thousand dollars and an online promotional presence to promote their recipe. Full details are available at the signup table and online at our website. Good luck to you all!" He stepped down off the podium, and several people gathered around to ask him questions.

Amanda couldn't help the sudden rush of adrenaline that coursed through her body as the information sunk in. This could be exactly what she needed to save the bakery. Twenty-five thousand dollars was a heck of a lot of money, but combined with the online campaign, it was so much more. Marketing was the key to help her grow by reaching new clientele and making the bakery profitable again.

Amanda yanked on Jennifer's sleeve. "Did you hear that? This is the answer."

"What do you mean? The answer to what?" Her friend's forehead scrunched up in confusion.

"The bakery. You know I can't keep going the way I am. I'm going to enter the contest, and I'm going to win. It'll save the bakery." She couldn't wait to tell Grandpa.

"I think it's a wonderful idea. Just don't get your hopes up too high. The man mentioned it's statewide, and that means a lot of recipes. Every cook in the state will be sending something in hopes of winning that kind of money."

"I know. But it's a sign. Me being here tonight, the contest being announced here. It's the perfect solution. I just need to create something spectacular."

Jennifer shook her head and smiled. "If anyone can do it, you can. You've already got my vote. But are you forgetting one teeny-tiny factor?"

"What's that?" Amanda gazed at her friend, not at all following her.

"You don't like chocolate."

"I don't hate it. It's just not my thing. It shouldn't stop me from testing a few recipes to find the perfect one." Too much chocolate one night when she was eight had cured any desire she had for the sweet treat most of America thrived on. It was the night she'd come home from the hospital only to discover her father had walked out of the house, leaving to start a new family. The memory of having her heart broken and an aching stomach had been enough to cure her of ever craving chocolate again.

"Make sure I'm on your list of testers. You know I love your cooking." Jennifer grinned.

"You'll be one of the first, I promise." Amanda nodded, gazing around the room. The place was packed. "There's an excellent turnout this year. A lot more kids than I expected."

"But understandable. Check out all the new things there've added. It looks as though every corner of this place has something set up for fun and games. Parents probably consider this an opportunity for free babysitting."

"There is that." Amanda grinned.

"*Ooh la la.* Check out that guy." Jennifer poked her in the arm and pointed across the room. A gorgeous hunk of a man stood there alone, looking lost and out of place. Most people were milling about talking to each other, but not this guy.

Their gazes locked, and for one second, Amanda recognized the flare of appreciation in his eyes, but then she looked away. "It's a guy. So what?" The last thing she needed to do was encourage her friend. For all Amanda knew, it was one of the men Jennifer had sent here. More reason to stay away. Men didn't just drop in at the Heart to Heart festival as the place wasn't exactly the hot-spot mecca for singles.

"You need to get over that jerk Greg. Stop letting him run your life." Jennifer crossed her arms and squared off with Amanda.

"He's not running my life. I've chosen to focus on the bakery. I see nothing wrong with that. Not everyone has to date. I'm happy the way I am." It wasn't to say that her life was perfect, but it was better than the pain that came with trusting someone with your heart, only to then have them stomp on it.

"If you say so. But I still remember little Amanda planning and preparing her wedding when she was seven years old. Don't look now, but that guy and Tanner Wilson are headed this way. I wonder how they know each other?"

"So, he's not one of your setups?"

"Um, no. I've never seen the guy before."

"Guess it's time for me to make an exit." Amanda turned to leave but found herself held firmly in place as Jennifer grabbed her arm.

"Stop running away. If you're determined not to date, then you shouldn't be worried about meeting people. One does not have to be synonymous with the other. You don't have to be unsociable." It wasn't often Jennifer went into preaching mode.

"Yes, mother." Amanda stopped resisting and accepted the inevitable. Besides, her friend was more than likely right.

"Fancy meeting two of the prettiest ladies in Hallbrook, and on Valentine's night of all nights." Tanner chuckled. He leaned forward and hugged Jennifer, dropping a friendly peck on her cheek, and then doing the same with Amanda. They'd all grown up together since kindergarten, and Tanner was one of those happily married men who smiled at life.

"Hey, Tanner. Where's Missy tonight?" Amanda didn't see them out and about often apart. True love. The two of them were a great example of when things worked out right. But Amanda's parents were a far greater reminder of what happened when things fell apart, and then there was Greg. He never even made the commitment of marriage before he was off and running.

"Her mother's coming over later to watch the kids, and then I'm taking her out. This is Kevin Thompson, the newest addition to Turlington High's staff. He works with me in the science department and is the new chemistry teacher. I thought it would be nice to bring him out to meet some other people from town, and this is where it's happening tonight."

The man reached out to shake her hand, and their eyes met and held for the second time that evening. A piercing green, the color reminded her of emeralds. "It's nice to meet you, ma'am."

"Amanda Tillman. Calling me ma'am makes me sound old." His handshake was firm and warm, his large hand engulfing her own.

"Then Amanda it is, for you are certainly not old." She admired the way he smiled and how the corners of his eyes crinkled. Dressed in jeans and a cable-knit sweater, he looked relaxed and comfortable. Far more comfortable than she was dressed in her volunteer special.

"And I'm Jennifer. Her best friend who already has a date tonight. Are you single, Kevin?" She shook hands with the man.

Amanda groaned. This was precisely why she'd wanted to run when she'd had the chance. Jennifer wasn't shy about anything. "Don't answer that. I'm sorry. She's a bit forward." Amanda shook her head and shrugged. The poor man's look of comfort vanished in a split second.

"Yes, Kevin is single. And so is Amanda. Imagine that. And it's Valentine's Day." Tanner clapped a hand on Kevin's back and beamed.

"You mentioned you were bringing me here to meet people, Tanner, not women. Had you been clearer, we might've avoided this awkwardness." The man might be uncomfortable, but he didn't sidestep the issue. She appreciated a man who could speak his mind and hold his own in any situation.

"Ignore them," Amanda told him. "This one—" she pointed at Tanner, "—is happily married and has been ridiculous in his efforts to promote the matrimonial state for everyone else ever since. And this one—" she pointed to Jennifer, "—just got engaged. And you have no worries with me because I'm not interested in dating or relationships."

Kevin nodded. "Then I guess we're on the same page." He smiled, his pearly white teeth beaming back at her with genuine relief, a sight that made her heart race a bit faster. The man was far too attractive for his own good.

"All the more reason for the two of you to hang out together tonight" Tanner wasn't backing down after the apparent rebuff.

Kevin shook his head and sent Tanner a warning look. "I think I'll have a look around. It was a pleasure to meet you, ladies. Have a nice evening." Kevin turned and walked off, not waiting for an answer.

"He's a great guy, and although I've just met him, I think he's going to fit in Hallbrook just fine. You might want to reconsider your stance on relationships and scoop him up before somebody else catches his eye. Just so you know, I brought him over to meet you because I noticed him checking you out." He winked and then walked away, leaving Amanda speechless.

"I knew it. You need to give that hunky man a chance." Jennifer wanted her to have what she had, but her friend simply couldn't accept Amanda wasn't in the market for a soul mate.

"Attractive and dreamy green eyes do not a partner for life make." Amanda moved to the next snack table and started refilling the bowls.

"Well, there's a start. You've admitted the guy is attractive, and that he has dreamy eyes. Tanner and I will just have to find a way for you to get to know one another? Don't you worry, between the two of us, we'll figure something out."

"That's what I'm afraid of. Don't you have somewhere to be?"

Jennifer glanced down at her watch. "Oops, it's time for me to go. My chariot awaits," she teased, dropping a kiss on Amanda's cheek before she scurried away.

Amanda shook her head, unable to believe what had just transpired. And if her friends were going to push them together as a couple, imagine what the matchmakers in town would do if they got an inkling to meddle. She'd do well to steer clear of Kevin for the rest of the night. Jennifer and Tanner were enough to deal with already.

Chapter Two

♥

KEVIN WOULDN'T HAVE EVEN agreed to come to this event if it hadn't been for his daughters pleading with him to go in order for them to hang out with their new friends. Since they were all adapting to being new in town, he didn't have the heart to tell them no. It was important for the twins to try and fit in. Heck, they were doing a far better job of it than he was.

He'd met Tanner, one of the other science teachers, the first day he arrived at Turlington, and they'd hit it off. Kevin wasn't big on talking about his personal life. Still, Tanner knew enough to know he had his hands full with the twins and getting adjusted to a new town as a single parent. Apparently, the phrase single parent meant something different to Tanner than it did to Kevin.

But then, Tanner didn't know Kevin's ex-wife or her propensity to dictate people's lives in order to control them. Relationships were out of the question if he intended to maintain full custody of the girls. A small price to pay the way he saw it.

He looked around the room to find the twins. Several older couples were out on the dance floor waltzing, but most of the people were standing around in groups, chatting away as if they didn't see each other all the time. Kevin spotted the twins at the basketball toss with their friends, laughing and having fun. He wished he could say the same for himself. Not that there'd been anything wrong with meeting Amanda. She seemed like a sweet woman. Her brown hair curled around her cheeks in loose waves and reached down to her shoulders. Her blue eyes had taken him by surprise, the cobalt shade unique. A man could get lost in those eyes if he wanted to—which he didn't.

He spent the past half hour managing to steer clear of her, unwilling to have them both put on the spot again. It was only so many times you could say no without sounding rude, and Amanda didn't deserve that sort of treatment. Part of him wanted to leave but taking the girls away early would be met with opposition, not to mention it wouldn't be fair.

Kevin spotted an empty table and moved to the corner of the room to find a seat. The table was set up with fancy white porcelain dinner plates, crystal glasses, red and pink napkins, and several heart-shaped decorations. The sign next to the table announced there would be a silent chef dinner and auction. He'd never heard of one of those before. He scanned the paragraph and was suddenly interested. A six-course meal he didn't have to cook sounded like a dream come true.

Not to mention, it would give him something to do while the girls were off having a good time.

The rules were easy enough. Eat and enjoy. Bid on your favorite course. Highest bidder for each course won a home-cooked meal by the secret chef who prepared it. A home-cooked meal sounded amazing. It would give him another night off from his mom-and-dad duties, something he desperately needed.

With Victoria in Paris on a modeling gig, there wasn't much chance of him getting a night off anytime soon. He'd agreed to the no-dating-relationship terms she set forth for him to have full custody, and a year later, was still good with the arrangement. Even if he was worn out at times playing the dual-parent role. He couldn't imagine not seeing the twin's smiling faces every day; an affliction Victoria didn't share.

He'd met his ex-wife their first year in college, back when he was naïve and completely enthralled by the gorgeous woman in art class who made it clear she was interested in him from day one. At the time, he hadn't realized she was the class model. With each line he'd sketched onto the canvas, he'd fallen deeper and deeper in love. A marriage, twins, nine years and a divorce later, he was finally happy. Tired, but happy.

He glanced across the room. The twins were having fun, or so it would seem. There was no reason for him not to join in the silent auction fun.

Kevin paid his entry fee, signed up, and let the parents of the twins' friends know what he was doing. Their reassurances to keep an eye on the girls allowed him to relax. This was a surefire way to pass the evening and not worry about anyone trying to set him up with someone else. He'd be too busy eating, and food was something he almost always enjoyed if he wasn't the one doing the cooking.

It was a short wait until the dinner began, and Kevin made his way back to the table to join the others who had gathered for the feast. A man stood at the far end of the table, a mic in hand. The people in the group fell silent, waiting for him to speak.

"I'm Jack Johnson, for those of you who don't know me." The man glanced in Kevin's direction. "Thanks for joining us for the secret-chef dinner and auction. We appreciate your registration donations, and in return, I guarantee you will have a fabulous meal. And some of you will be lucky enough to get two meals out of the deal. Just to make sure everyone's clear on the rules, you only get to bid on one course. So, pick your favorite, bid on it, and the highest bidder wins a home-cooked meal from the secret chef that prepared that course. Any questions?"

"What if the foods no good?" a heckler called out.

"You know me better than that, Phil. I always get the best chefs." Jack grinned as others around nodded in agreement.

"Did you go to Lancaster then?" The man guffawed. There was always one in the crowd.

"I think we have plenty right here in Hallbrook. Just remember it's for a good cause, guys. Your stomachs." Everyone laughed, and the moment was diffused.

The meal started with a fancy flatbread with a warm spinach-artichoke dip that was amazing, the cheesy mixture bursting with flavor. Kevin would've enjoyed an extra helping, but unfortunately, they were limited to one serving. Next was the salad. It was another excellent dish, the vinaigrette, a perfect touch of tangy lemon and creamy spices.

Some of the guys talked quite a bit, mostly about people, or farms, or things happening in the area that he knew nothing about. Their conversation more than made up for his silence. It was the perfect opportunity to learn what was going on in town, and no one seemed to notice his lack of response.

Each course continued to impress Kevin, the meal far better than anything he'd eaten in a while, considering at home he prepared all the meals himself. There hadn't been much time for eating out as they'd only settled in town a few weeks ago and were still trying to get their bearings. The girls struggled, having to adjust to a new school and make new friends. Not to mention their discontent with the situation in general. At ten—almost eleven—it was understandable they were still upset about the divorce, more so with their mother out of the country. Victoria didn't call nearly as often as she'd promised, adding to the upheaval in the twins' lives.

"I heard you are the new chemistry teacher at Turlington," the man next to him spoke up. "Welcome to town, young man. Name's Parker."

Kevin looked up, surprised to find all eyes on him as conversation ceased. "Thanks. And, yes, my daughters and I just moved here. It's a big change from the city, but a nice one."

"Glad you feel that way. Folks around here are tight. You need anything, you just need to ask." Everyone nodded their heads in agreement.

Kevin breathed a sigh of relief. No intrusive questions, just a good old-fashioned welcome. For the first time this evening, he found himself relaxing and glad he'd come to the festival. It was a big step in the right direction to meet people in the community. "Thanks, I'll remember that. Might come in handy when I need to escape from the madness of my twins." He grinned, knowing there wasn't a man at the table that would willingly volunteer for the duty.

"If that's what you need help with, I reckon you ought to call the missus. Menfolk around here aren't exactly nanny material," the man joked. It was no more than Kevin had been thinking.

The others all took turns introducing themselves as the final course was cleared and the dessert was brought out. Just looking at the cheesecake made his mouth water. Topped with raspberry sauce, drizzled with melted white chocolate, and then dusted with dark chocolate shavings and finished with a mint leaf to decorate each piece, the dessert was a work of art.

"This looks delicious." Kevin picked up his fork, eager to take a bite.

"I agree. And I bet I can guess who the chef is on this one." Parker grinned as the others joined in with hearty laughter.

"Probably not a difficult guess. All things considered, of course," another man chimed in.

"Wouldn't go wrong bidding on this dessert," one of the other guys spoke up, adding his two cents.

"Why, who is it?" Kevin asked, interested in bidding. The dessert was one of the best he'd tasted in a long time.

"That would be breaking the rules. Not allowed to eat and tell. But I can say this…if you want to win this secret chef, you better be bidding high." Parker spoke up, quick to remind everyone of the rules. Kevin also recognized the challenge, knowing he wouldn't be the only one bidding on the dessert. They didn't realize it, but Kevin liked a challenge. And this one was for charity, which made it even better.

They would try to outbid him, but he was just as determined to win the bid as they were. With a home-cooked meal at stake, he had far more to gain than the others. It was all a matter of outsmarting them, and it all boiled down to how high would they go.

A couple of guys approached and handed out the ballots to the dinner patrons. Kevin kept his board covered as he filled out the spaces. As everyone turned in their bids, he pretended to keep thinking, twiddling his pencil over the paper as if trying to make a final decision. What if his bet was too low? The donations were for a worthy cause, and the prize was a good cause for him.

Kevin started to hand in his ballot but pulled back at the last second, adding a one in front of his original bid. *That ought to do it*. He nodded with satisfaction as he handed the ballot back to the official. He shot a grin at the others. "Sometimes, it pays to be last."

"Sometimes, it pays to be in the know," Parker quipped.

Kevin didn't have a clue what the man meant.

Jack appeared at the head of the table again. "Thank you, everyone, for joining in the fun tonight. We will be announcing the secret-chef auction winners in about fifteen minutes. Stick around so you can meet your secret chef if you had the winning bid and set up your dinner date."

Kevin wouldn't exactly call it a dinner date, not with his twins there. He just wanted a home-cooked meal. But at this point, you could call it anything you wanted, as long as he scored the fabulous dessert chef. Anyone who could cook a dessert as tasty as the cheesecake he just devoured, had to be amazing when it came to cooking an entire meal. "I'm going to go check on my twins. I'll be right back."

"Sure thing. Just make sure you get back for the announcement. You don't want to miss this part." Parker chuckled.

The man was talking in circles, but Kevin wasn't about to miss the finale. By increasing his bid, he felt confident in the win. Not many people would pay such a high amount for a six-course meal in their home, but then most people weren't raising twin trouble single-handedly.

The girls were busy getting their faces painted and not likely to need him anytime soon. He returned to the table area and joined the large group of people congregating together to hear the results. Course after course was announced, the chef coming forward to stand by the winner. Loud cheers erupted after each one, everyone getting into the fun of the auction.

"And now for the final course, dessert. We had some surprising results, but the most remarkable one was a bid of one hundred and seventy-five dollars. A collective gasp rippled through the crowd.

Kevin smiled and nodded, knowing it was his bid that won.

"Kevin Thompson, meet your secret chef, Amanda Tillman." The crowd cheered, but Kevin tuned them out as he tried to grasp what he'd just heard.

Amanda. No way. He shook his head in disbelief. It couldn't possibly be the same woman, but as the brunette with cobalt eyes stepped forward, he knew it was true. He just paid a hefty price to have the woman he'd avoided all night come to his home and cook dinner for him and the girls.

Unbelievable.

There was no way this would end well.

Amanda couldn't believe it when she heard Kevin's name. She hadn't even known he was signed up for the secret-chef dinner. He must've been a last-minute entry, and now, well, this was a disaster. She'd been roped into participating in this event, her stupid inability to say no putting her in this position in the first place.

The man had spent the entire evening avoiding her, so him winning her secret-chef services was the last thing she'd expected. But it wasn't as if she had a choice, she had to honor the commitment. Luckily, it was just one dinner. She'd make the best of it, the same way she always did. Once upon a time, Kevin might've been the type of guy she was interested in, but not anymore, no matter how attractive he was or how nice his smile. Meeting him on February Fool's Day was a big, fat sign to stay away, something she'd gladly do after she fixed this one meal.

The two of them moved off to the side.

"Congratulations on winning the bid. It looks as though you're stuck with me. For a guy who openly made a point he wasn't interested, making a bet like you did makes me wonder. You're not having second thoughts, are you?" She had to be sure, and since he was a straight shooter, it was best to serve him up the same.

"Hardly. Your dessert was amazing, and that's what I bid on. I had no idea it was you." He shrugged.

"But a hundred and seventy-five? That doesn't sound like a bid for somebody who doesn't know who they're getting." Narrowing her eyes, Amanda watched closely for any sign he wasn't telling the truth.

"No, but it does sound like a bid a guy made to make sure he got the person who cooked the dessert. Something I was completely assured would be in high demand. It sounded as though the bids were going to be coming in high, and I just wanted to make sure I won it."

"So, is this a winning thing or a dessert thing?" Even though neither option was flattering to her as a woman, they were acceptable choices.

"Maybe both." He shrugged again, unsure of himself. "Honestly, the guys made it sound as if they all knew who the secret dessert chef was and that they would be bidding high for the privilege of one of your home-cooked meals. You have quite a reputation."

"And who told you this?" she persisted, wanting to know the truth. Something sounded fishy.

Kevin pointed across the room at the older man who stood in the center of a group of men laughing.

"You're kidding. My friend, you've been had. That's Tanner's dad, Parker Wilson."

"Well, I'll be. Didn't see that one coming. Some of the comments make more sense now. Can I at least hope your cooking is as wonderful as they say it is?"

"You won't be disappointed." Her answer might sound overly bold, but it was the truth and there was no sense downplaying the fact she could cook.

"It's for a good cause, so it's fine. Any chance we can do this dinner Sunday evening?"

"I can if you're sure about this." Amanda was hoping he'd back out, but her chances were slim to none.

"The one thing I'm sure of right now is that I paid a hundred and seventy-five dollars for a dinner, and I'm looking forward to it. Or at least I better be." He chuckled. "Oh, and there'll be four of us for dinner, including you."

She hadn't expected to be included as a dinner guest, nor had she expected it to be a dinner party, but the more, the merrier in this case. It would make it a lot less awkward to be around the guy who made her heart race a tiny bit faster with each smile he sent her way.

Chapter Three

♥

"Good morning, Cuppy." Amanda reached down and patted her dog on the head before continuing to the kitchen for a much-needed dose of caffeine by way of coffee. She poured a cup and took a few sips, savoring the robust chicory flavor as it fueled her brain with a wake-up call.

Today was going to be a busy day between dealing with the demands of the bakery and then her secret-chef obligation for Kevin's dinner party. Luckily, she'd had the foresight to pick up all the groceries for the meal yesterday, which had allowed her to complete early preparations for the beef Wellington. It was picture perfect and ready to go in the oven.

Now that the Valentine's rush was over, the bakery was back to its all-too-quiet mode, and back to its closing time of five o'clock. Diana, her part-time helper, would be able to come in at the last minute and cover for her today. Amanda wouldn't have much time to clean up and get to Kevin's place by four, but she'd make it happen.

"Jennifer is going to come over and let you out later today and to feed you. I'm sure you don't mind." The dog rubbed up against Amanda's leg, her tail wagging. Cupcake loved it when her friend visited and took the time to play with her. But lately, with Jennifer's love life in full swing, she'd had less and less time to spend at Amanda's. "I'll be home early, I promise."

"Woof. Woof." Cupcake nuzzled her hand, demanding more rubs. From the minute Amanda had laid eyes on the dog at the shelter, she'd fallen in love with the chocolate Lab. And for the past two years, Cupcake had managed to wrap Amanda around her paw.

"Yes, I know, you hate being alone all day, but I've been busy lately." Amanda fed the dog and let her out in the backyard to run and potty. Short on time, the dog's walk to the park wouldn't happen today. Amanda would make it up to her in the morning by allowing extra time. The pastries and donuts needed to be in the oven by six, and she was already running behind schedule, trying to make sure she had everything she needed for tonight.

She dressed warmly in her hat, scarf, and heavy winter jacket, hoping to ward off the chill as she went to start the car and load the two bags of her supplies she'd organized earlier. Amanda knelt beside Cupcake, who'd followed her to the front door. She kissed the dog on the forehead and gave her a big hug. "See you tonight, girl. Be good for Jennifer."

Mornings were always the busiest, but day after day, Amanda showed up in time to bake her fresh pastries, donuts, loaves of bread, and desserts. The first batch was ready by the time the bakery opened and the first customers started trickling in. With each lull in traffic, which was far too frequent, she baked more goods to replenish what sold.

By late morning, Amanda had started on tomorrow's creations. Some were tried and true favorites she made every day, others, she changed up for uniqueness. Everything refrigerated nicely, waiting for her to bake them fresh in the morning. It was a never-ending process, but one Amanda loved. The joy of measuring and sifting and rolling was soothing. Her mother used to have a way of making it fun, and even now, Amanda could still see her smiling.

The people in Hallbrook had loved her mother, her kind heart making everyone she saw feel special. Amanda had tried to follow in her footsteps, and things had been going well, at least until the Glen Haven bakery opened. Her mother was no longer here to turn to for advice, and Amanda had no choice but to put all her hopes on the contest. She prayed her mother would help guide her to pick the right recipe to help save the Sweeter Side of Life bakery.

Ever since the contest was announced, she'd racked her brain for something to submit but had come up empty-handed. The biggest disappointment had been not finding something in her mother's recipe book. Jennifer was right, it was hard for a non-chocolate lover to decide on an award-winning chocolate recipe.

Her gaze landed on her grandmother's recipe book on display on a corner shelf behind the counter. It was one her mother had used frequently, and one that Amanda used on occasion. It gave her an idea. Maybe there would be something unique and special in it that she could make her own.

She took the recipe book down off the shelf so she could go through it when she had a few minutes, or to at least take it home for later tonight when she was snuggled up in bed. It would make for excellent night-time reading.

The overhead door chimes jingled as a customer ambled in.

"Good morning, Mrs. O'Malley." The woman was a pillar of the community, her volunteer work having touched many lives here in Hallbrook over the years. Amanda's mother had once told her Agnes O'Malley had been one of her first customers and a regular ever since.

"Good morning, dear." Mrs. O'Malley made her way toward the register, her pace slow and steady.

"How are things going at O'Malley's Charm?"

"The boys are managing it just fine. Can't say I miss working there all the time. Even Frank is finding it easier to quit meddling in how they run the place and is spending more time enjoying our senior years."

"That's great to hear. Maybe he can take you somewhere special this spring?" Amanda said as

Mrs. O'Malley peered into the glass case, checking over today's choices.

"You know me, I just like to stay put. More than enough here in Hallbrook to keep me busy. Speaking of, I saw you at the Masonic Lodge last night, but I didn't get a chance to talk to you. What do you think of the contest they announced? You're going to enter, aren't you?" She pushed her glasses back on her nose and peered up at Amanda. The woman wasn't much above five feet tall and was a total sweetheart.

"Absolutely. I was just thinking about it and trying to figure out what to make. So far, I'm not having much luck." Amanda shrugged, letting out a deep breath of air.

Mrs. O'Malley frowned, one finger tapping her chin. "I remember when your mama made a chocolate cake and the whole town couldn't stop talking about it. I don't know why she quit making it, but it sure was delicious."

Amanda shook her head. She hadn't heard the story before, not even from her mother. "You know mom. She was always one to keep trying new recipes and creating new things. She loved to play with ingredients to see what she could come up with."

"True. But still, it's a shame. Maybe you should look through her recipes and see if you can find it. You wouldn't have been more than a couple of years old, I reckon, when she made it. I think it had some creamy caramel and nuts on the top. But then don't go by that. My memory isn't what it used to be." Mrs. O'Malley smiled, the wrinkles of her face deepening.

Amanda picked up the old recipe book and held it up for inspection. "I've been through mom's recipe book and didn't see anything like what you're talking about. I was going to go through my grandmother's recipes as my bedtime reading material. Hopefully, it'll be in here because the recipe sounds perfect for what I need, and it sounds like it has already been taste tested," she joked.

"I hope you find it, my dear. Now, I'll take three of your lemon scones and two of the old-fashioned sugar donuts. You know Frank, he won't be happy if I don't bring those home for breakfast before church." Mrs. O'Malley grinned and shook her head.

Amanda bagged the order and rang it up on the register. "Thanks for the tip about the cake. I hope I can find it."

"Always glad to help." Mrs. O'Malley held out a twenty to pay for her order, and Amanda counted out her change. "So, when are you going to Kevin Thompson's house to cook that dinner?"

"Tonight, actually. I guess everyone in town knows about that, too."

The older woman winked. "How could they not know about it with Parker Wilson running around town claiming he and Tanner set it all up."

Amanda had suspected as much, but to have it confirmed still came as somewhat of a shock. "What do you mean?"

"Well, I heard it from Sally Little over at the diner, who heard it from Parker, that Tanner asked him to try and do some behind-the-scenes match-making. You know Parker. That man is always up for a challenge. They made sure no one else outbid Kevin. I heard he could have bet a dollar and still would've won. This town enjoys a good love story and you know it." Mrs. O'Malley grinned, the twinkle in her eyes telling that she was one of those people.

"There is no love story. I don't have time for such nonsense, and you know it. All my time is wrapped up in the bakery and trying to keep it open. That bakery in Glen Haven has given me enough worries without adding man worries to the mix." It was the truth, but nobody seemed to be listening. It was as if they all had romance on the brain this time of the year. Who knew February Fool's Day would be contagious?

"You've always been a smart girl. Can't say as I blame your attitude after living with Frank for thirty-five years, but married life does have its upsides. A lot of them. Not always perfect, but I highly recommend it. It's all about finding the right guy. You're young. Give it time, and for the record, Kevin does seem like a nice guy." Her grin widened.

"Well, apparently, he's as uninterested in a relationship as I am. The matchmakers in town need to let this one go. What's the old adage? Barking up the wrong tree."

Mrs. O'Malley chuckled. "Okay. I'll see what I can do to spread the word, but sometimes this town has a mind of its own." She waved and headed for the door. "See you in church."

"Absolutely." Everyone knew Amanda closed the bakery for one hour on Sundays. She was unwilling to give up listening to the pastor's message but wanted to catch the after-church crowd. And this morning, she especially needed words of hope and encouragement and faith that everything would turn out okay.

She considered calling Kevin and breaking the whole thing off, letting him know he had every right to back out of his contribution and the deal. But then she reasoned that nobody had made him do what he did. And the Masons did need the money, so it was all for a worthy cause. The right thing to do was to see this through, and in doing so, prove the town wrong. When it came to love, they needed to realize you couldn't go around matchmaking people and playing with hearts.

After the church crowd dwindled, time dragged slowly, Amanda stressing over tonight's dinner par-ty. Typically, she and Grandpa would have been hav-ing their big Sunday dinner, but she'd had to cancel on him this time. Of course, he understood and was all too willing to have her cooking for a single man, probably hoping she'd make an impression with her culinary talents. Like many townsfolk, he didn't agree with her decision to focus on the business and not date.

Amanda used her free time to examine the recipe book. Page after page, she searched for the chocolate cake recipe Mrs. O'Malley had referred to. The recipes in the book were in no particular order, and she'd been through almost the entire book before she found what she'd been looking for. Without a doubt, the caramel nut cake was the one, the relief at her discovery overwhelming.

She scanned the recipe and frowned. There didn't seem to be anything special about it. Basic chocolate cake with a scrumptious topping. Maybe it was the wrong recipe. There was only one way to find out, and tonight was the perfect opportunity. She changed out the ingredients in the oversized bag she'd prepared to take to Kevin's for the ones in the cake recipe.

There'd be no torte tonight, just good old-fashioned chocolate cake.

Right at a quarter to four, Diana arrived, ready to take over. Other than a few short notes, everything was ready, and Amanda left in a hurry. She drove to Kevin's, the address not far on the outskirts of town. It was the old Crofton house, people who'd long since moved away from Hallbrook. The Victorian home had been on the market for quite some time, and it was great to see it sold. It was a big house for a bachelor, and more than she'd want to keep up with, but maybe Kevin enjoyed his space.

She knocked on the door. Kevin answered almost as if he'd been waiting for her to arrive.

"Hey there. Come on in. You're punctual, I like that." His kind smile reached his eyes, softening his features. She loved the shade of his green eyes and was curious if they ran in his family, but under the circumstances, there was no way she'd be asking him. That would be getting too personal, something she was determined not to do.

"When you own a bakery, punctual tends to be an admiral quality. Don't want to keep people waiting for their morning pastry and a strong cup of coffee since that's all that separates them from a good and bad day sometimes," Amanda teased.

"Point taken. I can attest to the fact sugar and caffeine can go a long way. Here, let me take one of those." He reached out and took a bag off her shoulder.

"Thanks." She followed him into the house and down the hall. The old house had fared well over the years. The beautiful hardwood floors were freshly polished, and the walls painted an off-white. Pictures lined the hallway like a real home and not a bachelor pad.

They entered the kitchen, and the room was a pleasant surprise. For a bachelor, this was quite impressive. The stainless-steel appliances and over-size island were a baker's dream.

"Just set your things down here." He pointed to the island. "Make yourself at home, and consider this your temporary kitchen. If you need anything, ask, and I'll see what I can do to find it, but other than that, I consider this my night off."

"No worries. I love to cook, and tonight is for a good cause. I'm sure I have everything I need."

"This is awesome. I'm really looking forward to a home-cooked meal. And I just wanted to say thanks in advance, in case things get hectic and I forget."

Amanda understood completely. People who didn't cook always appreciated an enjoyable meal without having to leave the comfort of their home. "You're welcome in advance." She grinned.

"Do I get any hints as to what's for supper?" Kevin leaned up against the counter as she unpacked.

"Supper. I think this lends itself more toward what we call dinner. Supper is far more casual than what I have in store for you tonight. You paid an exorbitant amount for the meal, and I thought you deserved something fancy. I fixed Beef Wellington as the main course with brussels sprouts and carrots as the side dishes. I've got a wonderful spinach and artichoke dip with bread triangles as an appetizer. And for dessert, there will be a special chocolate cake to tempt you." She grinned, waiting to see what he thought of the menu. She'd wanted it to be perfect and had spent quite a bit of time making her selections.

"It all sounds delicious. Maybe a tad over-the-top." He shrugged, shooting her one of those sexy smiles that always seemed to set her heart to racing. He crossed to the island and looked over everything she'd laid out. "The chocolate cake for dessert is sure to be a big hit, although it doesn't sound as if it should be in the same category as the rest of the meal.

"Well, from what I've heard, this is the most amazing chocolate cake, and there's nothing ordinary about it. It should fit right in."

"From what you've heard?" His gaze locked with hers.

"Yes, I never made it before. But if it makes you feel any better, it has caramel and nuts on the top to make it different. Special." She hadn't stepped away and forced her attention back to unwrapping the meat she'd prepared and rolled yesterday.

"Now there's a combination that works for me. But why make it tonight? Still seems out of line with the rest of the menu."

Amanda stopped what she was doing to gaze back at him. It's not as if the whole town didn't already know her situation. "Under normal circumstances, I might have made some fancy torte, or mousse, or something along those lines. But the contest they announced at the Heart-to-Heart festival is one I plan to enter. And one of our locals told me about this cake recipe my mother used to make, and she reported the whole town couldn't get enough of it. So, I found the recipe. At least, I'm pretty sure it's the right one because it actually turned out to be my grandmother's recipe. I decided to make it tonight and try it on you and your dinner guests."

"Well, I'm not sure that me and the girls will be the best judge of the merits of a chocolate cake, but

I'm more than willing to give it a go." The man's smile went straight to her heart. The guy was a charmer, and there was nothing more to it than that. The last thing she needed to do was mistake his natural charm for interest.

"The girls?" She knew he was having a dinner party, but she hadn't expected it to be with a couple of women. She rolled her eyes, realizing his charm was cliché.

The kitchen door swung open, and two young girls ran into the room.

"Who is she, Dad?" The first girl stopped suddenly, her hands on her hips as she looked back and forth between Amanda and her dad. *Dad.* Something else she hadn't known or expected. The *girls,* it would seem, turned out to be daughters. Amanda wasn't sure which was worse, two daughters or two dates? Either one meant the guy was far busier than she'd expected.

"This is Amanda. I met her at the festival the other night. I won a meal cooked by her. Isn't that awesome? You get something other than my bad cooking for dinner tonight."

The second girl stepped out from behind her sister, mimicking her stance with hands on her hips.

"Why would she do that?" The twins were identical, or almost. It was immediately obvious which one was the leader, and which one was the follower.

"Because I asked her to." Kevin shook his head. The guy was clueless about what the girls were asking. They looked about ten years old, and at that age, would have an opinion on everything. Especially a woman their dad brought home.

The scowl on the girls' faces deepened. Amanda realized there was something worse than two daughters or two dates. It was called twins. The identical faces glaring at her were a force to be reckoned with, their attitude toward her presence clear.

"Hi, girls. My name is Amanda Tillman. I own the Sweeter Side of Life bakery in town. It's nice to meet you. You should stop in to check it out. There are treats for everyone's tastes. And just so you know, what your dad meant to say, was that he bid on an auction item, and it turned out *I* was the auction item." *Ouch.* That sounded way worse than Kevin's comment.

"What she means is that I bid on a secret chef, and I got her," Kevin reassured the girls.

The twins didn't budge, the frowns practically pasted on their faces. "We don't need her to cook dinner for us. Your food is perfect, Dad," the bolder of the two twins responded.

"That's not what you tell me most every night I cook, but it's nice to hear you say it now. I thought it would be an awesome change to have a wonderful home-cooked meal. Amanda has a fantastic menu planned for the evening. And you both need to be more gracious." His rebuff wasn't well-received, and the girls' scowls deepened.

"Amanda, I'd like you to meet my daughters, Lacy and Macy." He pointed to each one as he said their names.

Macy was the one she'd identified as the bolder of the two twins. She stepped forward. "Well, I'm not really hungry, so maybe I'll sit this one out in my room," she huffed.

"You'll do no such thing. If you're not hungry, then don't eat, but you'll sit at the table with the rest of us while we do." Kevin's voice had taken on a level of frustration she'd not heard from him before.

"I'm not hungry, either." Lacy echoed her sister's sentiments, but the slight tremble of her lip gave away that she didn't mean a word of it.

Kevin grimaced but didn't say anything.

"There's chocolate cake for dessert," Amanda added, trying to diffuse the situation. She wasn't above bribery since they weren't her kids.

Both girls' eyes lit up at the mention of chocolate cake, but it was Macy who was quickest to recover. "Chocolate cake is boring."

"My mom used to make us fancy desserts. Like mousse," Lacy added.

Used to. An indication the girls' mother wasn't in the picture anymore, which matched up with the town's determination to pair her and Kevin. Her heart went out to the twins. It would be hard for them at this age not to have their mother around. It was a time when Amanda had looked up to her own mother for everything, and she couldn't imagine not having her there.

"Their mother is in Paris. We're divorced," Kevin offered by way of explanation. "And I'm sorry the twins have been rude. This isn't like them, I promise. I'll have a word with them in private and hopefully correct their attitudes. If you'll excuse us. I look forward to your dinner. And feel free to join us in the living room while it's cooking. You're not required to stay in the kitchen. In fact, I'd enjoy it if you joined me for a glass of wine."

Kevin was up to something, but whatever it was, the girls weren't happy about it, their faces turning even more sour if such a thing were possible. They stormed out of the room, the swinging door moving back and forth several times before it settled into the closed position.

Kevin shrugged and shook his head. "Sorry." He followed the girls, leaving her alone to get on with the dinner preparations. This was going to be a long night.

The kitchen was laid out well. Surprisingly, he had plenty of cookware, and she had no trouble locating what she needed. Most of it looked brand-new, but at least he had them, not to mention he stored things neatly and orderly, much the same way she did.

Amanda fixed a tray with the artichoke dip after warming it in the oven while she started to work on the other courses. She prepared the salad artfully, making the top look like a flower in bloom with the various colored sweet peppers of red, yellow, and green. The balsamic vinaigrette dressing she made was one of her own, and she hoped they appreciated it as well. She removed the artichoke dip from the oven and turned the dial to the correct temperature for the beef Wellington.

It wouldn't take long for the oven to preheat, but while it did, she started to mix up the cake batter. Step-by-step, she carefully measured each ingredient, wanting it to be perfect. She set aside the caramel and nuts as the final addition to what she hoped would be a winning recipe.

It wasn't long before Kevin returned to the kitchen. "I really am sorry about the girls. They aren't happy with the divorce, even less now that their mother's in Paris. They see her in video chats, but not nearly as often as she promised. I've reassured them you're not here as my date, and that I'm not trying to replace their mother. But I'm sure you know how girls can be, considering I'm pretty sure you were one at some point." He chuckled.

His attempt to lighten the situation wasn't missed, and Amanda felt sorry for him. A man dealing with twins at their age would not be an easy task. And it was a task that would get harder and harder in the years to come. Babies and young girls had nothing on teenagers.

"Don't worry about it. It's nothing I can't handle, or that I haven't dealt with. Not the dating part," she stammered to correct the wrong impression she might have given. "I deal with kids coming into the bakery all the time, and everybody has their own particular likes and dislikes. Whether it's a person or pastry, it amounts to the same thing. Kids don't like it when they don't get what they want. And, understandably, they want their mother."

"Thank you for being so gracious about all this. I meant what I said, however. Feel free to join me in the living room, and I'll have a glass of wine waiting for you while dinner is in the oven."

"I don't know. It might upset the girls even more. Their reaction was straightforward. It's called animosity." Amanda wasn't here to make waves, nor did she relish a stressful evening. It might be best to hang out in the kitchen. Out of sight.

"I know, and I might have suggested it in the first place to aggravate them and show them who's boss, but now that I've had time to think about it, the offer is genuine. It would be enjoyable to have someone to talk to other than twins who are bent on ruining my evening."

Amanda picked up the roasting pan, the meat skillfully prepared with a layer of filling perfectly rolled throughout the roast. A chef's masterpiece.

Kevin moved quickly, opening the oven door for her.

She slid the pan inside and set the timer at forty-five minutes. Amanda turned back toward the island counter, not realizing how close Kevin was, her hands coming up to keep them from bumping into one another. "Sorry."

"No problem," he murmured, his voice dropping a notch. An awareness crackled between them. It was the same awareness Amanda had felt and tried to ignore the night she'd met him.

"If you're sure about the wine, I wouldn't mind joining you. But I don't want to cause any problems."

"I'm sure." He nodded.

"Okay, then. I'll just be a minute. I need to finish making the dessert. That way, I can put it in the oven when the meat comes out."

"It looks as though you've already made the cake." He reached up and brushed the pad of his thumb against her cheek. "Chocolate." He licked it off his finger. "I'm a chocoholic, what can I say?" He grinned.

"Well, that makes one of us." She laughed, but the sound came out more like a tinkle, a school-girl-crush kind of laugh.

"What do you mean? Who doesn't love chocolate?" he teased.

"Me. It's not to say I don't care for it, it's just not my favorite. And I certainly don't crave it. It's one of those take-it-or-leave-it foods." She looked away, fiddling with the bread arrangement on the appetizer platter, finding it easier to breathe without the close proximity.

"Then why are you making chocolate cake?"

"Because the Anything Chocolate contest requires a recipe to use chocolate. And I need to win this contest." She shrugged. They'd moved on to a much safer topic, and the distance between them allowed her brain to actually think coherently.

"You mentioned that before. Why?" He leaned against the counter and waited.

"There's a new bakery in Glen Haven. Things have gotten pretty tough since they opened. My mother used to own the bakery before she passed away, and I have a lot of great memories working together with her as she taught me all about cooking and creativity and the business. I can't stand the idea of closing the doors, but I may not have a choice. The bank is only so forgiving and close to calling the loan. That's where the contest comes in." Talking about it made her sad. She pushed the memories aside, intent on making sure the meal tonight was perfect. One step at a time was her motto.

"I'm sorry. I wish there was something I could do to help. Hopefully, you'll win. I know your dessert the other night was incredible." Kevin winked, causing her heart to skip a beat.

"Thanks for the vote of confidence. Too bad you're not one of the judges," she joked, trying to lessen her level of awareness.

"Yeah, I probably wouldn't be a fair judge. Like I said, I'm good about the eating part, but I'm not sure I can tell the difference between good chocolate cake and bad chocolate cake. To me, it's all chocolate, so therefore, it's a winner."

She picked up the appetizer tray and handed it to Kevin. "You have a lot to learn." She let out a deep sigh. At least he was honest. Many guys weren't interested in the fine art of cooking, so she shouldn't be surprised. "I'll be out in just a minute. Can you take this in for me? And feel free to start eating. It's better when it's hot."

"Sure thing." Kevin walked out of the kitchen, using one hand to balance the platter and the other to push open the door.

She moved to the sink to rinse her hands and then dried them on the towel next to it. It took her a few minutes to finish up the batter for the cake, check on everything else, and then head down the hall to join the others.

Kevin looked up as she entered the living room. "There you are. This is amazing stuff. I love the tangy, creamy texture."

"I'm glad you are enjoying it." She smiled, moving to sit in the armchair on the other side of the coffee table.

Kevin stood and handed her a glass of wine. "I hope red's okay. I was thinking since you were serving beef, it would be a better choice."

"It's perfect. Thank you." Amanda glanced at the two girls sitting stoically next to their father on the sofa, each with an untouched plate in their lap. "What do you girls think? I remember I used to love spinach-artichoke dip as a child."

"We're not much into spinach, but thank you any-way." Macy's stilted voice and raised chin were indi-cators her animosity hadn't lessened in the slight-est.

Kevin shook his head. "Since when don't you eat spinach?" he called Macy out on her lie.

The girl's face flushed red from embarrassment. "Since it's mixed with artichokes. That doesn't sound like anything a normal kid would eat." The corner of her mouth curled up in distaste.

"It sounds gross, to be honest," Lacy added, agreeing with her sister. *The twin pact.*

"That's fine. Hopefully, you'll enjoy the salad. That might be a tad less gross and more normal." She smiled, trying to relate to the girls in a way to break the ice.

"May I get a drink of water? I'm thirsty," Macy asked while at the same time nudging her sister with her elbow.

"Me, too," Lacy added hastily.

"Of course, but you need to come back here as I've asked and sit with us and talk. This is a family dinner, and Amanda has gone to a lot of trouble to fix a meal for us."

"Yes, Daddy." Macy shot Lacy a grin that Amanda didn't miss.

She'd bet her next piece of lemon torte the girls weren't coming back. And she didn't give up lemon torte easily. "Don't worry about them. I really do understand, and you don't want to push them too hard."

"I just can't let it get out of hand. They've been struggling to get their schoolwork done and don't always listen. Clearly." He shook his head, lines of frustration grooved deeply on his face.

"Give them time. How long has it been? If you don't mind my asking, that is."

"Their mother and I divorced a little over a year ago. Long enough for them to get used to the fact she's not going to be around all the time. She's a model, and it's her photoshoots that are important to her." Kevin settled in against the back of the sofa and sipped his wine.

"That's a shame. Under normal circumstances, I'm sure they're lovely girls." Not that she'd seen them as anything other than strong-willed children who pushed their limits often.

"They are." Spoken like a true father. It was rather sweet.

The two girls moseyed back in the room, each carrying a cup of water and sat down. The fact they returned was surprising. Even more surprising, was the fact they picked up their plate and took a bite of the previously renounced spinach-artichoke dip.

"This is good. Different, but good." Macy glanced at her sister, urging her with a slight tip of the head toward the plate to do the same.

A look of relief flooded Kevin's face. "See girls. Sometimes you just need to try things. Thank you for doing that, Macy," Kevin said, smiling at his daughter.

"I like it, too," Lacy chimed in.

"Good. Just don't fill up on it. Amanda has an amazing main dish she's cooking, something I'm quite sure you've never had before."

For the next half hour, Kevin talked to the girls about school. The girls relaxed, going off into a lengthy discussion about their new friends, their new teachers, and of course, the troublemakers.

Macy was also quick to point out those kids didn't bother her because she was more than capable of handling herself. Amanda realized these young girls were growing up faster than they needed to. Divorce had a way of doing that to children, and

Amanda's heart ached for them both. It was wonderful though, that the twins had each other to muddle their way through the changes.

Amanda could still recall the long, lonely nights after her father walked out. She'd been just about the age the twins were now. Her mother used to cry herself to sleep, and Amanda had no one to talk to. Having a twin would've been amazing.

A sudden, shrill alarm sounded from down the hall. Amanda shot to her feet, her gaze immediately going toward the kitchen as she took off running, hoping for the best, fearing the worst.

Chapter Four

♥

KEVIN FOLLOWED AMANDA DOWN the hall and raced into the kitchen. The shrill alarm struck fear in the heart of every parent, but at least he knew where the kids were in case there was a fire. The smoke was thick, causing him to cough, but luckily, there was no sign of fire.

Amanda opened the kitchen window as Kevin opened the back door, locking the spring into the open position.

"I'm sorry. I don't know what happened. This doesn't make any sense." She waved a towel in the air, trying to get the smoke outside. "It's ruined, oh my gosh, it's all ruined. She flung open the oven door, letting a fresh rush of smoke escape into the kitchen. "The beef Wellington is burnt to a crisp."

"Don't worry about it." Kevin was more concerned about getting the smoke under control and the alarm off. It took close to ten minutes to clear the smoke, but the lingering odor was strong.

"What do you think happened?" he asked, stopping to survey the charred meat in the roasting pan.

"I have no idea. Beef Wellington cooks at 375°. This isn't even remotely possible. Maybe your oven is defective?" Amanda looked up at him, frustration in her expression. He knew without a doubt she felt horrible, and he almost hoped it was his oven if it would make her feel any better.

Kevin checked the dial. "You had it set at 550 degrees. That's not a faulty oven. That's a faulty operator." He grinned, trying to make light of a bad situation. Anyone could make a mistake. And it's not as if he'd never burned anything. Maybe not to this degree—but still.

"I'm sorry. I've never done that before. I feel awful."

"So much for a relaxing night off from playing dad. The guys at the lodge will get a huge kick out of this." Amanda didn't seem to share his humor. It was a lot of money, but it could have been worse. He was just happy the house hadn't caught fire.

Kevin headed for the living room to let the girls know everything was under control.

They followed him back to the kitchen. When they saw the meat, the girls pointed and bust a gut laughing. "That doesn't look like anything we'd eat. Are you sure you've cooked before?" Macy asked, her question out of line.

"I have, and trust me, this has never happened before. I'm so embarrassed. And I'm so sorry." Amanda answered the rude question before Kevin had a chance to make Macy apologize. He needed to have another long talk with the girls about their manners.

"Yeah, you should be. Our mom never burnt anything like this. She's a great cook. Maybe when she comes home to visit us, she can cook for Daddy and us. May she could even give you lessons," Lacy added.

"That's enough, girls," he snapped. His patience had worn out. "It was a mistake. At least we have dessert. We still have a salad for dinner, and Amanda can bake the cake. Right?" He looked up at Amanda, hoping he was right.

"Yes, definitely. Let me get it in the oven now that the smoke has cleared. We can have the salad and even finish the appetizers. It won't be long until the cake is done. Hopefully, it will make you forget all about burnt meat." She smiled at the girls, trying to find a way to make things right.

"I can't imagine salad and chocolate cake making up for beef Wellington, but I'm willing to let you try," Kevin teased. Anything else would make it worse.

This was nothing short of a hundred-seventy-five-dollar disaster, and the problem was, Kevin wasn't so sure it was an accident. He'd hate to think the twins had anything to do with it, but based on their attitude toward Amanda, it was a concern. The fact they'd been in the kitchen earlier meant they'd also had the means to adjust the temperature. Just one more thing he'd be sure to discuss with them tonight—after Amanda left.

"If you're willing, I'd love the opportunity to redo this dinner. I know how much it meant to you." It was just another example of her kindness.

He was torn between the fact she deserved a chance to make things right for her own sake, and what he suspected to be the truth. But the swaying factor was the main course had held great promise as she'd slid it in the oven, and not even tonight's disaster could stop him from wanting another chance to try it. It was a meal that was way out of his league.

Even the opportunity to relax and talk with another adult had been a welcome change from just watching Disney movies or some other kid's channel with the girls. "You don't have to do that, but I'm game if you are."

"Really, Dad. Lacy and I could cook better than she can. We can cook dinner when you don't want to," Macy fumed, glaring at her dad. Her attitude served to reinforce his belief. If Amanda returned to cook another meal, he'd have to keep the twins in sight, and out of the kitchen, just to be on the safe side.

"I think she deserves another chance to make up for this. And just think, with another meal, comes another dessert. It sounds as though we're on the winning end of the bargain." He grinned, hoping to get the girls on board and to ease up.

The twins giggled. He shook his head, unsure of what to think but worried he was about to find out.

"By the time you are finished your salads, I'll be back with the cake. I just need to melt the caramel and finish putting on the toppings." Amanda got up and headed for the kitchen.

"Did you two have anything to do with the oven dial being turned higher?" he asked as soon Amanda was out of earshot. Kevin watch them closely, looking for any sign of guilt.

"What do you mean, Daddy?" Lacy asked.

"We got water. We wouldn't do something like that." Macy shrugged, giving him the I-can't-believe-you'd-ask-that look.

"And you haven't done anything to the cake?" There was nothing wrong with asking, and he wasn't accusing. He wanted to believe his kids wouldn't do something so mean, but lately, they'd been getting up to more and more mischief.

"Of course not," Macy insisted, glaring at her sister.

"Good, I'm glad to hear it. I would be disappointed if you had anything to do with burning dinner." He'd let them stew on that for a bit before broaching the subject later.

It wasn't long before Amanda returned carrying a plate with one of the most delicious-looking chocolate cakes he'd ever seen. Sure, he told her he wouldn't be able to tell the difference between good and bad, but his eyes told him the answer before he even tasted it. He hadn't been lying when he mentioned chocolate, caramel, and nuts were his Achilles' heel. "This looks amazing."

Amanda set the plate down and cut four servings, handing them each a piece. She watched as he took his first bite, waiting to see his reaction.

"Oh, wow! This is incredible. I lied. I *can* tell the difference. This is by far the best chocolate cake I've ever had." Kevin smiled and then proceeded to shove another bite in his mouth. He glanced at each of the twins to gauge their reactions, only to discover they were both watching him intently, their faces scrunched up as if they'd eaten something horrible. Except that judging by their untouched pieces of cake, it wasn't possible. "Eat up, girls. It's killer. I think this proves Amanda can cook."

"I haven't tried this recipe before, but I have to agree with you and Mrs. O'Malley, this cake is amazing. And I don't even like chocolate. It's so moist and flavorful. I definitely think this is contest worthy," Amanda exclaimed.

The twins looked back and forth between them, a baffled expression on their faces. They glanced at each other and shrugged. Macy picked up her fork and was the first to take a bite. And then another. Lacy was quick to follow suit, neither girl saying a word but making quick work of finishing their slice of cake.

"If we were doing the judging, I'd say you have a winner." He smiled, reaching out to cut another slice.

Chapter Five

♥

AMANDA STILL COULDN'T BELIEVE last night's disaster. In all the years she'd been cooking, nothing even remotely close had happened that could compare. Unless you counted the cookies that she'd burnt when she was nine. And that was because Jennifer had come over and they'd watched the latest teenage singing sensation on TV. This wasn't at all the same thing.

At least Kevin had given her a chance for a redo and to save face. It meant spending more time in his company, but it couldn't be helped. She'd be the laughingstock of Hallbrook if word got out. Kevin had been a good sport about it, the girls, not so much. Amanda was sure it wouldn't take long for them to tell the other kids at school, and then they would tell their parents, and then they would tell other parents. That was the way things worked in small towns. Which is precisely why she wanted to fix the situation, and fast.

The highlight of the night had been the cake. Her grandmother's recipe was nothing short of delicious, and her mother's addition of caramel and nuts stepped it up to amazing. Always one to find ways to change things up for extra flair, her mother had made cooking special.

Up extra early, Amanda managed to freeze her way through Cupcake's early morning walk and then brought her to the shop. The dog would have to remain locked in the office if Amanda didn't want any trouble with the health department, but it was the best she could do. The cake had to be finished in time for today's customers to taste test it and give some last-minute reviews before she submitted the recipe to the contest people.

Amanda held out a doggy treat. Cupcake gently took it from her hand, the dog's silky tongue lapping at her fingers. Satisfied, the dog ambled over to her Sherpa bed where she curled up to work on the treat. Amanda left the office, smiling at her furry friends' antics.

She might have named the dog Cupcake, but Cuppy ate anything with the word cake in it, which was another reason to keep her in the office. Otherwise, she'd be twenty pounds heavier, and the vet would be giving Amanda heck. Chocolate cake on the other hand, would make the dog sick, making the two of them perfectly suited for each other since she wasn't a fan of chocolate anyway.

Amanda mixed up a double batch of cake and poured them in the pans. While they baked, she put the finishing touches on some of her other daily treats and placed them in the glass case. She unlocked the door just as her first customer arrived looking for a dose of caffeine and sugar.

"Good morning, Captain James. You're early this morning." Amanda smiled.

"Late night call with the rescue squad. I'm hoping you've got the extra bold Jamaican stuff to help keep me awake." He yawned.

"I do. Made medium and bold. Monday mornings tend to be rough on lots of people. Do you want a scone with it?" Amanda ordered the coffee directly from Jamaica, and it was the same bold coffee beans she'd ground up and added to her grandmother's recipe to boost the flavor of the chocolate cake. It was her way of making the recipe her own—something her mother had always told her to do. And it had made Kevin's response all that more satisfying.

"Naw, nothing fancy. How about a couple of those baked sugar donuts you always have? Bet they're fresh out of the oven this time of the morning."

"They sure are." Amanda handed him his coffee and donuts, rang up his order, and counted him back his change. "Have a great day."

"Thanks. A quiet day at the fire station would be nice." He waved as he left the bakery.

Amanda removed the cakes from the oven as the timer went off, placing them on the cooling rack. She heated the caramel over the stove on low heat, letting it melt until it was creamy. She drizzled the caramel on top of the cake and then scattered the nuts across the top. The nuts would stick better in the gooey mixture as it cooled.

For a non-chocolate lover, Amanda was surprised at her own urge to sample a small slice. She cut off a piece and laid it on a plastic plate. Eyes closed, she breathed in the fragrant chocolate and opened her mouth to sample the cake, savoring the moment. Rich chocolate with a hint of coffee, creamy caramel, and robust nutty flavor all mingled together in her mouth. "Hmmm," she sighed, but as she swallowed, the cake seemed to stick in her throat.

Maybe her mouth was dry. She drank some water, then tried again, this time forcing herself to focus on the texture of the cake and not so much on the flavor. It still left something to be desired. It was dryer and cakier, making it thick as she tried to choke it down. She didn't remember the texture from last night's cake being like this at all.

Something's different. Too bad the leftover piece she'd kept for herself was at home in the refrigerator. She must've messed something up, but there was no way she was serving this to her customers. Not until she figured out what she'd done wrong. It was disappointing, and just one more thing that wasn't going right.

Amanda shook her head, frustrated with the change of events. She pulled out her phone and dialed Jennifer, needing her advice. "Good morning. I know it's early, but I need to talk to you. Are you alone?"

"Of course, you know me. Still an old-fashioned girl. Ask me that question after we're married," she joked. "Maybe then I'll have a different answer."

"I'll remember that. If only to embarrass you. I need to ask you something. Get your advice." Growing up together for as many years as they had, the teasing between them never stopped. It's part of what kept their friendship fun, never knowing what to expect from the other.

"Shoot."

"I'm sure eventually the news will get around town, but last night was bad. I burnt the Beef Wellington, almost setting Kevin's kitchen on fire. All under the watchful eyes of his twin ten-year-old girls—who hate me, by the way." That summed up the evening in a nutshell. All except for the small moment of awareness that had passed between her and Kevin. Something neither one of them wanted but hadn't been able to prevent.

"Sounds as though it was a miserable evening. What happened? That's nothing I've ever known you to do before." Jennifer was genuinely sympathetic, something Amanda needed at the moment.

"I've asked myself that a million times, but I can't come up with an answer. I did everything just right. The oven was set to 550 degrees. I swear I turned it to 375."

"Well, maybe you're just stressed over the busi-ness and made a mistake. You need to let it go. It's not a big deal, and after the next big thing to happen in town, your cooking disaster will be for-gotten." Under normal circumstances, this would be true.

"I've offered to redo the meal because I felt so bad. That means more time away from the shop, but knowing what he paid for the dinner, I couldn't not offer. I was just surprised he accepted. I think he felt sorry for me. That and I made an incredible chocolate cake for dessert." Even the girls had given in and eaten the cake and had seconds. Apparently, their animosity toward her didn't include her cake.

"Well, there you have it. The evening wasn't a total loss." Jennifer chuckled.

"Maybe not from that perspective, but I wanted to make the recipe again and test the cake out on the customers. I want to enter it in the Anything Chocolate contest."

"What's the problem?"

"Last night, it was a winner. This morning, I can't recreate it. It's not the same and I didn't change a thing." Amanda paced the walkway behind the display case, her phone trapped between her ear and shoulder, freeing up her hands to refill the pastry plates.

"Maybe you need to take a break and step back. You've been under a lot of stress lately."

"That's not it." The recipe wasn't rocket science. It was a basic cake recipe even a ten-year-old could make.

"Then tell me what you think it is. I sense you have more to say on the subject."

Amanda did, but it wasn't good. "Just remember I'm using you as a sounding board, not making an official declaration. But I told you those girls didn't like me, and at ten, they're old enough to be mischievous. What if they turned up the oven dial? They did go in the kitchen for water and came out acting all weird." The more Amanda recalled the incident, the more she was convinced she was right. But the last thing she could do was accuse them of anything. They had enough trouble in their lives without her adding to it.

"Sounds like twin trouble to me. But even so, it doesn't explain your cake."

"I know, and I'm going to try to make it again. But the girls were hesitant to eat cake last night. Maybe they did something to it, too."

"But they ruined your beef Wellington. To hear you tell it, the cake was perfection. It's not likely they could perfect anything you were making, and their motive would be to ruin it, not make it better. Recheck your ingredients, your oven temperature, and everything else. You must be missing something."

"You're right, I'm overthinking it. But I do know one thing, when I go back to Kevin's house and cook this next meal, you can be sure I'm not going to be sitting in the living room having a glass of wine and socializing. No one's going to touch the oven without me knowing it."

"Wine? You didn't say anything about wine. Tell me more."

"There's nothing to tell on that end. Kevin and I are just two friends who shared a glass of wine with what was supposed to be dinner." Technically, not even that. They were auction winner and chef. That's all.

"Let me know how it goes. I'll be rooting for you. Sounds as though you have your hands full."

Jennifer made sense. It was unlikely the kids were the culprits. Why would they ruin one thing and make the other one better? She needed more time to figure this out, but time was something she didn't have. The recipe had to be submitted in a little over a week.

Maybe the answer was to just ask the kids straight out, but then Kevin might not appreciate her questioning them or her being suspicious. The man had enough problems with the twins without her adding to them.

Amanda flipped the "Back in 10 minutes" sign on the front door and left through the back to take Cupcake on a walk. They both could use some fresh air.

Chapter Six

♥

THE DOORBELL RANG, AND Kevin couldn't help but glance up the stairs, hoping the girls would be on better behavior this evening. The last thing he needed was a repeat performance. He opened the front door and quickly grabbed one of the bags from Amanda.

"Thanks for doing this. It's nice to know the twins didn't make you go running for the hills, never to be seen again." He grinned, taking her coat and hanging it on the coat rack. It had only been three days since he'd last seen her, but they'd been three full days rife with problems at work and problems with the girls at their school. Amanda's presence would be a welcome relief to having the same discussions night after night with the twins about staying out of trouble and keeping up their grades.

"The thanks all go to you for giving me a second chance. I swear, tonight you'll get to relax the way you wanted. You *do* deserve it. I didn't realize that first night that when you remarked there would be three of you, that you were talking about twin daughters. I can't imagine how hard it's been on you as a single parent trying to settle in a new town and into a new job." Amanda picked up her bag, and they headed for the kitchen.

"It has its moments. Honestly, they can be a challenge, but then life is one big challenge." And no matter what those girls threw at him, he'd take it, because he loved them and because he knew they were acting out because they were upset with him and their mother.

"Great attitude." Amanda set her bag on the counter and Kevin set the other one next to it.

He started to unpack everything, making small talk until he was comfortable making his exit to head for the living room, intent on kicking up his feet and relaxing. The girls were still studying and cleaning their rooms, which meant peace and quiet for the short term. "What's for dinner tonight?"

"I thought about doing the same meal, but then I couldn't get the picture of that poor pathetic roast out of my head, so I decided something else is in order. Something more in line for ten-year-old girls and a grown man." She organized the ingredients in small groups, her efficiency satisfying to a chemistry teacher who liked everything exactly right when it applied to experiments and in regular life.

"Other than spaghetti, pizza, and hamburgers, I can't imagine what that would be?" He grinned.

Amanda's hair fell loosely across her shoulders, and she quickly pulled it back into a ponytail, using a band from around her wrist. The soft, graceful lines of her throat reminded him of a swan. Sleek and elegant.

"Shrimp macaroni and cheese. It's all the rage now." She batted her eyelashes and grinned, daring him to challenge her. Amanda had to be yanking his chain.

"I'm sure the girls will like the mac and cheese, but I'm not so sure about the shrimp part. And as for me, the shrimp sounds tasty, but not the mac and cheese mixed with it. Call me a traditionalist." It sounded awful. He'd lost out on beef Wellington for fishy macaroni and cheese? Hardly a fair trade-off.

"You won't know until you try it. I've got another salad to go with it, and I made another chocolate cake." She cast a questioning glance in his direction.

"But we still have some from the other night. I wouldn't let the girls eat it because they brought home a couple of bad test grades. I thought perhaps they should spend more time studying than being rewarded with cake."

"The hard taskmaster, are you? But in answer to your question, it's because I tried making it again, and it's not quite the same. I was hoping you three could tell me what's different. *If* you can tell the difference. It's great you still have a leftover piece, because then you can compare the two."

"Maybe you're missing the smoky flavor," he teased.

Amanda tossed a hand towel at him. "Haha. Are you the entertainment for tonight?"

"Someone's got to be. Your variety of entertainment is just too smoking hot," Kevin continued to tease, this time moving out of range for her to make him target practice, especially with a knife in her hand.

"Enough. You're not going to let me live that down, are you?" The pretty flush on her cheeks was becoming and had nothing to do with the heat in the kitchen. He liked the way she couldn't hide her emotions.

"Probably not." He grinned. "Do you need anything else? Otherwise, I'll fix us a glass of wine, and you can join me, the same as last time. It was pleasant until all heck broke loose."

"I've got the salad all fixed, and the macaroni and cheese is ready to go in the oven. You can even watch me set the dial for 350." She grabbed his arm and led him toward the oven, letting him witness her setting it to the correct temperature.

"Okay, then. Temperature verified. Does that mean you're ready for a glass of wine? I can open a bottle of white to go with pasta and fish." He scrunched up his nose.

"It's not fish, it's shrimp. Big difference. I'd love a glass of wine, but I prefer to stay in the kitchen this time. That way, I can keep an eye on everything. Wouldn't want to chance a repeat." She shrugged. "Besides, I still need to mix up the cake batter."

"Whatever you want to do is fine by me. But I've already checked the oven temperature. It's all good, and the timer is set." Kevin had looked forward to the evening for the past three days, and not just for the cooking. There were no two ways about it, he enjoyed Amanda's company.

"Still, I'd prefer to stay here, where I belong." She wasn't budging, not that he blamed her.

"Then I'll stay here with you. No reason the two of us can't have a glass of wine together. Although we should be careful, because the people in town will think this is a second date, and we already know what they're up to. If we keep meeting this way, they'll have us married in no time at all," Kevin teased. It was fun watching the expressions on her face as she processed his words.

"I don't—"

The girls entered the kitchen, almost bounding through the door, cutting Amanda off. "Who's getting married?" Macy asked the question without hesitation, not caring that she was letting it be known she'd been eavesdropping.

"Not me, that's for sure," Amanda replied quickly. "I don't have time for such silly nonsense." She dumped the flour in the bowl and stirred, not even bothering to look up at him.

Silly nonsense. Coming from Amanda, the words sounded odd. The girls slid onto a couple of barstools next to each other, watching every move Amanda made.

"That's good. It is nonsense, isn't it? I've seen the way the boys are with some of the girls at school, and they're making complete fools of themselves," Lacy spoke up, her words causing Kevin to do a double-take. Since when did the twins even notice boys? He wasn't ready for this—not by a long shot.

"Funny you should say that. I call Valentine's Day, February Fool's Day. You and I think a lot alike." Amanda nodded, her smile directed at Lacy.

Kevin wasn't sure he wanted Amanda's line of thinking foisted onto his daughters. He wouldn't say anything because it would be counterproductive at this point. Sometimes, it was better to keep his mouth shut, and this was one of those times.

"I see you've made dinner again. What is it this time?" Macy asked. Kevin was happy she'd checked her attitude at the door.

"Mac and cheese." Amanda poured the batter into a rectangular cake pan and popped it against the counter. Seemed like an odd thing to do. Maybe for good luck, he inwardly laughed.

"It's kinda hard to ruin that." Macy nodded.

"Yummy," Lacy chimed in.

"It is yummy. It has four kinds of cheeses and some shrimp mixed in." Amanda glanced up from what she was doing to check out the twin's reactions.

"Shrimp?" The girls exclaimed in unison. "Yuck!"

"The shrimp and mac is quite a popular dish, but it is kind of a grown-up thing. It might be beyond what you two enjoy, but you can just pick out the shrimp. Or maybe try one, and if you don't like it, take out the rest. The mac and cheese is something I'm sure you'll enjoy. All kids do." For not having children of her own, Amanda was pretty well-versed in how to handle them. *Reverse psychology.* Maybe it was something he should try sometime.

"We have a rule that new stuff has to be tried. Just one bite won't hurt you." Kevin jumped in, not about to let this conversation get out of hand.

"We're not little kids. I just haven't had shrimp before, and it doesn't sound like it belongs in anything as good as mac and cheese." Macy sat up straighter on the stool as if to prove her point.

"Try one bite, and if you don't like it, push the rest to the side. It won't hurt my feelings. It's why I thought the meal choice was perfect for tonight. Satisfies both young and old alike. Hey, Macy, will you hand me that towel, please?" she asked, pointing at the blue cloth closest to Macy.

His daughter looked at her, a question in her eyes, but she didn't say a word. Instead, she picked up the towel and handed it to Amanda. Kevin was impressed and pleased.

"Thank you." Amanda wiped her hands, refolded the towel, and placed it next to the sink. "I was hoping you two could help set the table tonight. I heard you had trouble at school today, and maybe if you help me out, your dad will let you off the hook this time."

Lacy hopped off the stool. "I'm on it. I don't like it when he's grumpy with us."

"Thanks, Lacy." Amanda opened the refrigerator and removed the salad. She spooned it into four bowls. "I brought several kinds of dressing because I wasn't sure what you'd want. But salad and pasta always go great together."

Neither girl said a word, but Macy slid off her stool and joined her sister, carrying plates and silverware to the dining room, as well as the dressing Amanda put on the counter.

"I'm impressed," Kevin marveled as the swinging door closed behind the girls. You got them to help and didn't even need me to step in and tell them to."

"They're sweet girls. I imagine they're just having a hard time expressing themselves during this difficult period." Amanda shrugged, defending the girls. Even after all she suspected they'd done to her and her dinner.

"If you say so. I'm just glad it worked. I'm looking forward to a peaceful meal." The timer went off, and Amanda picked up two potholders, carried the casserole from the oven, and set it down on the cooling plate.

"We can eat the salad as a first course. It will let this cool a few minutes, and the flavors will set up better."

They all sat down to eat the salad, and silence ensued. It was awkward, but not in the way he'd expected. It felt like a family meal—except they weren't family. Or at least Amanda wasn't. The girls had only taken a few bites when Macy set her fork down with a clatter.

"I need to get water. I forgot. Lacy, are you coming to get yours." A glance passed between the two that spelled trouble, one he'd seen before. There was no way he was letting them go to the kitchen alone.

"I'll get—" Kevin started to stand.

"No, sit down. This is your night to relax. I'll get the drinks for the girls. You all enjoy your salad." Amanda's smile made him think something was up, but he wouldn't ask in front of the twins.

"We don't mind getting our own," the twins tried again, coming to their feet.

"And I don't mind getting it for you. I'll be right back." Amanda was halfway to the door, putting an end to the discussion.

The girls sat, another strange look passing between them.

It wasn't long before Amanda returned and handed them each a glass of water.

"Thanks," the girls mumbled.

"Your welcome. And I'll be right back with the mac and cheese."

Amanda set the casserole down on a potholder in the center of the table. It smelled good, even if it did look funny. Not that he'd say anything of the sort to the twins.

Kevin took up a smaller than normal helping and gestured for the twins to serve themselves. He took a small bite, surprised to find he liked it. The second bite was bigger, and by then he was hooked. "This mac and cheese is the best I've ever had. Never would've guessed those two foods would mix," Kevin said, right before taking another bite.

"In cooking, I'm always finding times when a surprise ingredient turns out amazing. Some things, you just never know until you try. What do you girls think?" Amanda asked, pausing to hear their answers.

Macy shrugged. "I don't know. It's different, but I'm eating it. Guess that makes me a grownup." She shot a dare-you-to-doubt-me look at Amanda, challenging her earlier statement.

"I ate a couple of the shrimp, but the thought of the squirmy things swimming in the ocean bothered me." Lacy scrunched up her face, her shoulders shaking in revulsion.

"See, everyone has a different opinion, and that's okay. I'm just happy you both tried it. Luckily, we have more dessert. But I need your help with something. I made the same chocolate cake that I made here the other night. I'm trying to enter it in a contest, but it just isn't coming out the same, and I can't figure out why."

The twins glanced at each other. Kevin didn't miss the slight shake of Macy's head. Now more than ever, he was positive they had something to do with the burnt beef Wellington. Although what it had to do with the cake, he had no idea.

"I was going to have you three taste it and tell me what you thought. But now your dad tells me you still have some from the other night, so I thought maybe we could compare them, and you could tell me what you think is different. I really need your help."

"Sure thing," Macy spoke up first.

"Can I help you get anything?" Kevin asked, pushing back his plate after his second serving of mac and cheese.

"No. I'll just clear these dishes and be right back with dessert. I just need to put the topping on the new cake to make them the same. Just give me a few minutes."

True to her word, Amanda returned less than ten minutes later with a slice of the old cake and four slices of the new. She divided up the older piece into four, putting enough for a couple of bites on each person's plate.

"I hope you all can help me with this." She eyed the girls directly, which made Kevin stop and pause. Did she really think the girls could help her? They were ten. Unless she suspected, what he was pretty sure he already knew.

The girls took a bite of the new cake. They looked at each other, their noses scrunched up. "It's, umm, okay. Just dry." Macy took another bite of the older dessert, and if anything, her frown deepened.

Kevin took a bite of each and compared them, trying to understand his daughter's reaction. She was right. The original cake was moister, and contrary to his teasing, the difference wasn't a smoky flavor. "I agree the first one is better. Surely you must be able to figure it out from the recipe."

"One would think. But I've done it twice now since then, and it's not working. And I'm just wondering if something was added that I don't know about. I'm not upset or anything if anyone did, but I am wondering if you girls added something when you went into the kitchen?" Amanda stared at the girls as she waited for an answer.

"Are you accusing the girls of messing with your cooking?" It was a stupid, knee-jerk reaction. She really did suspect the twins, but no more so than he did.

"Well, let's go over the events of the evening. The temperature on the oven did get raised to 550 degrees. I don't think it was magic, and I don't think it was me. I know the girls were upset that I was here, and the only logical explanation is they had something to do with it. And if they had something to do with that, then maybe they had something to do with the dessert." Amanda folded her arms in front of her chest and sat back, waiting.

The girls looked guilty, but it didn't mean anything. He wanted to believe they wouldn't do such a thing. "Girls, did you have anything to do with either of these things that Amanda is asking you about?"

"No, Daddy. Of course not." Macy answered for them both, but neither one of the twins looked him in the eye.

"Let's assume you're correct about the oven situation because let's face it, they're not acting as if they are innocent," he said, disregarding Macy's denial. "But if they ruined your beef Wellington, why would they make your cake better and not want credit?"

"I don't know, but that's what I was hoping to find out. If they added something and made it better, I really need to know what it was if I want to submit the recipe." Amanda didn't budge, her gaze still locked the girls. She was clearly waiting for some big confession.

"Girls, do you have anything you want to tell Amanda?"

"Sorry about the oven, Miss Amanda." Lacy shifted in her chair, poking her fork over and over into the cake, decimating it.

"Sorry." Macy shrugged.

Kevin shook his head. He'd known the truth but hadn't wanted to face it. His angels weren't as angelic as he wanted them to be. It also left him feeling guilty for letting Amanda make a second meal. "Anything else?" He glared at them, willing them to tell the truth.

"Nope." A shuddered expression crossed Macy's face. There'd be no other confessions tonight.

"The both of you can be excused. I'm disappointed, and we'll talk about it later after Amanda leaves."

The girls left the room without so much as a goodbye or a second look.

"I'm sorry. I suspected as much, but I kept hoping I was wrong. A father wants to believe his kids wouldn't do something of that nature. This whole thing with their mother has them acting out in ways I've not seen before, and honestly, I'm not sure how to handle it."

"It's in the past. I forgive the twins. And I understand where they're coming from. Go easy on them tonight." Amanda stood and started stacking the dessert plates.

"You're a forgiving person. And sweet. After all they've said and done to you, you're still on their side. I find that amazing." He gazed at her as if truly seeing her for the first time. More than her blue eyes and brown curly hair. More than her soft cheeks and pretty lips. He saw a woman filled with kindness, someone who radiated a special kind of inner beauty.

"I'll talk to the girls tonight to try to get more feedback. I'll see if I can get any sense about whether they are innocent with regards to the cake. I feel awful about what they did to you, and it's only fair that I help you figure things out. So, I have another suggestion. As you know, I'm a chemistry teacher. Why don't we take what's left of the original cake and see what we can figure out by running some tests on the ingredients?"

"Do you mean that? You'd do that?" Amanda's eyes lit up with excitement.

"Absolutely. Just let me talk to the kids first, and I'll get back to you tonight or tomorrow. Then we can set something up if need be."

"Thank you. And for the record, you are doing a wonderful job with the girls. Don't beat yourself up."

After she left, he thought about her words. The problem was, he wasn't sure he agreed with her. He made his way upstairs, determined to face off with the burnt-Beef-Wellington culprits.

Chapter Seven

♥

AMANDA TRIED ON THREE outfits before she was satisfied with her appearance. It's not that she was dressing to impress, quite the opposite. She wanted to appear completely normal. Unaffected. She settled on a pair of jeans and a thick knit sweater with a turtleneck underneath. Warmth was far more important than impressing Kevin.

She wasn't surprised when he called her last night to let her know the twins hadn't revealed anything. It didn't mean they weren't guilty, only that they weren't fessing up. Amanda agreed it didn't make any sense they would do something to make the cake better—but it was the obvious answer.

If Kevin could figure out what was different, she would be forever grateful knowing it could help save the bakery. Who would have thought one day she'd find herself back in a chemistry classroom? It had been one of her least favorite subjects in high school, even though time and time again, her mother had been quick to point out baking relied on the chemical reactions between ingredients. Amanda tried not to think about it in those terms, afraid it would take the fun out of something she loved so much.

Amanda pulled on her heavy winter coat and fur-lined boots and grabbed Cupcake's leash. The dog was waiting by the door, tail wagging, ready for her early morning run. "Easy, girl. I hope you don't plan to make this a long venture. It's freezing out here." She buried her face in the fuzzy warmth of her scarf to fight the chill.

She waved at Mr. Avery as he made his way down the sidewalk to get his newspaper. Not many others would be up and out this early to get the Hallbrook news. But considering his wife was the editor of the paper, Amanda didn't think he had much choice.

"Cold morning to be out. This is earlier than normal for you. But I reckon folks at the bakery will be happy you don't let the cold keep you home." He smiled, reaching down to pick up the newspaper.

"Jennifer's handling the shop this morning. I have an errand to run over at the high school." Her friend Jennifer never seemed to mind helping, preferring to be paid in pastries, which was more than okay in Amanda's books. It was hard enough to pay Diana her part-time hours, but the student's help at the bakery wasn't something she'd give up easily. After all, it was usually Amanda's only time away from the shop.

"The school, you say. Wouldn't have anything to do with that young fellow you've been seeing, does it?" Mr. Avery grinned, the twinkle in his eyes enough to keep her from taking offense at the assumption.

"I'm not seeing anyone. I'm meeting Kevin Thompson. He's a chemistry teacher who's helping me figure something out with the recipe for the contest."

"Sounds like a newfangled date to me. Even has food involved." The old man chuckled, his breath forming the whisper of a cloud in the chilly air.

"Don't go feeding all the rumors around town. There's enough as it is. Maybe you could help set the record straight." Ever since the festival, people had been asking her about Kevin. And half the town already knew about the burned dinner, just as she'd expected. And somehow, people figured the bakery was a good place to talk about what was going on and grill her for answers. Always in a cordial but nosey way, of course.

"I'll do that once *I know* exactly what the record shows. Have a nice day, Amanda." He waved and headed back up the snow-covered path to his small cobblestone house.

Amanda huffed in exasperation and shook her head. *Why won't anybody listen? We're just friends.* She tried to keep Cupcake in check, not wanting to become a fall victim on the icy sidewalk because of the dog's early-morning enthusiasm. She couldn't afford to miss chemistry class.

They reached the park, and Amanda removed the dog's leash, turning her loose inside the fenced area. "Go play, Cuppy!" There was no one else here yet as it was barely even light outside. Streetlights cast a glow across the snow-covered grass. Amanda grabbed one of the plastic poopy bags the town provided and kept an eye on the dog. Bouncing up and down on her toes, trying to keep warm, each breath she exhaled looking like a smokestack. Cupcake ran around as if the cold didn't bother her, more interested in chasing any squirrels or birds that happened to get too close.

Jennifer would be arriving at the bakery soon, and Amanda needed to get a move on. Luckily, her friend worked from home and had been able to help her out again today. "Cuppy!" Amanda gave a whistle. Cupcake stopped immediately and turned back to her, pausing a second before bounding her way. "Good girl." She patted the dog on the head and reclipped the leash on her collar, tucking the plastic bag in her pocket for next time. "Let's get back to the house where it's warm." Amanda urged the dog forward, moving faster for the return trip.

With the dog back in the house, Amanda made her way outside to the cold car, starting the engine and waiting a few minutes before flipping the heater on high. The high school wasn't far from her house, but one morning walk was enough. She drove the short distance and parked, grateful she found a front row spot. Amanda grabbed the two labeled containers with the samples of cake and made her way into the brick building.

There weren't many people milling about yet, but she knew her way around having gone to Turlington High years ago. Down the hall, and to the right, she made her way to the science wing. More specifically, the chemistry lab where she was meeting Kevin. She pushed open the door, relieved to see him already here, just as he'd promised.

"Good morning. Thanks for doing this" Amanda removed her hat and shook her head to free her hair. She ran her hands through it, trying to eliminate the static electricity.

"Good morning." Kevin's voice was huskier in the early morning, the sound warm and pleasing. "I just hope this works. I can't apologize enough for the twins and what they did. Figuring this out for you would help even the score."

"Say no more. I told you, they're just kids. What do you want to do first?" She took her coat off and laid it on his desk.

"If you write down a list of your known ingredients, we can rule those out, and I'll check for something not on the list. You get to hang out and watch, and I'll do the work."

"Here's the recipe. Each ingredient is on there, except for my ground coffee beans. I don't mind being your assistant chemist." Amanda moved to stand next to Kevin and handed him the index card.

"That will work. Normally, the assistants I have are the kids, so my expectations are pretty high for you." He grinned. "When we test food, we typically start with the Benedict solution and test for sugars. It's the easiest. But in this case, I'm pretty sure we already know there's sugar. It is a cake, after all."

Amanda nodded in agreement. Cake without sugar wouldn't be cake.

"I want to try a Biuret solution and test for proteins. I'll need a piece mashed up from the samples, but make sure you don't get a part that's touched your caramel and nuts to avoid contamination."

"That sounds as though your testing for meat."

Kevin chuckled. "Proteins come in a lot of forms, but I doubt we'll find steak in here." He shook his head and went back to work. "This is called a Biuret reagent. If the sample turns the solution to purple or pink, there's protein present. Nothing on your ingredient list has proteins."

She mashed up a sample, put it in the test tube, and then handed it to Kevin. "This is kind of cool."

He mixed the sample and the solution and held the test tube up to the light, putting a white index card behind it.

"Look. No color. There aren't any traces of protein, which rules out more ingredients. Another test we can try is for any kind of fat and fatty acids. No, on second thought, there's oil in the cake, so that won't work. Maybe it would be better to do a test on the specific molecules."

"You're the boss. You lost me back when you started talking about Benedict's solution to test for something. I think of Benedict's solution as iodine to put on cuts as an antiseptic." Amanda shrugged.

"Iodine can be used for that purpose, so technically, you're not wrong. But the solution can test for starch as well."

Kevin continued to test several tiny pieces of the original cake, performing a series of intricate tests. Amanda watched him in fascination, his totally focused and serious face proof he enjoyed what he was doing. Apparently, she wasn't any more help than his students, but then chemistry, and science in general, had never been her thing. And neither was math. She had a high appreciation for anyone who could excel at both, and clearly, Kevin was one of those people.

They laughed and talked about the antics of the twins, in between his periods of serious focus. It gave her a greater appreciation for what he faced every day, and she couldn't help but admire him for what he was doing. Giving up a lucrative job as a chemist at a food plant in the city to teach in a small town was no small thing, but he'd done it to give his girls a better life. It was a job that gave him the ability to focus on his career and still have the time to fill his dual-parenting role.

A student entered the classroom. Amanda glanced at the clock, surprised to see that first-period was over and the kids were arriving for the next class. It was disappointing they hadn't figured out a thing.

"I'm sorry. We've got labs today, and I need to set up their stations. I've tested quite a few compounds with molecular tests, but I'm just not getting a match. I'm trying to stick with things one would commonly find in a house. My house, to be specific. I don't know. Just give me a few minutes, and I'll be back."

"Go on. This should be fun to watch you in action. I haven't stepped foot in a classroom since I graduated." She couldn't stay much longer anyway, having promised Jennifer she wouldn't be long.

"At least you won't be tested on what you learn today. You'll get off easy." Kevin chuckled, moving away to talk to the early students arriving and enlist their help. It was no surprise they all looked at her with curiosity in their gazes, and several times, she caught Kevin glancing her way, his gaze warm and caring, something that caused her to flush with pleasure.

True to his word, he returned periodically to work on the cake sample, but more often than not, he was tied up helping the kids with their labs. He was a dedicated teacher, and the kids seemed to love him.

A shrill ringtone sounded, breaking into the general buzz of the lab. Everyone stopped what they were doing and glanced around as the phone continued to ring.

"Who brought a phone into lab class? You know it's against the rules." Kevin looked around at each of the kids, checking to see who would make a move to silence the phone.

The sound was coming from the direction of Kevin's desk, and Amanda glanced in that direction, knowing her jacket was there. She noticed a phone lying on the desk, its screen lit up. Thankfully, it wasn't hers. "Umm, I think it's yours." Amanda winced, pointing at his desk.

He grinned. "So it is. I must have forgotten to turn it off this morning. I was clearly distracted." Kevin shot her a wink. "Do I have to stay after school for detention?"

The kids all burst out laughing as Kevin made his way to the front of the room. He played back a message, his facial lines deepening with each second. He shook his head and pocketed the phone.

"I've got to leave, everyone. I'll have Mr. Wilson stop in and oversee the lab as you finish up the experiment. Try not to explode anything. Please. And there'll be a quiz on it tomorrow."

The kids all groaned. Kevin moved back to his desk, shoving some papers in his briefcase before holding her jacket out for her to slip on. "I'm sorry this didn't work out." Kevin reached out and took her hand. "I wish there was more I could do. It's the girls. They're in trouble at school again, and I've got a meeting with the principal. I think they're working their anger out on everyone around them, not just you. It's not right, but nothing I say seems to have any effect."

"Is there anything I can do to help?" she offered. Not that she was an expert on kids.

"Adopt two girls?" he joked. "I've got to run."

"Don't worry about a thing. Maybe I'll find another recipe or just give up." It was the last thing she wanted to do, but it didn't seem as if she had much choice.

"Definitely don't give up and don't change recipes just yet. There's still time." Kevin squeezed her hand.

"Not much. Get going." Amanda gave him a push toward the door. "The principal's office awaits."

Chapter Eight

♥

KEVIN DROVE TO THE elementary school, furious with the girls. Enough was enough. Trading places was the oldest prank in twin history, but doing it during testing was outrageous. He used the few minutes it took to drive between the schools to take a few breaths and calm down. This could be on their permanent record unless he could talk the principal into leniency based on the circumstances. They were ten, almost eleven, but this was a serious charge.

He walked into the building, his long strides covering the distance quickly to take him to the principal's office. The two girls sat in chairs outside her door, their heads low as they awaited his arrival. They looked up at his approach, smart enough to appear sorry for their actions. Not that it would get them out of hot water.

"You two have a lot of explaining to do. After I talk to the principal." He used his dad-like stern voice, wanting to give them more to think about. Kevin walked past them and knocked on the door.

"Come in." Beckoned into the principal's office. A place he hadn't been since...well, high school. A memory that helped soften his heart even more toward the girls. He'd been no angel in school, but then, they were getting into trouble a lot younger than he'd been when he was sent to detention for skipping classes. He entered the office, shaking his head.

"Thanks for coming over so quickly. Have a seat." The principal pointed to the chair in front of her oversized desk.

"I'm so sorry for the trouble, Miss Martin." The woman was the epitome of the image one thought of for a principal. Coiffured hair in a tight bun. Wire-framed glasses. White silk blouse with a red bow, the only splash of color against her blue suit. And a sharp, angular jaw that helped to portray the stern effect she was after. *Mission accomplished.*

"Please, call me Evelyn. We are both educators and adults." The corners of her mouth lifted in the barest hint of a smile.

He nodded. "Evelyn, the twins have a lot going on, and their mother just told them she isn't coming home for their birthday. I know it's no excuse, but I'm hoping you'll let me handle this at home." No sense skirting around the issue. Kevin plunged right into the thick of the situation.

Evelyn shook her head, lines of tension deeply etched across her forehead. "I don't know, Mr. Thompson. It's the first time they've done something like this, but it's a serious matter. These were state reading and math tests. From what I gather, they decided to each study for one and take each other's place in class. That way, they had less study time and got better grades on both tests. It's a well-thought-out plan, but not what we expect from our students. Their intelligence needs to be applied in a positive direction. I can't condone this activity, and I'm leaning toward suspension."

"Suspension? You've got to be kidding me. They're in fifth grade, for Pete's sake. I'll talk to the girls, and you can make them retake the test. I can assure you there won't be any repeat of this behavior. They're going through a difficult time, between their mother being out of the country and our divorce a little over a year ago. Can't you cut them some slack since it's a first offense? Please." Kevin wasn't above begging, not when it came to the girls. And how would it look to have his daughters suspended from school, and him being new in town and a teacher? He'd have to take time off from his job to babysit them—his job at school, no less.

Evelyn jotted down notes on the two files in front of her. She pushed her spectacles back on her nose and looked up. "I'm quite aware of your situation, and I sympathize. I do." She shrugged and let out a deep breath. "But what message do we send to the children if we don't hold them accountable for their actions?"

"One that says we understand kids make mistakes, and that we expect them to be responsible for those mistakes and not make bad choices again in the future. And having them retake the test would do exactly that, and they would know there'd be no leniency the next time around. They would know the consequences. They're ten years old, not sixteen." Kevin leaned forward, placing his hands on his knees as he waited for the verdict. *Please, Lord, let her understand.*

Evelyn sat quietly, the tapping of her pen against the desk the only sound in the room. "It's against my better judgment, but I'm going to agree. I know you're just getting settled in Hallbrook, and it's a huge adjustment. For all of you. I trust you'll take care of the situation tonight and explain to them the gravity of what they've done. This Saturday, I expect them here in my office at noon. I will personally oversee them taking both exams." She leaned back in her chair; her gaze fixed on him.

"I will have them here at noon. Thank you ever so much. I promise you this won't happen again." They were the words he was expected to say, but unfortunately, it wasn't a promise he had complete control over. That would be up to the twins.

"The girls will remain in school and need to return to their classrooms."

"Thank you." Kevin stood and quickly left the office. He stopped in front of his daughters and shook his head. "I'm disappointed in you two. We'll talk about what's going to happen tonight after school. For now, you need to go back to your classrooms and stay out of trouble."

The twins nodded. "Yes, Daddy," they spoke in unison, their sullen faces enough to touch his heart. Kevin wished he had a magic wand and could make everything right for them, but so far, one hadn't magically appeared. Before the divorce, they'd been angels, but they were growing up and had strong opinions of their own. He watched as they walked down the hall and turned the corner before he headed back to Turlington High.

The day went by slowly, and at times, it seemed as though everything that could go wrong in the lab did. From spilled liquids to a broken Bunsen burner, to a minor test-tube explosion, he was relieved when the three o'clock bell rang. Except today, he had to go from kids that didn't listen at school, to his own kids who didn't listen at home.

He pulled up in front of the elementary school and waited. He spotted them as they cleared the front entrance, breaking into a run to get to the car. There was no evidence of the trouble they'd been in today and faced tonight. They'd gone on their merry way through the day and played with their friends, but that would change the minute they walked through the front door at home.

"I got picked as the head of the dodgeball team in school today." Macy strapped on her seatbelt and leaned forward, excitement in her voice.

"That's great. Just remember to always be fair in whatever choices you make for everyone." He was proud of her and wouldn't let today's trouble sour her achievement.

"Yes, Dad." Macy nodded.

"How was your day, Lacy?"

"It was fine." He glanced in the rearview mirror just in time to see her eyes darken and her face scrunch up. "Other than the kids all asking me if we were getting kicked out of school. Are we?" She grabbed the headrest of the front passenger seat and leaned forward.

"Not this time." He arrived back at the house and parked in the driveway. "You girls need to put your things in your room. Come downstairs and grab a snack, and then meet me in the living room. It's time for a family meeting," Kevin said, using a tone that brooked no argument.

They looked at one another and took off running. He used the time they were gone to figure out what to say. Over and over, he played out the twins' recent transgressions. The oven shenanigans with Amanda had been wrong, but cheating on state testing? Definitely going from bad to worse.

As for Amanda, he felt bad because he'd gotten her hopes up about figuring out the missing ingredient and he'd failed. The sad expression in her eyes spoke way louder than her actual words trying to convince him not to worry. Once again, it would seem the girls were muddling things up for her. There had to be something more he could do.

Kevin paced the living room while he waited. An idea hit him, one that just might work. He pulled his phone from his pocket and called Amanda. "Hey, it's Kevin."

"Hi there. Is everything okay with the girls?" Leave it to Amanda to be worried about them. She always put others ahead of herself, even when she was struggling.

"No, not really. I'll tell you about it sometime, but not now. I'm waiting on the imps to come downstairs and face the music. But I had an idea about the recipe and figuring out the missing ingredient, which by the way, I'm more convinced than ever you're right and the kids had something to do with it." It was only fair to tell her the truth.

"What's your idea?" she asked, hope tinging her voice.

"Common sense and deductive reasoning. If we review what's in my pantry and rule out the known ingredients, the ones eliminated by today's tests, and the obvious wrong choices, we can start narrowing the options based on probability. It's got better odds than looking for a needle in a haystack." Not to mention, it would give him a chance to see her again. Something he wanted more than he realized, even if it wasn't the smartest thing he could do.

"That sounds like a great idea. When can we do it? I've only got a week before the deadline."

"How about tonight? The girls will be grounded, and I'll have plenty of time without having to worry about them getting in more trouble."

"Are you sure that's a good idea? I sense they don't approve of me being around," she tried to tease, but there was far too much truth to her comment for his liking.

"It'll be fine. Trust me." At least he hoped it would be.

"That sounds great then."

"And maybe while you're here, I can pick your brain for other ideas on what to do with the girls. I'm clueless."

"I can try, but it's not as though I have kids, so I'm no expert, either." He needed all the help he could get, and the best kind of help would be the female kind. Women had a special knack for understanding kids.

"The girls are coming downstairs, and I need to talk to them. How does seven sound?" He glanced up at the twins, who were eyeing him with interest over the stair banister.

"Perfect. See you then. And thanks."

Kevin wasn't sure how the girls would take Amanda coming over, but based on the way they'd acted today, it was a non-consideration in his book. The two of them trudged slowly down the stairs and plopped on the sofa.

"Aren't either of you getting a snack?" Kevin asked, making sure they didn't have an excuse to leave the discussion once he got started.

"I'm not hungry." Macy folded her arms across her chest and flopped back against the sofa.

"Me, either," Lacy echoed, duplicating her sister's grand theatrics.

"Fine. Have it your way. So, I'm going to do the talking, and you're going to do the listening. There's nothing you could say about what happened today that could justify your actions. What you did was wrong. I know you're not getting suspended, but only because Miss Martin was gracious enough to give you a second chance. Not everyone gets those second chances. Cheating is cheating. It doesn't matter if it's a state test, a quiz, or when you're playing a game. It makes people not trust you. And trust is one of the most significant character traits people want in friendships, work, or in any relationship for that matter. Without trust, there's no real connection to people.

I get that you two are twins, but using that to your advantage in a wrong way will hurt you both. Something you should think about. I don't know which one of you suggested this crazy idea, but you need to think about more than yourself. You need to think about your sister. Because both of you would've taken the fall for this one. The way it stands now, Miss Martin has agreed for you to go in this Saturday and retake both tests under her direct supervision."

"Saturday? That's our weekend. She can't make us do that," Macy exclaimed.

"She can, and I agreed. Consider it detention. It's taking responsibility for your actions and paying your dues. The principal is going easy on you. *This time*. Next time, it'll be an automatic suspension, and I doubt there will be anything I can do to change the outcome. And *that* would affect your permanent school records and possibly your futures." It was basically the same lecture he'd received every time he'd gotten into trouble at school when he was a kid.

"Doesn't sound light to me." Lacy twirled her hair around her finger. "I'm supposed to meet Ariel at her house, and her mom is gonna let us bake cookies." Her pout tugged at his heart, but not enough to open the door to get her way. Not this time.

"Sorry. You'll have to tell Ariel some other time. As to your punishment at home, that's another story. You both are grounded for a week." He rubbed the back of his neck as he delivered their sentence.

"A week? That's not fair!" Macy jumped up, hands on her hips, looking far too much like her mother.

"What's not fair is Miss Martin having to give up her Saturday to monitor you because of what you did. What's not fair is that the other kids had to study twice as hard as either of you to pass the exams honestly. Something neither one of you were willing to do. So, don't talk about fair. For one week, you go nowhere after school."

"Feels like jail time to me. Whatever happened to second chances?" Macy asked, her sullen attitude nothing less than he'd expected.

"Speaking of second chances, you're both going to get one with Amanda and I hope you'll use the opportunity to making things right with her."

The girls looked up at him, a question in their eyes.

"I've invited Amanda to come over." He had a feeling they wouldn't be happy about it, but neither of them were in a position to influence his decision.

"Her again?" Macy shook her head and rolled her eyes.

"Yes, her. Again. Now, more than ever, I'm convinced she's right, and that you added something to her cake. I don't know what or why, because whatever you did made it better. Amanda's done nothing to you, and she's not trying to step in and take your mother's place. She's just a sweet lady who cooked us dinner, one that you girls ruined. Amanda's trying to keep the Sweeter Side of Life bakery open by winning a contest, and she really needs to know what you added. Now, if either of you wants to tell me what the ingredient was, I might consider reducing your sentence." Cutting a deal might not be the smartest thing on his part, but heck, if it worked in the legal system, why shouldn't it work for him?

"I'll be in my bedroom." Macy stood and headed for the stairs, Lacy following suit. Sooner or later, Lacy would need to think and act on her own, or her headstrong sister would end up running her life.

"Well, here's the thing. I mentioned you are grounded, but I didn't say doing what. And I've decided you're going to sit in the kitchen with Amanda and me while we work on the recipe. If we need a hand, you'll help. And if you choose not to, then I'll just keep adding more days to your grounding. The choice is yours. I'm expecting you to put aside your differences and play nice. It's exactly what your mother would expect you to do." It was true. Victoria wouldn't allow them to be rude any more than he could. She might not be up for a mother-of-the-year award, but she wasn't totally clueless.

"Well, she's not here, so that doesn't matter." Lacy's bottom lip trembled as she spoke.

"Our meeting is adjourned. You two can go to your rooms and start studying for your exams. Dinner is at six, and Amanda will arrive at seven."

"Fine," they mumbled, stomping back up the stairs. The slamming of their bedroom door was an indicator neither of them got the play-nice message.

Amanda arrived at Kevin's promptly at seven. She knocked hesitantly on the door, unsure of the reception she'd get.

It was Kevin who answered, looking pretty amazing in blue jeans and a thick black sweater that molded his chest.

"Come in. It's freezing outside." He pulled her inside and closed the door, shutting out the cold wind.

"If it wasn't for the lure of the secret ingredient, nothing could've gotten me out in this weather tonight." She stomped her snow-crusted boots on the mat, small white clumps falling away. "Let me take these off. I don't want to track water all over your floor."

"Sounds perfect." He took the bags she held and moved them out of the way. "Let me help you with your jacket first." Kevin helped her out of her coat and hung it in the nearby closet.

Amanda unzipped her fur-lined boots and carefully placed them on the mat. "Let's just hope it's a more productive evening than it was this morning. I brought what I needed since I didn't know what you have on hand." Kevin looked good, too good if there were such a thing. Not that she was interested because her focus had to remain on the business, not to mention, the self-preservation of her heart.

"I had a talk with the twins, and it didn't go so well. But just so you know, I've told them they need to be in the kitchen while we're working so I can keep an eye on them. And that they have to be our helpers."

"That's pushing them a little hard, don't you think?" *Poor girls.* "Today has certainly been a rough day for them."

"Maybe so, but the rough day was of their own choosing."

"Girls, Amanda's here. Time to come downstairs and help us," Kevin hollered up the stairs.

"Hi, girls. I hope you don't mind me being here. Your dad was thoughtful to volunteer his time to help me."

They glanced at her in surprise and then at each other as if just realizing something. "Hi," the twins spoke in unison, rounding the corner and starting toward the kitchen, leaving Kevin and Amanda to follow.

"Can I get you a glass of wine?" Kevin asked as he took two glasses out of the cupboard.

"No, thanks. Water would be great though. I can only stay long enough to mix this cake together and get it baked. I need to let Cupcake out for her last potty break for the night. I called Jennifer, but she's out with her fiancé and couldn't help."

"Water it is then. Will one of you girls get Amanda a glass of water, please?"

Lacy's mouth dropped open in shock. Macy, on the other hand, pursed her lips in defiance. Amanda was about to tell them never mind when she caught the shake of Kevin's head. His warning stopped her cold, but it was his grin that made her toes curl. The man was up to no good, but they were his kids.

Amanda was surprised when Lacy did as she was asked with no rebuttal. The girl handed her a glass of iced water and returned to her stool without a word. "Thank you, Lacy."

The young girl eyed her with interest, her eyes questioning. Amanda didn't have a clue about what was going on and gave up wondering. There'd be time enough for that later.

"What can I do to help? It's only right that I'm your assistant since you were mine this morning." Kevin grinned.

"When did you see her this morning?" Macy asked, cradling her chin in her hands for support as she watched them, a scowl on her face.

"You wouldn't tell us the ingredient, so I had her come to the science lab this morning. We worked together, trying to figure it out." Kevin was doing his best to make a point, that much was obvious. Except she didn't want to be his point. The girls disliked her enough as it was.

The twins looked at each other and rolled their eyes.

"If you'll chop the nuts, that would be a big help. Other than that, I can easily handle the rest. It's just a matter of measuring ingredients and stirring them all together. Oh, and if you want to grease these cake pans with oil, you can do that. Just use a paper towel." She handed him everything he need-ed, and he went straight to work without complaint.

"Sounds easy enough. Girls, if you watch Aman-da, you might learn something about cooking. Her pastries and desserts are the talk of the town."

Amanda laughed, knowing he was referring to the Wilson's plan to set him up with her at the auction. Kevin was doing a good job trying to en-gage the girls, but they were having none of it. He kept the conversation rolling, filling Amanda in with tales of the science lab and of the twins, much to their consternation. But it did help cover the awkwardness of the girls' silence.

"Oh, darn it. I didn't realize I was this low on sugar. I hope you have some." She looked at Kevin expectantly.

"I'm pretty sure we have plenty of sugar." He nodded and then looked at the girls.

"I just need enough to top this measuring cup off. Macy, can you handle that for me?" She was trying to find a way to make friends with the girls.

Macy resisted just long enough that Kevin had to step in. "Remember what I told you. One week can get a whole lot longer."

She shrugged, taking the measuring cup from Amanda and headed for the pantry.

"I'll help her find it," Lacy added.

The girls returned moments later, surprisingly more amiable than when they entered the pantry, immediately setting off alarms in Amanda's head. She glanced down at the measuring cup Macy held out to her.

Based on everything else they'd done, she knew better than to accept the offering without question. Amanda wet the tip of her finger with water and dabbed it into the white crystals. She licked her fingertip. *Salt.*

The girls would have to be more original than that to get one past her now. Enough was enough, and the guilty looks they shot her way were all the proof Amanda needed to know the mistake was intentional.

"That's the oldest trick in the book, girls. And with all your tomfoolery lately, I wasn't about to fall for it. Think of all the time and food that would have been wasted. You're too old for these antics." She let out a deep sigh, hoping Kevin wouldn't be upset with her for taking charge.

"You're not our mother, and you can't correct us. Tell her, Dad." Macy stood, her feet apart, hands on her hips, glaring at Amanda.

"I'll tell her no such thing. I can't believe you tried another prank. You owe her an apology."

"You can ground me to my room forever. I'm not apologizing." Macy turned and stormed out of the room.

"Me, too," Lacy added, following her sister.

"I'm sorry. I know I keep saying that when it comes to the twins. And there's only so many times I can make excuses. But their birthday is this coming Tuesday, and they just found out their mother isn't planning on coming back to see them, even after she'd promised to try and make it. They've taken the news hard, and I think that's why they've ramped up their shenanigans. I think they're worried you want to take their mother's place and it upsets them. It's only natural for kids to make the leap, even if there's not a grain of truth to it." Kevin shook his head, frustration vibrating from every inch of his tense frame as he leaned back against the counter.

"I feel sorry for them. It's probably not a good idea that I make things worse, and my being here does that. I really appreciate everything you've tried to do to help, but I don't think this is working. I should leave and let you deal with the twins. They need you." She laid her hand on his arm, urging him to go after the girls and find a way to make things right.

"You're one heck of a woman, Amanda. You're forgiving with all that they've done. And I love the determination you have to save the bakery. It makes me want to help you more. I would agree with you that perhaps now's not the right time to have you around the girls, but I don't think it should mean I can't help you. Why don't I make a list of the ingredients I find in the house that are possible, and I'll meet you at the bakery. We'll see if we can figure this out together."

Amanda liked his persistence, even if it was slightly misguided. He didn't need to feel guilty, the twins old enough to make their own decisions and be responsible for their mistakes. "In that case, I accept. But let's not upset the girls anymore. Figuring out this recipe is important, but not to the point that it hurts them. They have enough going on in their life that they're trying to deal with without me making things worse."

Chapter Nine

♥

AMANDA HADN'T HEARD FROM Kevin since Thursday night. Not that she'd expected him to have time to help her any further, but she'd held onto a tiny ray of hope they'd figure out the missing ingredient. With only days before the deadline, it was time to pick another recipe. She poured through her mother's and grandmother's cookbooks again, searching for something else that would work. She wasn't a quitter and would enter no matter what, even if it wasn't the recipe she wanted to use.

She'd have to find the time to make the new recipe today at work. Hopefully, Jennifer would be over later tonight since it was Hallmark movie night, and her friend could be her taste tester for the new dessert.

The weekend had given her plenty of time to think about the twins, especially during church. She hated the trouble they kept finding themselves in. It brought back memories of a time when Amanda had felt lost after her dad left. Not that the twins' mother had left for someone else, but still, Paris was a long way away, and her job was demanding.

Amanda could never put her career over her children, but some people did, and some people found a way to make it work. But her being halfway around the world wasn't working for the kids. What they needed was something to make them feel special. Sometimes, a little extra love went a long way in a hurting child's heart.

"Hey, Cuppy." Her baby girl trekked into the room, nudging Amanda's leg with her nose, wanting to be petted. She scratched around the dog's ear and down her shiny brown coat of fur, pulling her close for a hug. Amanda drew back and stared at Cupcake, an idea taking shape.

After a quick kiss to the dog's head, Amanda stood. "I've got it. I'll make the girls cupcakes for their birthday to take to school tomorrow. Maybe they just need an extra dose of kindness."

The dog nudged her hand more as if in agreement. "You're the best for inspiration."

Amanda let the dog outside in the backyard for a quick run and potty break, knowing she would need extra time at the bakery to get everything done. Fifteen minutes later, she pulled up and parked just down the street, leaving customer spots open that were closest to the bakery. She left the sign flipped to *closed*. Minutes mattered on today's tight schedule. She headed for the kitchen and flipped on the ovens to preheat them, eager to get the first batches for today's inventory baking. Then she would have time to get started on the cupcakes.

It took her an hour to make two dozen red velvet cupcakes and two dozen chocolate cupcakes. While they were cooking, she lifted the oversized basket of baking decorations off the shelf, searching through them for the perfect idea for each of the girls. After much deliberation, she chose her favorites and set them aside.

The timer went off for the oven and Amanda moved the cupcakes to the cooling rack. Glancing at her watch, she realized there was barely enough time to make the torte. Left with no choice, she bagged up the decorations to take them home with her.

Amanda closed the bakery right at five o'clock, loaded down with cupcakes and decorations. After putting everything in the back seat of the car, she started to pull out of the parking spot, stopping suddenly as she remembered the torte in the refrigerator. She backed into the spot again, letting herself back in the bakery to grab the dessert. It didn't take long, but it was precious time lost. Signature creations took time and couldn't be rushed.

Her cellphone rang just as she entered the house. After setting all the boxes and bags down, she tried to remove it from her pocket, her cold fingers not making it easy. The lit-up screen identified Jennifer as the caller. "Hey, what's up?" Amanda unwound her scarf from around her neck and hung it on the hall closet doorknob, her hat with it.

"I'm sorry, but I need to cancel on Hallmark night. Will's not feeling well, and I promised I'd take him some chicken noodle soup."

"Well, darn. I needed you to try a dessert for me. Maybe you could stop by and pick it up, and the two of you could do a taste test. That actually works out great, because then I can use the rest of the night to finish the toppings on some cupcakes I'm making." Suddenly she had lots of free time, Amanda letting out a deep sigh of relief.

"For the shop?" Jennifer knew she didn't usually work at home for the bakery's inventory.

"No, for the twins." Amanda smiled, wishing she could see Jennifer's expression.

"Oh? Is there something I should know?"

"No. I just feel bad for the girls. It's their birthday tomorrow, and their mom's not around. I decided to do something special for them." It was a perfect idea, and she couldn't wait to see the kids' expressions. Maybe this would put the girls and her on the same page going forward.

"Sounds to me as though someone's getting more and more involved with the Thompson family. Speaking of, how is Kevin?" Her voice had turned more curious and more intense.

"I wouldn't know. I haven't talked to him in four days." It was the truth, so Jennifer needed to keep her feet on the ground. Kevin wasn't flying her to the moon and back just yet. And Amanda, well, she wasn't even buying a ticket for the excursion.

"Four whole days? Goodness, it's over," Jennifer teased.

"It's over because it never started. I don't know why you keep pushing me in his direction."

"Because he seems like a great guy, and Tanner speaks highly of him. And you deserve someone nice." Amanda couldn't help but agree, at least the part of deserving someone nice. Kevin was a really good guy and a wonderful father, but self-preservation keep her silent on her opinion. Jennifer would be like a freight train if she sensed any growing attraction between her and Kevin, and she'd turn a blind eye to all the reasons it wouldn't work.

"He was just helping me with the recipe. It's called guilt. His twins sabotaged my auction dinner."

"Say whatever you want, but I think running a chemical analysis on your cake goes a bit above and beyond an apology. I'll stop by and get the dessert in about fifteen minutes. I never say no to free food if you're doing the cooking."

"Perfect. And thanks." Amanda flipped on the TV and turned it to tonight's Hallmark movie. Thankfully, they were past all the Valentine's Day movies. She turned up the volume and sat at the kitchen table facing the living room so she could see the TV as she decorated the cupcakes.

Jennifer didn't stay but a few minutes when she picked up the chocolate torte, other than to take the time to extract a promise she'd take pictures of the cupcakes. Her friend's curiosity was still in hyperdrive, but luckily, girlfriend duty called.

The cupcakes turned out perfect. One at a time, she created twenty-four miniature masterpieces for each of the girls. For Lacy, she carefully topped the red-velvet cupcakes with two-tiered donut-shaped swirls of pink icing, topped with a strawberry and chocolate heart. She stuck a green leaf next to the strawberry and placed a solid chocolate heart on the side, setting each one on a lacy doily for added effect.

Amanda decorated Macy's chocolate cupcakes with a butterscotch cream-cheese frosting swirled like ice cream on the top. She added tiny white, milk-chocolate balls and a star on each one, finishing them each off with a piece of a miniature Kit Kat bar like a straw. Sweet and fun, but not as fancy.

It took her far longer than she'd intended, but it was well worth it. Satisfied with the way they'd turned out, she hoped the twins would be pleased when she dropped them off early knowing they could take them to school. She also hoped Kevin wouldn't mind the early morning intrusion, her doubts stemming from the fact he hadn't been in touch with her. She was looking forward to seeing him again, but only to see how things had been going. He'd made a lot of sacrifices for the girls, attesting to what kind of man he was, and she wanted things to work out for him.

Kevin looked up as the girls stumbled into the kitchen, rubbing the sleep from their eyes. "Good morning, girls. And happy birthday to you both. Today's a special day. It's your second double-digit birthday."

"It's just another day. Nothing special about a day we're grounded. Now, if we were in Paris, maybe this would be a special birthday." Macy shrugged, unaware of the pain her words drove into his heart.

He was just never enough, no matter what he did. Victoria was their shining star right now. They didn't understand it was their mother's choice to be in Paris. That her choice was to put career over family. It's not as though she wanted the twins with her, but he'd never tell the girls. It was better they stay mad at him.

"Paris would be amazing. Think of all the beautiful dresses the women wear. Oh, and their fancy coats. It would be a dream come true." Lacy's eyes twinkled as she pictured the fashion palace of the world.

"I can't give you Paris, but I do want to make your birthday special. What would you girls like to do after school? I know technically you're grounded, but I'll lift it for today. We need to do something to celebrate. Call it a hiatus of sorts." He grinned, dropping a kiss on the top of each girl's head.

"Or you could just lift the entire grounding and call it a birthday present," Macy pushed.

"Or not." Kevin was tired of having to hold the line and be the disciplinarian all the time, but someone had to do it.

"Could we go to dinner? Maybe catch a movie. What about ice-skating? We could call our friends and see who could meet us there." Lacy's suggestions sounded like fun, which were much-needed options after Macy's wishful thinking.

"Macy? Any ideas?" Kevin tried to draw her into the conversation, but the stiff line of her back was an indication of where she stood on the matter. It was her way or the highway.

She shrugged. "I don't care. Just whatever." He wasn't going to do this her way, and with her attitude, she'd be hitching a ride all the way to her bedroom. *But not until tomorrow.*

"I guess that settles it then. I'll check and see what's playing at the theater and then we can decide. I'll pick you up after school and we can come here to change for dinner and a night out. I'm making you a pancake special this morning. They should be done in a few minutes. Get some orange juice, and while you're at it, grab the maple syrup and whipped cream, will you?"

"Okay," Lacy replied, jumping down off the barstool and heading for the refrigerator. Surprisingly, Macy followed her sister and did as she was asked.

Kevin took the whipped cream from Lacy and returned to the counter where he'd put a couple of special Mickey Mouse pancakes on each plate. He sprayed two whipped cream eyes and a mouth on each one, dropping chocolate chip pieces in the center of each eye, and a trail of them in the mouth like teeth.

"Ta-da!" He handed them each their plate. "Happy birthday to my two favorite girls."

The twins looked at each other and then back at their plates.

"Cute, Dad." Lacy smiled.

"Maybe next year, we could graduate to grown-up pancakes," Macy added.

"Point taken. It's hard to believe you're both eleven."

"Not until 3:25 this afternoon. 3:30 for knucklehead over here." She nodded toward Lacy.

"I remember all too well, trust me. But in my book, today's your day all day. It won't be long before you're both driving and bringing home boyfriends, and then you'll be off to college."

The twins rolled their eyes.

"Geez, Dad. It may seem fast to you, but to us, it's forever," Lacy added.

They may have thought their Mickey Mouse pancakes were a bit immature, but it didn't stop them from chowing down.

The doorbell rang. Everyone looked toward the kitchen and then at each other in surprise.

Kevin glanced at the clock on the wall. 6:15 was early for anybody to be visiting. "I'll see who it is, and you two finish your breakfast."

"Maybe Mommy's here to surprise us." Lacy jumped up out of her seat and raced around Kevin, Macy hot on her heels. There may be a strange visitor at their door, but he'd be willing to bet the girls grounding status it wasn't Victoria. She'd never been a morning person, not to mention, Paris was a long way for her to come without advance notice. The girls would be disappointed, but there was nothing he could do about it.

Macy yanked open the front door.

Kevin was surprised to see Amanda standing there, bundled up like a snow bunny, two large containers in her arms.

"Oh, it's you." His daughter was out of line, but he'd let it go for the moment. The downcast expressions on the girl's faces as they trudged back to the kitchen nearly broke his heart.

"Come in, Amanda. What a surprise to see you this morning." He closed the door behind her, a wave of sweet jasmine floating his way.

"Sorry to barge in on you so early. I wanted to wish the girls a happy birthday and to bring them a special treat." She glanced down the hall, a pained look on her face.

"Really? You shouldn't have gone to any trouble. But since you did and you're here, I guess it's too late to stop you." He grinned, taking one of the boxes from her. "Follow me, they've only gone back to the kitchen to finish breakfast. They thought you might be their mother paying a surprise visit," he said by way of explanation for the girl's rude behavior.

He pushed open the kitchen door. "Girls, Amanda's here to see you, not me, and she's brought you something." Two heads swung around and stared at him as if he'd lost his mind.

Both girls frowned.

"Happy birthday, Macy." Amanda removed a plastic cupcake tree container from the box and set it in front of his daughter. "And happy birthday, Lacy," she added, setting the second tree in front of Lacy. "I wanted to do something special for you both, so I made you cupcakes to take to school today."

"Why?" Macy asked, her eyes narrowing as she glanced back and forth between him and Amanda.

"Because kids love to share birthday cupcakes with their classmates. At least, they did when I was in school." Amanda smiled. She was trying hard where the girls were concerned, and it was a pity they couldn't find it in their hearts to stop seeing her as a threat. Nothing could be further from the truth.

Macy's eyes narrowed. "Why would you be nice to us? We burned your dinner, and we haven't been nice to you."

"Because I understand what you're going through and why you do the things you do—I was a young girl once upon a time, too. I choose not to hold grudges, preferring instead, to offer kindness as a better avenue."

"Or is it because you want to marry our dad?" Macy asked, getting straight to the heart of what was bothering her.

"Macy, knock it off," Kevin interjected, this time unable to hold his tongue. The next step was to send her to her room without finishing breakfast, something he preferred not to do today of all days.

"No, I'm not looking to marry your dad. I don't know how many times I must tell you that before you believe me. I'd rather we all be friends. And friends do nice things for each other. Do you want to see the cupcakes? I decorated them last night.

I'm really pleased with the way they turned out." Amanda smiled at the girls and reached for the cupcake trays.

"No, thanks. We'll see them at school, I'm sure." Macy snapped.

"We've got to go get ready. We're running late. Come on, Macy, let's go." Lacy grabbed her sister's arm and yanked her in the direction of the door.

The look of disappointment on Amanda's face was heartbreaking. He could only imagine the time she'd taken to go out of her way to do something like this for the twins, and in return, they were acting like spoiled brats. It was times like these that he considered grounding them for life. "Thank you for doing this. And I'm sorry for the way they're acting."

"I debated whether I should do it or not, but I wanted to make up for their mother not being here. I should've stuck by our plan and stayed away. I'm the one who's sorry. I've upset them on their birthday. Maybe I should just take the cupcakes with me."

"No. I've got to take the girls to school this morning and I'm sure the cupcakes will be greatly appreciated by the other children. I did notice she admitted she'd see them at school." He smiled down at Amanda.

She nodded. "If you're sure, then okay."

Kevin was positive it was okay, because if not, he'd make it right anyway.

Chapter Ten

♥

THIS MORNING STARTED OUT as a bust, only to be followed by another slow day at the bakery. It didn't help that it had been windy and cold, keeping most people home or at least, not in the mood for sweets and treats. Unfortunately, fewer customers meant less sales, excess inventory, and more time to worry about the future.

It wouldn't be long before Amanda would be forced to cut Diana's hours. The high school student didn't get many hours now between her schedule and Amanda's limited resources. The girl depended on the extra cash to pay for her athletic equipment and Amanda hated to disappoint her, but there was no way around the inevitable unless she won the Anything Chocolate contest.

The problem was, with the recipe she'd be forced to submit, Amanda wasn't holding out much hope of winning. It was a good recipe, but not good enough to beat everyone else in the state of New Hampshire. The bank letter she'd gotten this morning was a cold, hard reminder of her financial situation and another dose of reality. It was time to start thinking of what would happen when the bakery closed.

Cupcake wandered over and sat by her feet, leaning against her legs. "Hey, girl. What do you think I should do? I could always go over to O'Malley's and see if they need another server. Or maybe I should check in Glen Haven." But Glen Haven was probably no better than Hallbrook when it came to employment. "I'm just not sure what to do. And I've got you to think about."

Woof. Woof.

Amanda hugged her sweet baby, drawing strength. Lancaster was her best bet for finding employment, but the roads in the winter were never reliable which would make it hard to leave Cupcake alone all day, unsure whether she'd be able to get back and forth. "There's just got to be something

I can do." Cupcake nudged her leg, and Amanda responded by patting her head and her side.

"Mom managed to keep the place afloat. Why can't I? I had really hoped the contest was the answer. I thought with an online presence and master marketing program, we'd put ourselves on the map and make things work. But I don't have the kind of capital it takes to do that on my own. But don't you worry, girl. We'll figure something out. I promise." Amanda's eyes filled with tears. It was one thing to say the words, another to believe them.

Woof. Woof.

"Come on, let's get you some dinner. I've got some leftover pizza I can reheat for mine and some scrumptious turkey with gravy for you." Amanda made her way to the kitchen and opened a can of dog food and portioned out Cupcake's dinner. Covering the rest, she put it in the refrigerator and grabbed the Styrofoam box with leftover pizza. Not an exciting dinner, but it would have to do. She turned on the oven, preferring to reheat the pizza that way. Microwaves always made it too mushy.

She grabbed herself a glass of water and sat at the table, waiting for the buzzer to indicate the oven was preheated. Her cell phone rang, and Amanda stood, crossing the kitchen to retrieve it off the counter. The name on the lit up screen shocked her.

Kevin.

"Hello," she answered as she tried to control her racing heart. This morning he'd had no choice but to see her and it had been awkward, but this—he was the one calling her.

"Hey, Amanda. I hope I'm not disturbing you?"

"No, not at all." Leftover pizza didn't qualify as doing anything that couldn't be disturbed.

"I know this is going to sound really odd, and I won't blame you if you say no, but the girls are asking if you can come over and see them. And before you say anything, I realize that based on this morning's behavior and the way they've acted toward you in the past, there's no rhyme or reason to the request. But they won't tell me what it's about, and they made me promise I'd call."

"And you always honor your promises, don't you?" He was a man of honor, something she'd picked up on right away. *Why did he have to be so perfect?*

"I do. Will you come over? I hate to ask for you to come here, but when I offered to bring them to your place, they balked. Maybe it's the new eleven-year-old hormones." He chuckled.

"Careful, mister. Don't go blaming hormones for things you can't understand," she joked. "They weren't overly happy with my visit this morning, and I'm not sure I'm up to more of the same treatment. It's been a pretty lousy day, but I'll make an exception because it's their birthday." The last thing she wanted to do was go back out in the cold, but curiosity wouldn't let her say no. On the bright side, at least the wind had died down.

"Thank you. I wish I could say you won't regret it, but with the twins lately, I have no way to know." Kevin was honest to the core.

What he didn't understand was that the girls were becoming young ladies, and the transition could be mind-boggling. "I'm a big girl and I can handle myself."

"I'm sure you can. You seem to do quite well when you set your mind to something."

Mutual appreciation never hurt anyone. It made her feel all warm and fuzzy that Kevin seemed to understand her. "Thanks. Coming from you, that means a lot to me. I feel the same about you. I know the twins may be a handful now, but trust me, they'll come around."

"In about seven years, right?" He chuckled.

"I plead the fifth on that. When should I come over?"

"Now?" he asked, the wishful question in his voice almost laughable. It was as though he never thought she'd agree.

Amanda glanced at the oven and then back at the pizza on the counter. *Dinner could wait.* "See you in a few minutes," she said and then hit the disconnect button. Amanda turned off the oven, tossed the pizza back in the refrigerator, and headed for her room, Cupcake close on her heels. "I'll be back shortly to take you for your walk. I'm more than positive this won't take long."

Amanda went to the closet and changed her shirt into a more casual sweater, something more flattering than the button-up blouse she'd worn to the shop. She ran a brush through her hair twenty times, determined to give it some lift and shine. After adding a few dabs of makeup and a dot of her favorite perfume, she was ready to go.

She put on her boots and coat and made her way to the car. Luckily, the car engine was still warm enough that when she flipped on the heater, lukewarm air blasted her. At least she wouldn't be an icicle by the time she arrived at Kevin's. She backed down the driveway and headed up the street toward his place. The upside of her visit was she'd be able to pick up her cupcake containers if the girls had remembered to bring them home.

Amanda pulled into the driveway and put the car in park. She carefully walked up the sidewalk, testing each step for slick spots until she reached the porch. *Tap. Tap. Tap.* The front door knocker was easier to use than removing her glove and exposing her hands to the cold while she waited. To her surprise, it was the twins who answered.

"Hello, birthday girls. I heard you wanted to see me, so I came right over." Amanda kept a cheerful expression on her face despite the inner trepidation she was feeling.

"We've been talking, and we want to ask you something," Lacy spoke first, but it was difficult to gauge her attitude.

"It's too cold to stand outside." Macy grabbed her arm and pulled her inside. "We need to talk," her non-committal voice with the attitude to match, in perfect sync with her twin.

"Yeah, we need to talk." Lacy echoed.

Amanda moved inside and closed the door. She removed her scarf and hat and turned to face them just as Kevin walked into the room. Unsure what to expect, she was relieved to see him.

"I thought I heard voices out here. You got here fast." He shot her a smile that warmed her heart. "Girls, why don't we let her take off her jacket and get settled in the living room instead of bombarding her in the foyer with whatever mission you're on." He was trying to help and was probably more than a little curious what they were up to.

Makes two of us.

"We need to ask her something first, Dad. Wait." Lacy spoke up, holding her finger to her lips to shush him.

"Your cupcakes were a big hit at school. Apparently, around here, you're the queen of cupcakes. We didn't expect everyone to be nice to us. They thought it was cool that you are friends with our dad." Macy was doing the talking, and so far, without any of their normal disapproving tones.

Amanda relaxed. "I hadn't heard that title before, but I must say, I kind of like it." She grinned. The question remained, did the twins? They were acting strange, and Amanda didn't have a clue what was going on.

"Well, we've been talking, and we wanted to ask you something important." Macy was still taking the lead.

"Yeah, something very important," Lacy added, nodding in agreement.

"I'm listening." Amanda watched them closely as she tried to figure out where they were headed with this conversation.

"Who am I?" Macy asked.

Talk about *out of the blue*. It was an odd question, especially given the request Amanda come over on a cold night for the asking. "Is this a trick question? Are you two trying to play a joke on me?" She wasn't gullible where the twins were concerned, at least not anymore.

"No trick. Just answer the question." Lacy spoke up, a hopeful smile on her face.

It was the smile that put Amanda at ease. "Well, that's easy. You're Macy, and you're Lacy." She pointed to each of the girls, not questioning her response.

"How do you know us apart every time? Most people at school can't tell the difference, and you've only known us for a few days," Lacy asked.

The girls waited; the intensity of their expressions surprising.

Kevin, on the other hand, stood back and watched the scene unfold. He looked just as confused as she was or in this case, had been.

Everything fell into place with Lacy's question. "Is that what this is all about? That's easy." Amanda shrugged. "Just because you are identical twins, doesn't mean you're identical in every sense. You're both still unique, and those differences are shown in your personality, the way you carry yourselves, and in the way you speak."

"Is that why you made our cupcakes different?" Macy asked, her gaze never leaving Amanda's face.

It was like being under twin microscopes.

"Well, yes. I've already explained I see you both as unique. I tried to decorate the cupcakes in a way that complemented your individual qualities. Lacy's, for instance, were more feminine—no offense, Macy. But she tends to prefer things to be neater and prettier, more bows, lace, that kind of thing. Lacy keeps her hair perfectly in place, and her shirt tucked tightly into the waistband of her school clothes.

You, on the other hand—" she turned back to Macy, "—you are more confident, and usually the first one to speak up. You prefer things to be done just right. No frills. But I also know how much you enjoy chocolate and butterscotch." Amanda wasn't sure where all this was going, but it was the longest she'd talked to the girls in an almost normal conversation. Strike that. This was the first time they'd had a normal conversation.

"Butterscotch? How would you know that?" Macy's forehead wrinkled in confusion.

"Because the few times I've seen you, you've always had a pack of butterscotch lifesavers in your hand or nearby." They were small observations, but apparently important ones.

The girls looked at each other and shrugged, then looked back at her, soft smiles on their faces.

"Do you know you're one of the only people who's really noticed those things about us? Even our own mother still gets us wrong sometimes." It was Lacy who spoke up this time, surprising Amanda with the truth.

"Well, I'm sure she's just busy. Her career is demanding, and maybe she's just not good at noticing details. But it doesn't mean that she loves you any less. You do look a lot alike."

"But you can tell the difference," Macy chimed in.

"Yes, I can." She nodded.

"It was nice of you to go to the trouble to make them for us, and we're sorry we were so mean to you this morning. And for all the other mean things we've done." The girls waited expectantly for forgiveness, hope in their expressions.

Amanda's eyes welled up with tears. After a long day, their words were soothing to her heart and soul. At least something was finally going right. "Thank you for the sweet and heartfelt apology. I'll let you in on a secret though, I had fun making the cupcakes and I'm so glad you enjoyed them. You only turn eleven once, you know?" Amanda teased, the girls taking a second to catch on to her joke.

"We had a good day today because of you. And now, we have something we want to show you." The two girls looked at each other, nodded, and headed out of the room.

Amanda looked at Kevin for guidance. He shrugged, and the two of them started to follow the girls.

Macy stopped and turned back. "Wait here," she said, taking charge and pointing at the sofa. The girls headed for the kitchen, leaving the two of them alone.

"This is bizarre," Amanda said, looking at Kevin to see what he thought of the whole thing.

"I agree. I had no idea, but I'm rather pleased. Just when I think everything is going downhill, they do something to renew my spirit. This is one of those times." His eyes crinkled at the corners; his smile genuine.

The girls were talking as they ambled back into the room, stopping in front of Amanda.

Macy handed her a jar of vinegar. "This is what we put into your cake. We just thought you should know, and we don't want you to lose the bakery." They looked at their dad briefly, who rewarded them with a smile.

"You've got to be kidding?" Amanda said, shaking her head. "How would vinegar make the cake better?"

"We wondered the same thing. I'm sure you can guess we didn't mean to make that happen." The twins had the good graces to appear remorseful.

"Thank you for telling me, but there has to be something else. This can't be it. Maybe another clear bottle or something similar. Maybe corn syrup?" That was something she hadn't thought of before. She turned to Kevin. "Do you have corn syrup?"

"I wouldn't know what to use it for, so it's safe to say we don't." Kevin shook his head and shrugged as if he wished he had a better answer.

"This. Is. It." Macy stood there, hands on hips, insisting she was right. "I added three shakes into the batter and then stirred."

"Are you sure?" Kevin spoke up and repeated the question.

"Yep. Make it and see what happens," Macy said, her positive attitude gaining ground with Amanda.

"Thank you, so much. I will make the cake with vinegar, just as you say. If this is the ingredient, you may very well have helped me save the bakery. If I win the contest, that is." Amanda grinned, filled with renewed hope. *Vinegar.* It was nothing she'd ever used before in any of her recipes—at least not in any of her sweets or treats.

"You did a nice thing, girls. I appreciate you taking responsibility and stepping up to make things right." Kevin hugged the girls, telling and showing them how proud he was of their actions.

"Thank you, Dad," both girls cried in unison.

"Now, I'm sure Amanda has plenty to do this evening, and we should let her get home. Not to mention, we have some birthday festivities to start." Kevin looked her way for clearly hoping for support.

His earlier tension had vanished, and Amanda was happy for him and the girls. She nodded. "I can't wait to go home and try the recipe with some vinegar. I'll call and let you know how it turns out. I promise." Amanda stood to leave and made her way to where she'd draped her coat over the back of a chair.

"Wait. We want you to come with us tonight," Macy asked, her sister nodding in agreement.

Kevin stood there speechless, a stunned expression on his face, probably one that matched her own.

To go from begrudging buddies to besties and hanging out was a huge leap. And spending the night hanging out with Kevin and the girls was a huge risk. She'd already figured out she was attracted more to Kevin than she wanted to be.

Teamed up, Kevin and the girls were heart-warmers that could melt any frozen heart, including hers.

"Thanks for the offer, but I really should work on this cake tonight." It was a good, solid excuse, one that would keep her out of trouble.

Kevin glanced her way, their gazes locking. It looked as though he wanted to say something but changed his mind, instead, grabbing his jacket out of the closet.

"It's our birthday. You have to say yes. We're going to dinner and then ice-skating and then a movie." Lacy smiled, willing her to agree.

Ice skating was the last thing she wanted to do. It was something she hadn't done since she'd fallen and bumped her head, earning her a trip to the hospital. It was also the night she'd come home from the hospital and discovered her dad had walked out on them and wasn't coming home.

"Please, Miss Amanda?" Macy's expression tugged at her heart. This was a different side of the girls and she felt it was only right to meet them halfway in this new friendship mode they found themselves in.

"Okay, then, but it's because you all are being so sweet. That is, of course, if your dad doesn't object." Amanda looked to him for confirmation, unsure of what she'd see.

"If the girls want you along, who am I to object? The more, the merrier." Kevin shot her a wink. The man certainly had a way with the charm, and Amanda wasn't at all immune.

"I do need to stop at the house and let my dog out for a quick potty break if you don't mind."

"You have a dog?" Lacy asked, her eyes lit with excitement.

"I do. She's a chocolate Lab. Friendly, and I'm sure you'll love her." Amanda followed Kevin and the girls to the front door.

"What's her name?" Macy asked.

"Cupcake." Amanda said, trying hard to keep a straight face.

Everyone burst out laughing.

"How appropriate," Kevin joked, his grin widening. "Lead the way."

Tonight was one thing, but that's where Amanda had to draw the line. She was doing this for the girls. The last thing she needed to do was fall for him and the twins. That would spell triple trouble.

And there was no way she wanted to be a fool for love.

Chapter Eleven

♥

AMANDA PULLED INTO THE driveway, Kevin right behind her. The girls jumped out of his car and ran to the front door.

"Cupcake gets excited around new people, so be careful she doesn't jump on you," Amanda warned.

"It's okay. We can handle it. We love dogs, but Daddy won't let us get one. What good is it living in the country if you can't have a dog?" Macy shook her head in frustration. She might be the more outspoken of the two girls, but in this instance, they were both in agreement, Lacy nodding and looking up at her father.

"What I told you was, let's get settled into Hallbrook, and *then* we can reassess the situation."

"Grown-up talk for never gonna happen." Macy rolled her eyes while Lacy pouted, both obviously trying to figure out a way to budge their dad on the subject. Amanda suspected it wouldn't be long before the Thompson family had a dog. The twins would wear him down until he capitulated.

Amanda opened the door, and just as expected, Cupcake was there to greet them. "Easy, girl." She grabbed hold of the dog's collar firmly to keep her from jumping.

"She's so pretty. Cupcake's the perfect name for a brown dog with a pink collar. I love her big, brown eyes," Lacy said, petting the dog's head.

"Cupcake's a chocolate Lab," Amanda told them, while trying her best to calm the dog.

"Can Lacy and I take her for a walk? It'll be just like having our own dog. Sort of," Macy asked, kneeling next to the dog to pet her, earning a wet doggy kiss in the process.

Amanda laughed. "She's used to it just being me or my friend Jennifer taking her out and I'm not sure how she'll act. Instead, why don't you take her out in the backyard and let her romp around? I'm sure it will give her all the exercise she needs, and you can play with her." She glanced at Kevin. "It's fenced in," she offered by way of reassurance.

Kevin nodded. "Go for it."

"Yippee." The girls headed for the back door as Amanda flipped on the backyard flood lights.

"Come on, Cupcake. Let's go play," Macy called. The dog didn't have to be asked twice and happily ran after them.

"We can watch from the kitchen window if you prefer to stay inside where it's warm. This is a treat for me to have someone else take the dog out." She smiled, hoping he'd agree.

"Inside works for me, too." He grinned, following her to the kitchen. "Nice place. I love all the chair rails and crown molding. It really dates the house but in a nice way."

"Thanks. It was my mother's and it's where I grew up."

"Wow. I bet that doesn't happen often anymore." He shook his head, checking out the kitchen and inspecting the woodwork.

"Probably not. I love it here. Sometimes, it's as if I can still feel her presence. I may have to give up the bakery, but they can't take this place from me. It's paid for. My mother was adamant that no loan would ever tie up the house and its history. I've honored her wish although it hasn't been easy. I think that's what makes it more difficult when it comes to bakery. This house would be an option, but I promised. And—"

"A promise is a promise," he finished for her. Something else they had in common.

They stood next to each other by the window, Amanda all too aware of the energy between them. She wanted to ignore it, but it wasn't that easy. Not with his cologne drifting her way, the woodsy scent fresh and inviting and more than a little masculine. And then there was the man himself. The love he felt for the two girls outside shone in his eyes and lit his face with genuine emotion as he watched them play. The kids chased each other and the dog, oblivious to the cold and Cupcake was loving every minute of it.

"I remember once upon a time, playing outside like that with a dog I had as a child. Great memories. I get why you're not ready now, but you should seriously consider getting them a dog when you are. They're naturals with Cupcake, and it's a great way for kids to get exercise." No harm in trying to help the girl's cause.

"Don't let them hear you say that, or that's all I'll hear for days and weeks to come. Amanda said we should have a dog. Amanda said. Amanda said." He tried to mimic the girls' voices, and the corners of his eyes crinkled as he laughed.

"You sounded more like a parrot than your kids. But I promise not to raise their hopes or show I'm siding with them. I have enough on my plate without being responsible for your pet decisions." That wouldn't stop her from pushing the issue from behind the lines. For the girls' sake, of course. They were friends now, and friends had each other's backs.

He glanced at his watch. "We should probably get going. The skating rink closes at seven, so we need to go there before dinner."

"I'll go call the kids in." Kevin opened the back door and whistled. "Kids, let's go. Peterson's rink closes at seven."

The twins barreled through the door, followed closely by Cupcake.

"That was a blast," Macy exclaimed as she smacked her mittens together to knock the snow off them.

"It's not even cold outside when you're running around. I'm actually hot and sweaty." Lacy started to unwind her scarf.

"Leave your stuff on. You don't want to catch a chill going from hot to cold repeatedly," Kevin told them, showing off his expert parenting skills.

"Then let's go. Can we take Cupcake?" Lacy asked, Macy nodding in agreement. The adoration shining in their eyes was priceless as they petted Cupcake's head and back, the dog's tail thumping to show her mutual approval.

"I'm not sure that's a good idea," Kevin answered before she had a chance.

"Other people bring their dogs. It's a farm, not some fancy city rink," Lacy pleaded, her hand never leaving the dog as she rubbed Cupcake's head with her mitten-covered hand.

Amanda realized it was the perfect way to get out of making a fool of herself at the rink. Dog sitter and picture taker sounded a whole lot better than another skating disaster. "I'm okay with it. I'll grab her leash. We can drop her back by the house before dinner."

Kevin shrugged and shook his head. "Guess it's decided. I'm outnumbered three to one."

They headed out the front door, the girls taking Cupcake. The dog didn't have nearly the same amount of energy she'd had when they first arrived, and Amanda was positive the girls could handle her. She locked up the house while Kevin waited.

Keven placed his hand at the small of her back to guide her around the car to the passenger side, opening the door for her. It was a gesture that made her feel cherished, her racing heart seconding the emotion.

They drove to the Peterson dairy farm, where the old man set up a skating rink every year and decorated the barn for winter festivities. It was one of the ways he gave back to the community to thank the town for their support. The place was lit with pretty white lights as they twinkled against the darkening sky. At Christmas, the big evergreen tree next to the rink had been decorated with colorful balls and ribbon and a star at the top, but now, it was covered in red, white, and pink hearts. Kids and parents alike had gathered around for some local fun, despite the cold. A bonfire had been lit, and several people stood around drinking cocoa, while most of the others were on the rink or standing on the edge watching.

Which was precisely where Amanda planned to be. She walked with Kevin and the girls to the skate rental check-in booth. The girls waved at several friends they spotted from school.

"Good evening, folks. Great skate night. What sizes can I get you?" Henry asked, the jovial man always with a ready smile on his face.

"Hey, Henry. It seems busy night for a weeknight. I'll let them—" she gestured toward Kevin and the girls, "—tell you their sizes since I don't have a clue, and I'm not skating." Meeting the girls halfway meant coming with them, no one said anything about her getting on the ice.

"What do you mean you're not skating?" Lacy asked, her brow drawn tight. "You have to skate. That's why we're here."

"We're here for your birthday. Someone's got to stay with the dog, so I volunteer. It'll be more fun watching you with your dad." Amanda pulled Cupcake close as another owner and dog approached. Cupcake would want to play, and that wasn't in the cards with the crowded area.

"Maybe she's afraid," Kevin teased. He'd only gotten it half correct. It was the fear of falling and the humiliation combined she didn't want.

"You're not afraid, are you, Miss Amanda? Tell him," Macy defended her.

"I haven't skated much since I was a kid, and I'd be a bit rusty, but, no, not afraid." It was the truth. She wasn't afraid of skating. It was the falling part where the trouble started.

"What size, Amanda?" Kevin insisted. "We can take turns hanging back with Cupcake."

Judging by his grin, he more than suspected the truth and wasn't letting her off the hook easily. "Fine. Size eight, Henry."

The girls and Kevin rattled off their sizes, and Kevin pulled out his wallet to pay.

"I can get my own." She reached for her wallet.

"Tonight's my treat. You're helping the girls have a happy birthday." He pushed her hand away and laid a twenty on the counter.

Henry handed the girls their skates and grinned at Amanda. "Glad you two got that worked out. I've heard around town you been dating, and I must say—"

"We aren't dating," Amanda jumped in quickly to correct him. She glanced at the girls. Thankfully, they'd moved off to one of the benches to put on their skates and hadn't overheard.

"Well, then maybe you should be." Henry chuckled, handing Kevin his change.

"I've already got two females at home, and it's hard enough to keep up with them, what sane man would want to add another?" Kevin teased.

Henry laughed at the joke, the two drifting into their own male-testosterone space. "I hear you, brother."

Men. Amanda didn't see the humor. Women could say the same for men. Between toilet seats, cupboard doors, and picking up after themselves, men weren't a picnic all the time, either. But she'd let them have their fun because she knew from experience that guys would ramp up the teasing before letting go if someone tried to fight back.

She grabbed the skates from the counter and hurried back to the bench to put them on before she changed her mind.

"Watch us, Amanda. We love to skate." The twins took off, hobbling over to the edge of the rink before stepping onto the surface carefully. They were adorable in their matching sweaters, warm leggings, and fancy white winter hats which looked as if they could have come straight from Paris, and therefore, compliments of their mother. Lacy wore a pink sweater, of course, and Macy wore the red. Twins, and yet so unique.

"Be careful," she warned, thinking of bruised bottoms, broken bones, and cracked skulls. She shuddered to think of the dangers. The girls hadn't lied about their skating abilities. They ran into a few friends and were soon zipping around in a circle with the rest of the crowd, expertly maneuvering around slower skaters.

Everywhere she looked, people were laughing and having fun.

Kevin joined her. "You waiting on next Christmas to put those on?" He leaned in close and bumped her shoulder. "I promise I'll help you, and it'll be okay."

"I wouldn't want you to take on anything extra, you know, seeing as you're already overloaded with women."

Kevin chuckled. "We were teasing. Besides, it ended the dating conversation. Isn't that what you wanted? It's not as though he was paying any attention to your denial, whereas my comment put an end to it."

"Okay. There is that." Why did he always have to be right? At least she knew for sure they were on the same page. Even if his lack of interest wasn't flattering, it was honest.

"I'm going to skate with the girls for a bit, and then I'll get one of them to watch Cupcake. You are going to take a spin, and I'm going to help you. So put your skates on."

"I know how to skate, wise guy. And I can tie Cupcake's leash to the bench. I've a got a rug for her to sit on so she doesn't get chilled, so she'll be fine. Go on, and I'll do this when I'm ready. I'm having fun watching everyone. It's not often I get to relax and take in the flavor of the community much."

"Liar. Get up your nerve, and I'll be here." Kevin laughed as he skated away.

Nerve was exactly what she didn't have, although she had no intention of telling him. Memories of when she last skated here began spinning around in her head. Amanda shook her head, shoving the memories far into the recesses of her brain. She didn't want to think about them now.

The place was packed. Amanda glanced around, waving at several of her regular customers and saying hi to others as they walked past. Some stopped for conversation, but most were there for a purpose.

The twins waved as they flew by and Amanda marveled at how carefree they were. *Fearless.*

She knew Kevin was going to make her try, even if she preferred to sit tight and watch. There was only one thing left to do. She waited until they passed by again and then tied off Cupcake's leash. Amanda finished tightening the laces and made her way to the edge of the rink, determined to do this on her own. Memories of kids laughing at her, flooded her brain. She pushed the thoughts away, unwilling to cave to her memories.

Cupcake barked, and Amanda glanced back to make sure the dog was okay. She was yanking at her leash, trying to join Amanda, as if sensing her need. Amanda shoved one foot forward and tested the ability to move. Then the next. Again, and again.

She was skating. Maybe at a snail's pace, but she was doing it. The twins sailed past her, doing a one-eighty turn when they recognized her.

"Miss Amanda, yay!" They rewarded her efforts with happy smiles. Amanda was still getting used to the change in friendship status with the girls, although she had to admit, Cupcake had done won-ders pushing things to a whole new level.

"Here, take our hands, we'll help you." So much for everyone not finding out how pathetic she was at skating.

"Thanks, girls. You go ahead. I'm just getting a feel for it again. Next time around, will you check on Cupcake?"

"Sure thing." The two of them sailed off and joined more friends ahead.

"I won't give up so easy," Kevin spoke from behind her. She turned to answer, but the effort cost her as her feet slipped out of control.

"I've got you," he said, two strong arms coming around to help her regain her balance.

"Thanks, but I was doing fine." She grimaced.

"Not from what I saw."

"I almost fell because you startled me," Amanda insisted.

"And nothing to do with the fact you're a novice? Have you actually skated before?" Kevin asked, holding her close.

Amanda was seeing stars, but not the kind she had when she bumped her head. They were the kind you saw when it felt like the man you were with just hung the moon. She pulled back a little, trying to regain a sense of stability. *Physically and mentally*. "Yes, wise guy. I was little."

"Come on, let me help you." Kevin faced her, took her hands, and started to skate backward, helping her to glide forward.

"I look silly."

"Not to me. You look beautiful," Kevin said, his deep masculine voice rife with sincerity.

Amanda's skate tip caught on the ice. She looked up at him, unsure of how to answer. "Um, thank you, I think."

"Good answer. It was a compliment." He laughed. "Just relax. I'll lead you around and let you get a feel for what the skates can do."

It wasn't as if she had a choice, but the reality was, she appreciated him helping her. She also realized why, and it wasn't good. She was falling for Kevin, whether she wanted to or not, which could only lead to heartache for her.

All the more reason to keep her distance after tonight. But for now, she wanted to enjoy the pleasure of Kevin's company and the warmth of his laughter.

Seven o'clock arrived way too fast, and before she knew it, they'd dropped Cupcake off at her place and were headed to O'Malley's. It was a short drive but filled with chatter—twin style. Talking centered around skating and Cupcake. Her dog had always been popular with kids, and the twins showing up with her had garnered them extra attention.

After they were seated at a table and had ordered, the conversation changed to school and clothes, and afterschool activities and friends. Apparently, with twins around, there was never a shortage of subjects for discussion. It would seem grown-ups had a limited role in conversation and were merely there to confirm or deny what they were saying. It was the first time she could remember being out on a date with children.

No, not a date. Technically, this was just two friends getting together to celebrate the twins' birthday. Something she'd do well to remember. The twins might have put a temporary hiatus on their dislike of her, but if she showed any interest in Kevin whatsoever, it was sure to rile them up again. Something she preferred not to happen for their sake. The school wouldn't put up with too many antics, no matter what the situation. It would be a shame if they went too far. Tonight, she'd focus on the girls and prove to them there was nothing between her and their father.

"Miss Amanda, Dad's birthday is next week. Maybe you could teach me and Lacy how to bake, and we can make a cake. Something really cool and special."

"I didn't realize you had a birthday coming up." Amanda glanced over at Kevin.

He shrugged. "I prefer to ignore birthdays, but the girls don't seem to let the day slip past without some fanfare."

"Last year, I made him a tie. He doesn't wear it much, but sometimes he does. Although, I did notice that when he comes home, he's either not wearing it, or he's wearing a different one. I think he's trying to be nice and act as if he likes it, but I didn't do a good job."

Lacy's admission stunned Kevin, judging by the expression on his face. He'd been busted and now cornered. "That's not true, honey. Sometimes I have to take my tie off because I can't have it get near the chemicals. Other times, I change it because I don't want anything to happen to it." It was a gracious save on Kevin's part.

Lacy beamed. "Thanks, Daddy."

"Last year, I gave him a back massage. He really liked that," Macy joined in the conversation, not wanting to be left out. "I haven't decided what to do this year, but it'll have to be something pretty special. He's turning thirty and getting really old." She shook her head and frowned.

"Hasn't anyone ever told you not to tell the age of grown-ups?" Kevin asked.

"I think that rule applies after you turn fifty." Amanda winked at Macy.

"Can you help us figure something out, Miss Amanda? Maybe we can come by the bakery and talk about it after school." Lacy wasn't letting this one go. It couldn't hurt to say yes, and it's not as though making a cake would take long.

"Girls, let's just focus on your birthday tonight. Amanda's got a lot on her plate with this contest, not to mention a lot going on with her business. Let's not put her on the spot," Kevin admonished.

The twins shrugged. "Fine. We'll talk about it later." Macy winked back at Amanda.

It was her decision, and it rankled that Kevin answered for her. Did he not want them spending time together? At first, it had been understandable because the girls didn't want her around. But now? It would appear as if he were the only one who didn't want them hanging out together. Not that she didn't understand the dangers of it, but the benefits far outweighed the issues at this point. It wasn't as though she was pining for him.

They finished dinner, and Kevin graciously picked up the tab, refusing to allow Amanda to even leave the tip. Quite a few people had stopped by the table to talk to her, and there had been more than a few raised eyebrows at her dinner companions. By tomorrow, town gossips would have them marching down the wedding aisle.

Kevin drove to the movie theater, but they were surprised to see the place dark and no one around.

"It looks closed," Amanda reported. That didn't happen often. Around here, the movie theater was an iconic place that kept its doors open and was a great source for family entertainment.

"Let me check out the sign on the door," Kevin offered, putting the vehicle in park. He made his way to the front door, read the sign, and returned just as quick. "Frozen water pipes. They might not be open for days. Sorry, girls."

"That stinks!" Macy groaned.

"We could go back to the house and play games," Lacy suggested.

"Yeah! Games will be fun. Like charades," Macy quickly fell in step with her sister.

"I'm sure Amanda doesn't want to come back and play games." Was he hoping she'd say no? After all, she was the fourth wheel in their family circle.

"Please, Miss Amanda. It's still our birthday celebration, and you said yes earlier. You can't just go home in the middle of the party." It seemed Macy wasn't above using any tactic she thought would work.

"Sure. Sounds like fun." All she had to do was keep remembering this was for the twins—just to keep her head straight.

Amanda caught Kevin's surprised expression and flashed a grin in his direction. When they arrived back at his house, the twins bounded out of the car, eager to get the next stage of their special night started.

Once inside, Amanda and Kevin made hot chocolate while the girls picked out a game and set it up. She handed the twins their mugs, each one topped with marshmallows.

"You didn't add vinegar, did you?" Macy joked.

"Hardly. I'm not mischievous like two young girls I know," Amanda teased. The setup in the living room was cozy. *Family-ish.*

"*Hmmm.* This is yummy," Lacy said, as she tried to pick a marshmallow off the top.

"Okay, so we are going to play charades, and it's you two against us. The rules are that you have to act out something on the card you pick and see if your partner can guess it. There's no talking, but everything else is fair play." Macy looked pointedly at Amanda. "Any questions?"

"Did you pick this game because you two know everything about each other and know you're going to win?" She couldn't help but tease them. Adults against kids was always a family favorite, or it had been until her dad had left to play family somewhere else. The games had ended then, and she hadn't played since.

"Maybe. But it's fun to see grown-ups try. And we never have two grownups here anymore, so we never get to play charades. And it's one of our favorite games." Lacy was shuffling the cards and placed them in two stacks.

"Let the games begin," Kevin said, waving his arms in a grand gesture. "I hope you're better at acting than you are cooking beef Wellington." He winked at Amanda as he sat down beside her on the sofa.

"Haha. Old news and worn-out teasing, especially given it's been established it wasn't my fault. Let's just hope you can act, and that you're smart enough to guess right. Geeky chemistry teachers don't strike me as the acting type."

"Ouch." Kevin's pretend surprise at her put-down made her laugh. So far, there was nothing geeky about the man, but he didn't need to know that.

"We get to go first because it's our birthday," Macy announced. She jumped up and went to the front of the room and drew a card. She glanced at her sister and scrunched up her face.

"Hey, no early signals. Not until the clock is started." Kevin was quick to call them out for a rule violation. "They are good at this game and don't need special treatment, birthday or otherwise." He chuckled.

"Sorry." Macy didn't seem all that sorry, her Cheshire-cat grin making it look more as if she was pleased with herself.

Kevin flipped the timer, and Macy went into acting mode. She scrunched up her face again and then acted like a bird flying through the air.

"*A Wrinkle in Time,*" Lacy shouted, jumping up, positive she had it right.

"Yes!" Macy high fived her sister.

Kevin hit the timer button, stopping it.

"And we get five bonus points because we did it in under ten seconds." Macy pointed at the clock.

"I don't remember hearing about that rule before we started to play," Amanda quipped. "Are you making that up?"

Kevin shook his head and laughed. "Technically, it's a rule we added. House rule. But Lacy got that one faster because of Macy's early start giving out a clue. But we'll give you this one as a birthday special. And since Amanda thinks she's a great actress, I'll let her take the stage first." Kevin sat back, content to letting her make a fool of herself first more than likely.

"No pressure. Just a bit of advice, Miss Amanda. Remember, you're dealing with the science geek." Macy laughed as she took her seat.

Amanda looked at her card. *Sleeping Beauty* was the easiest one on the card, and Amanda was sure even Kevin could get it.

"Ready?" Lacy asked.

Amanda nodded, and Macy started the timer.

Lifting her arms, she danced around the room as if she was dancing with a prince, closing her eyes as she twirled when space permitted, aiming for the dreamy touch.

"*Shall We Dance*," Kevin shouted.

Amanda opened her eyes to glare at Kevin and shake her head. It was actually a good guess, but it wasn't the one she wanted. She laid down on the floor and placed her hands on her chest and closed her eyes.

"*Romeo and Juliet*," Kevin exclaimed. Amanda shook her head as she rolled to her knees and pretended to wrap her arms around a human form on the ground and lowered her head for a magical kiss.

"Dad, it's a kid's game," Lacy shook her head and giggled.

Amanda shot her a look of gratitude.

"*Cinderella. Beauty and the Beast*. How do I know?" Kevin remarked, exasperated at this point.

"Five seconds," Macy jumped up and started doing a victory dance.

Amanda stood and acted as though she poked her finger and fainted.

"Time," Lacy called out.

"*Sleeping Beauty*." Kevin jumped to his feet; positive he'd gotten it right.

"Too late," Macy reminded him, pointing at the clock.

Amanda shook her head and looked at the girls. "I see what you mean, it's not easy working with the scientist."

"What was all that gyration where you were on the ground trying to lift something up. I thought it might be Belle trying to raise the Beast." Kevin was intent on justifying his guesses, and Amanda couldn't help but laugh.

"It was the prince delivering a magical kiss. I had just played the role of the princess lying there asleep under the spell. The natural jump should have been to the prince awakening her," Amanda explained as if it all made perfect sense. It wasn't her fault Kevin didn't know Disney movies inside and out the way the girls did.

"I guess I don't have much experience with magical kisses." He smirked, sitting back to take another sip of chocolate.

Amanda had to laugh. She'd cut him some slack on that one because she'd never experienced a magical kiss, either. They were even on that score.

The rest of the evening played out in almost the same way. The girls won far more often than the grown-ups, although Amanda was sure her partner was giving them an extra birthday edge.

And she didn't mind at all. It made him seem all that much sweeter to her. Kevin Thompson was one of the good guys. A guy who would put others ahead of himself, even in competition. For him, it wasn't about winning, it was about loving.

Chapter Twelve

♥

KEVIN TOOK ADVANTAGE OF his short school day and headed for the Sweeter Side of Life to see Amanda. Last night had been fun, more fun than he'd expected. Although, to be fair, he'd never envisioned Amanda out with them in the first place. Whatever she'd put in the cupcakes for the girls must've had some sort of kindness magic, because the change in the twins was nothing short of amazing.

The only problem was if Victoria found out, but short of outright telling the girls not to say anything, he wasn't sure how to prevent it. And telling the girls would require an explanation he wasn't prepared to give.

He pushed open the front door, the bell jingling above his head. Amanda glanced his way, her smile filling him with warmth. "Hey, there. Thought I'd stop in and grab a pastry and coffee, and to say thanks for last night. The girls slept like a rock and I had a hard time getting them up for school this morning."

"I know the twins cornered you and you felt obligated to let me tag along, but I hope it wasn't too bad. I'm sure you wanted to enjoy the time with them alone."

"No, not at all. It was shocking, yes, but after I realized the sincerity of the offer, I relaxed and truly enjoyed the evening. Those two were hysterical." After they'd gone to bed, he'd replayed the evening in his head. He couldn't have imagined their birthday celebration being any better, and he owed it all to Amanda. Heck, before she'd shown up at his doorstep, Macy had barely been on speaking terms with him.

"It was fun, and they are great girls. Cupcake will be looking for her playmates today, I'm sure." Amanda came around the corner and handed him a cup of coffee and a plate with a pastry. "On the house. You went overboard paying for everything last night. This is called a lemon chiffon scone."

It wasn't his normal jelly-filled danish, but he'd try it. "Thanks. Honestly, it was the least I could do. You were such a good sport about everything—even skating."

"*Ugh*. I hurt in places I didn't even know I had this morning."

"Take a hot bath when you get home. You'll be fine."

"And you're an expert on this why?" The timer went off on the oven, and she moved back behind the counter to turn it off.

"Because it's the same thing I tell the girls for every ache and ailment they have, and it seems to work. Must be something medicinal in the heat and bath oils, I reckon. Speaking of medicinal, I want to know what you put in the cupcakes." He chuckled. "I need to invest in whatever ingredient it is. Better still, if you have a magic recipe, I can invest in that."

"Invest away, my friend. Throw money my way, and I'll tell you anything you want to know." The tinkling of her laughter was genuine and a sound he would never grow tired off.

"Your timing is perfect. I just finished baking the vinegar cake—if you can believe it."

"I can't. The way I see it, no baker in their right mind would add vinegar. Even the name sounds unappetizing." Sometimes it was better not to know the ingredients.

"Well, you're partially right." She grabbed a potholder and took the cake out of the oven.

"What do you mean?" Kevin leaned back against the counter to watch her work.

"I did some research after I got home last night while I was trying to unwind. I discovered that back in the Great Depression when there was a shortage of eggs, butter, and milk, people used vinegar. I've never heard of such a thing and don't recall my mother ever mentioning it. I looked through my grandmother's recipes again and you'll never guess what I found. There was a notation next to one of her cake recipes that mentioned using vinegar. My mother must've seen that and used it in the chocolate cake recipe."

"That's crazy. I don't understand it, but some things don't need to be understood. Like why chocolate cake tastes so delicious. Telling me there's vinegar in it could ruin it forever."

"Well, you're just in time to be able to tell me. Give it twenty minutes to cool off, and I'll put the caramel and nuts on it. Hopefully, you can stick around and do a taste test, since you're a chocolate lover."

He glanced at his watch. "I've got time. The girls get out at three. The high school had an early-release day. I still can't believe you're not a chocolate connoisseur and you're entering a chocolate contest."

"Me, too. My mother loved chocolate." A tender smile crossed her face as if she were recalling a fond memory. There was an inner peace within Amanda that drew him to her warm spirit.

"You must get your ambivalence toward it from your father then. It's not normal." He grinned and then took a bite of the scone.

Amanda's smiled disappeared. "I wouldn't know. He left when I was eight and never really spent any time with me after that. He had a new family to deal with. Pretty young wife and new children."

"I'm sorry to hear that." He'd give anything to take back the comment and for her warm smile to return.

"Don't be. I'm over it. And it gave me the chance to spend a lot of quality time with my mother. Time I wouldn't have had if he'd stayed in the picture and continued to make her unhappy." Amanda shrugged, shooting him a pointed look. She always had a way of looking on the bright side, something else he admired about her.

"Are you trying to tell me something?"

"Only if you're listening." She flashed him a smile and returned to stirring the caramel heating on the stove.

"I am." Kevin made the connection and knew she was right, but sometimes, like when the girls were acting up, he regretted the impact the divorce seemed to have on them.

"Good. It's important for the girls that you understand, sometimes people being apart is better than them being together. It doesn't make any sense, especially to the kids at first. But soon, they'll understand, and they'll appreciate the decision you made. Don't get me wrong, it broke my heart when my dad chose another family over my mom and me, but it was his choice. And I'm not going to let my happiness rest in his hands. I moved on."

She crossed the short distance to his side and laid her arm on his. "The twins will need to do the same. It's something they will eventually figure out on their own. At least for them, their mother is still in the picture. And that, more than anything, can be quite a healer when they're ready to accept the situation."

He shook his head. She was wrong, but then she didn't have all the information. "There's just so much they don't know, and if they did, it would crush them. How is that fair? As they get older, I prefer they were kept in the dark."

"I'm sure my mother did plenty to protect me from the reality of life. But the older we get, the more we see and understand without being told." Amanda moved back to the counter, flipped the cake over on the cooling rack, and continued to stir the caramel. "I take it from the twins' reaction to the idea of us dating that you don't date much?"

Kevin was suddenly alert. The conversation had taken a turn he hadn't expected. "Not at all. By choice. I'd rather stay focused on the girls." Not to mention, his promise to Victoria.

"But that doesn't help the girls to grow and understand real relationships. They get that by watching you. So far, all they have is divorce as a guideline, and that's not healthy."

"I guess that's for me to decide." The arrangement he had with his ex-wife was odd, but it worked for him. He'd do anything to protect the girls from an unstable childhood, and if it meant not dating, then he wouldn't date. Amanda didn't understand why he thought it was better to just play along with his ex-wife's rules. But the idea of the twins going back and forth to Paris with a mother who was more concerned for her own welfare wasn't anything he wanted for them. Young girls lost in the big city. What if they got caught up in the glitz and glamour, the same way as his ex-wife? He didn't want that life for them.

She nodded, a faraway expression in her eyes. "Touché. You're right. I just wish my mom had started dating again. Maybe then I wouldn't be so cynical when it comes to men and relationships." Amanda flipped off the burner and pushed the pan to the center of the stove.

"You? Cynical? I don't see that." Amanda's determination to succeed would outweigh any cynicism she could begin to muster.

"You wouldn't. I've had years to practice hiding it." Amanda drizzled the caramel on top of the cake, scattering the nuts across the surface in a circular motion. I'll cut you a piece now while it's still warm. Fingers crossed."

Kevin reached for the plate she handed him, their hands touching. Mesmerized, he gazed into her eyes. He knew her well, even if she didn't see what the world saw. Amanda was loving, warm, kind, and gave of herself to everyone she knew.

He took a bite of the cake. Perfection. Amanda was back on track with the award-winning recipe she needed for the contest. "Fantastic. I can't believe it. Even knowing it has vinegar doesn't ruin it for me," he teased, trying to ease the moment between them.

"Great. Even I can tell the difference." Amanda twirled around and grabbed the recipe off the counter, waving it in the air. "I've got the golden recipe!" She threw her arms around his neck, hugging him.

The light in her eyes as she pulled back and gazed up at him made Kevin want to hold her tight and not let her go. He loved the blush that tinged her cheeks as she realized what she'd done.

"Thank you. I can't wait to tell the girls. I'd like to name it Chocolate LaMa Cake honoring the twins. What do you think?"

"Llama?" It sounded worse than vinegar cake. The woman could cook, but she was terrible at names.

Amanda scrunched up her face, looking at him like he was short a few screws. "Oh, I get it. Llama. No, not the animal. The first letters of Lacy and Macy. LA and MA. Get it?"

She still hadn't moved away, and her mouth was proving to be a greater distraction than he planned. "I think you better stick to cooking and leave the naming to someone else. I'm not sure anyone's going to vote for Llama Cake, no matter how you spell it." He chuckled, trying to diffuse the ever-growing temptation to kiss her.

Amanda took another bite of cake, his gaze never leaving her mouth. He brushed a piece of chocolate from the corner of her lips with his thumb. Unable to stop himself, he lowered his head and kissed her.

The shrill tones of a phone ringing sliced through the air. They stepped apart quickly, like two teenagers caught necking in the locker room. "I'm sorry. I shouldn't have done that."

"I'm not." Amanda's fingers lay pressed to her lips as she stared at him, wide-eyed and confused. The loud ringing demanded attention and Amanda grabbed the phone off the counter. She moved away as she spoke, her back to him, her hushed tones barely audible. A minute passed before she turned back to face him, her eyes wide, her face ashen white, the phone still stuck to ear. "Hang tight, Grandpa. I'll be right there."

She hung up the phone and slid it in her pocket. "I've got to go. Grandpa's not feeling well. He never fusses, so I'm worried. He looked under the weather this week but kept insisting he was fine. I should have spent more time over there other than just dropping off food occasionally, but I've been so busy trying to hold everything together."

"Is there anything I can do?" Kevin helped her with her coat.

"I walked here. Is there any way you can drop me at his place? I can walk home after if everything is okay."

"Or you could call me, and I'll come pick you up when you're ready to go home." It would be dark and cold and was unnecessary for her to be out walking alone. Hallbrook might not be the city, but he still valued safety.

"Really? No, that would be hard with the girls, but it's sweet of you to offer." She shook her head and headed for the back room and started turning off lights.

"I tell you what, send me home with three pieces of cake for dessert tonight, and I'll take you any-where you want to go and pick you up and take you home. Deal?"

Amanda hesitated a second. "Deal. Can you finish getting the lights while I box it up?"

"Sure thing." Amanda didn't like to be a burden to anyone but this way, they were even and both happy with the outcome.

"I'll use the rest of this to test on the customers tomorrow to make sure you really are a choco-late connoisseur and not just someone wanting free desserts."

He chuckled. "Guess you'll find out which one. Until then, shall we go?"

"Yes." They walked out the front door, Amanda flipping the sign to closed and locking up behind them.

The moment between them had passed, but the memory of the kiss was still very much in his brain. It had been a moment of madness, the phone saving him from making a huge mistake. "No problem. We seem to be helping each other out quite a bit lately."

It wasn't long before they were in the car and he drove her to her grandfather's house, Amanda giving him the directions turn by turn. He pulled into the driveway of an older stately brick house, the place well-kept and the landscaping pristine. He'd noticed a lot of people in Hallbrook took pride in their homes and the community.

"Hope your grandfather is doing okay. And don't forget our deal. Give me a call, and I'll come to take you home. And if you need me to take care of Cupcake, just say the word. I'm sure I've got two babysitters for you that would be more than happy to help."

"You really are a nice man. Thank you." Her hand lay on his shoulder as she spoke, and Kevin found himself torn with the desire to kiss her goodbye.

Something I shouldn't do. He forced himself not to move.

Amanda slid out of the car and waved goodbye, Kevin watching until she was safely inside. He backed out of the driveway and headed down the street, the kiss forefront on his brain. *More like how much he wanted a second one.*

Dangerous territory for a man who stood to lose everything. He couldn't afford to jeopardize his custody of the girls, which meant no relationships, not even the appearance of one. Which is exactly what everyone would think if they'd seen the two of them together last night and today.

He needed to stay away from Amanda Tillman. She was a threat to his heart and his family.

Chapter Thirteen

♥

"GRANDPA? WHERE ARE YOU?" Amanda rushed through the front door and into the living room. Not seeing her grandfather, she ran to the kitchen. Still no sign of him. She started up the stairs, her adrenaline spiking when he didn't answer, fear forming a lump in her throat. Amanda was all the family her grandfather had left. It was her job to take care of him. She owed that much to her mother's sweet memory.

"Grandpa?"

"I'm right here. Quit your hollering." At the sound of his voice, she breathed a sigh of relief.

Amanda met him at the top of the stairs. "What are you doing up here? I thought you said you didn't feel well, and you'd wait for me on the sofa and not overdo things until I could check on you." His color looked a little off. She felt the top of his forehead to see if he was feverish.

"I've felt better. I'm a grown man and can make my own decisions." He pulled back when she started to roll up his sleeve.

"I just want to take your pulse, for heaven's sake. So, you're not having any chest pains now, and you don't feel lightheaded? I still think you should've called an ambulance and let the hospital check you out." They walked backed down the stairs, Amanda keeping a close eye on the stubborn mule.

"And I told you that you're worrying too much. It's just a case of indigestion. For all I know, it's the cheesy pasta casserole you dropped off last night. I ate it for lunch. Maybe it's your cooking that's the problem." He chuckled.

Amanda didn't laugh. "Now's not the time to joke about things like that. This could have been serious. And you need to pay attention, especially at your age."

"*Humph.* I'm in good shape for a man my age, so quit acting like a mother hen. I appreciate you coming over to check on me. You're a sweet girl, Amanda, but I only called you as a precaution, because I'm being careful. The ambulance would have been overkill. I'm not senile yet, young lady. Now that you've seen for yourself that I'm fine, I'm sure you can find better things to do." He sat in his recliner and picked up the newspaper.

"You know I'd rather be here with you or at the bakery. And I've been at the bakery all day, so you're the lucky winner of my time." She'd loved every minute with her grandpa when she was growing up, and that hadn't changed. He'd been the only male role model in her life after her father left.

"You're just sticking around to keep an eye on me. You can't fool an old man." He shook his head and chuckled.

"Or maybe, I fancy beating you at checkers," she teased, relieved his sense of humor had returned. He really *was* okay.

"Once in a while, you get lucky, but I don't think tonight's going to be your night."

"If you're sure you're okay, I'll set up the game and grab us some water."

"Fine. If you don't mind losing, I don't mind beating you." He grinned.

They spent the next couple of hours playing checkers, and true to his word, Grandpa trumped her every time. Checkers had never been Amanda's game, not like her mother. Her mother used to enjoy beating Grandpa regularly. Which is probably why he enjoyed beating Amanda even more.

Satisfied he was okay, Amanda felt it was safe to go home. Other than a couple of yawns, he looked just fine.

"How will you get home tonight? I saw who dropped you off through my bedroom window." He eyed her with curiosity.

"I was supposed to call Kevin, but I'm thinking it's too late for that, what with him having the girls at home to deal with. I think I'll walk home." It would be cold, but far more practical, all things considered. Kevin's kiss had befuddled her brain into agreeing to his deal, but now that she'd had time to think about it, she realized her mistake.

"If the man's expecting your call, you should call him. And how come you haven't told me much about this new beau of yours? I've had to hear about him from the neighbors."

"Because he's not my new beau." Hallbrook's gossip chain was alive and well, even if misinformed.

"That's not what I hear and trust me, I've heard plenty."

"The town gossips have it wrong, go fancy that. They are usually quick to judge what they see and slow to get the facts." Amanda shook her head and stood, easing into her coat.

"Seems like a right nice young fellow. A girl could do a whole lot worse."

"Gee, thanks, Grandpa. When I go husband-hunting, you'll be the first to know," she joked, pulling on her hat and scarf.

"Well, you're not getting any younger. You can't let that last jerk you dated ruin the rest of your life. Call your young man. Be brave. See what happens."

"It's my love life, and you need to mind your own business." It wasn't often Grandpa interfered, and she preferred to keep it that way.

"That's a two-way street, sweetheart. You let me take care of my health, and I'll let you take care of your own love life. I reckon I'm doing a whole lot better job on my end than you are."

"That may be, but it is still my life." Grandpa didn't know that she'd already given Kevin way more thought than was necessary after his kiss. Talk about confusing. She'd be a fool to forget that he'd told her he didn't date. Letting her heart get involved would be a huge mistake.

Halfway to the house, Amanda was second-guessing her desire not to call Kevin. It was far too cold to be walking outside, the chilly wind whipping right through her winter coat. There was no turning back now, and the sooner she got home, the sooner she could let Cupcake outside.

Think of anything but the cold. Or Kevin.

What she needed was a name for the cake recipe. Kevin was right, LaMa Cake did have a certain ick factor to it.

Kevin glanced at his watch, wondering what was keeping Amanda. He was tempted to call her but resisted the urge. He didn't want to give her the wrong idea. If she needed him, she'd call. Otherwise, whatever was happening was none of his business, other than saying a prayer for the man who Amanda clearly held dear in her heart.

"Daddy, we had a blast last night with Amanda. You're right, she's pretty cool. You should ask her if she wants to watch a movie with us tonight." Lacy edged closer to him, a soft smile on her face as she looked up at him in earnest.

Kevin was beginning to think he'd never understand the makings of the female mind. "I got the impression you two weren't keen on her hanging out here. Around me. I thought maybe your birthday was just a one-time deal."

"Oh, Daddy, we're allowed to change our minds about people when we get to know them," Lacy said, shaking her head as if at loss to understand why he was having a hard time keeping up the changes.

"She makes things fun," Macy added, joining in the conversation.

"And I'd love for her to teach me how to bake." Lacy smiled. "Please, Daddy, ask her."

The girls were impressionable, and Amanda had already managed to leave a huge one on them. It didn't matter that the twins had been the ones to beg Amanda to join in their birthday fun, it would still cause trouble with Victoria.

"I'm glad you both have an open mind and that you like her, but nothing has changed between she and I. We are friends—nothing more, the same as I've been telling you all along." A friend he'd kissed, but only once. There'd be no repeat performance if he could help it. "And living here all her life and running the bakery, she has lots of other people she needs to spend time with. Tonight, she's at her grandfather's house. He's not feeling well."

"Oh, that stinks. Maybe I'll draw a card for her grandfather." Lacy was a sweet girl with a gi-ant-sized heart. *Just like Amanda.*

"I'm sure she would really appreciate it. In fact, I'm waiting for her to call me. I'm supposed to pick her up at her grandfather's and give her a ride home. I dropped her off at his house earlier." It was more than he should have told them. He was doing a lousy job at keeping the two worlds separate.

"Cool. That was nice. Did Miss Amanda try the new recipe yet?" Macy asked, eyeing him with in-terest.

"In fact, she did. And vinegar was exactly what the cake needed, believe it or not. She told me to tell you both thank you very much. I even brought home some of the new cake for our dessert tonight."

"Maybe we could skip dinner and go straight to dessert," Macy offered.

His chocoholic daughter was thinking along the same lines as he was but being the parent in charge meant he couldn't give in to those wants and still set a good example. "I don't think so. Dinner first, and make sure your homework is done." The latter was an afterthought, but if it worked, he was all for it.

"She's going to win the contest. I just know it. Her cake is the best thing ever." The adoration in Lacy's voice was shocking.

"Amanda considered naming the recipe after the two of you, but I convinced her otherwise, or at least, I hope I convinced her not to use the one she was planning to submit." Kevin shook his head, recalling the conversation.

"Why would you do that? That would be totally awesome," Macy exclaimed.

"You haven't heard her idea. Chocolate Llama Cake. I don't think that sounds any better than Vinegar Cake."

The girls giggled. "I get it. Lacy and Macy. La and Ma. It's funny, but you're right, Llama Cake sounds kind of yucky." He couldn't believe the girls figured it without so much as a hint.

"It was great of her to think of us, and it would've been cool," Lacy added.

"I agree. But no matter what Amanda names it, I'm placing my bets on her winning."

"Do you like her, Daddy?" Macy asked.

He gazed at his daughter as he considered his answer. "I do. As a friend. She's one of the kindest, sweetest, most giving people I've ever met. It seems she takes care of everybody, putting them before herself. I think that's why I wanted to help her so much with trying to save her bakery."

"So I guess you *like* like her. Does she *like* like you?" Lacy asked. The innocence of the question caught him off guard. There was apparently a big difference between like, and *like* like, but it was nothing he would admit to the girls. The price would be too high if his ex-wife got wind he might have feelings for a woman.

"What's with the twenty questions about Amanda and me? I intend to stay focused on you two, and that's a full-time job. I don't have room for a relationship, so don't even start thinking that way."

"Oh, Daddy, we're not *that* difficult," Macy said, rebutting his comment.

"Walk in my shoes a few days, and you'll see what I mean." He winked, reaching over to tickle Macy. Lacy jumped on top of them both, and an all-out tickle session ensued. It was one game he always came out the winner, but he also knew when to call a halt.

"That's enough. We need to settle down and think about getting dinner. Who's up for pizza?"

"I think you should ask her out." So much for his change-in-subject tactic.

The girls were like bulls, pushing him in a direction he knew better than to go. "Where is this coming from?"

The twins glanced at each other and shrugged before turning back to him. "Mom has a boyfriend. She told us on the phone yesterday when she called." Macy frowned.

The news was quite a shock, but it didn't change anything. A boyfriend didn't stop her from filing for joint custody. "Is that why you asked Amanda to come with us last night?" Things were suddenly starting to fall in place.

Lacy shrugged. "Sort of. I mean, we loved Amanda's cupcakes, and it totally rocks she notices us for who we are and not just as twins. She's pretty, and we think you might like her, even though you won't admit it. We thought if you had a girlfriend, it would be better when you found out about Mom."

"Not to mention, we love Cupcake. If you hook up with Amanda, we get a dog." Macy grinned.

Kevin shook his head and laughed. Maybe it was time to get the twins their own pet, because dating a woman for hers, didn't seem right. It was time to rein in the girls and their fanciful notions. "A dog is not a reason to date someone and what do you know about hooking up? Never mind, I'm not sure I want to hear the answer. Please tell me we don't need to have a talk about the birds and the bees yet, you just turned eleven."

"Good grief." Macy rolled her eyes. "Spare us the sex lecture. This isn't the dark ages, and we hear plenty at school and don't need to hear it from our dad. Yuk." Macy grimaced.

Kevin wasn't sure if they heard about it in class or from friends, but either way he wasn't happy. It wasn't a subject he relished addressing with them either, so they agreed on that score. This sounded like a conversation Victoria needed to have with the twins. "Fine. As to a girlfriend, I don't need one, so you can get the idea right out of your head. I have you two as my sweethearts, and that's all I need." He moved to hug them, daunted by the idea they were growing up too fast.

"Yes, but we won't be living here forever. Lacy and I finally realize you and Mom aren't getting back together, and we want you to be happy, too."

Kevin smiled. He was blessed beyond belief, and it was moments like these, he knew why he'd give up everything to keep the twins happy and give them a stable life. "I am happy. I like things just the way they are. Let's order pizza, I'm hungry."

"What about Amanda?"

"She may have already made other arrangements to get home." Amanda's determination came with a dose of stubborn, and he wouldn't put it past her to walk home anyway, no matter what deal they made.

"Just think about what we said." Macy sounded far older than her eleven years at that moment.

"Okay." He stood and left the room, ending the discussion. Maybe he'd think about it in seven years when the girls went off to college. Until then, it would serve no purpose.

Chapter Fourteen

♥

AMANDA WAS GRATEFUL TODAY was one of the days Diana helped in the bakery. The handful of customers who came this morning loved the free samples of chocolate cake she'd offered. Their reactions were exactly what she needed, giving her the confidence to move forward with the contest.

"Give me a few minutes, Cupcake, and I'll be finished. We can go for a walk to the park, I promise." Amanda pulled up the website, typed in the information they needed and attached a copy of her recipe. In recognition of the girls' contribution to the success, she'd named the dessert "Twin Delight Chocolate Cake." Contrary to Kevin's opinion, she did come up with a great name after she'd had more time to think about it.

She pressed send and sat back in her chair, letting out a sigh of relief. Now all she could do was wait—and pray. Cupcake nudged her leg with her nose. "Okay, okay. I'm done."

It was a beautiful sunny day; the temperatures having risen into the forties. A jacket, mittens, and a knit cap were all she needed with her warm boots. Cupcake pulled her along, eager to get to the park. Halfway there, her phone rang. "Hold up, girl." Amanda pulled back on the leash, placing it between her knees to free up her hands. She yanked a mitten off and fished the ringing phone from the depths of the quilted pocket.

The sun glinted off the screen, and she couldn't see the name or number of the caller. "Hello," she answered, grabbing the leash once again and setting off toward the park.

"Hi there. It's Kevin." Of course, it was Kevin, she'd know his voice anywhere.

"What's up? Are the girls okay?" Staying focused on the twins was the easiest way to keep whatever was happening between them at bay. She enjoyed his kiss far too much, but he hadn't said another word about it. His apology still rankled.

"They're fine. I just thought we should talk. Just the two of us."

"What did you have in mind? Do you want to meet me at the bakery tomorrow? Or you could come to my place tonight." Probably not the best of suggestions, but it would be quiet.

"I was thinking more along the lines of dinner. Out of town. I don't want to give the girls any ideas or confuse them. Or give the gossips more than they can handle," he added. She could picture him grinning on the other end of the phone, his lack of love for the town gossip chain well known.

The mention of dinner made her heart race, but just as quickly, it came to a screeching halt. Dinner wouldn't just confuse the girls, it would confuse her, and she was confused enough at this point. The last thing she needed to do was put herself at risk of falling for Kevin harder than she already was. "I don't know. Like you mentioned, it's confusing to the girls. Maybe we should leave things the way they are now."

"One dinner won't hurt, and I really need to talk to you. The girls are at a friend's house working on a project and for a sleepover, so I'm free tonight.

Please, say yes." The sincerity in his voice left her considering her options.

Amanda wanted to say no, but the word wouldn't come. Instead, Grandpa's words flitted through her head, filling her with what would undoubtedly end up in misplaced hope. "If you think it's a good idea, that's fine. Just two friends having dinner. Right?"

"Right. Can I pick you up in thirty minutes?"

"Make it an hour, and you've got yourself a date. I mean, you've got yourself a dinner companion." *Idiot.* Her mouth seemed to have no filter. But either way, date or dinner companion, she needed the extra time to get ready. She turned Cupcake loose in the park, keeping a close eye on her.

"An hour it is then. See you soon."

"Wait," Amanda called out, trying to catch him before he hung up. She was curious where they were going considering it greatly affected what she'd choose to wear.

Silence greeted her on the other end. She'd pick something halfway between comfortable and casual to be on the safe side. Twenty minutes later, Cupcake was worn out and lying on her bed, while Amanda tried to find the perfect outfit for the impromptu evening planned with Kevin. She couldn't help the excitement filling her as the minutes ticked down, the memory of his kiss responsible for her racing heart.

After choosing her traditional black slacks, she vetoed the cutesy blue sweater, opting instead for a cream-colored blouse and a black string of pearls. Unfortunately, she'd have to settle for her calf-high, flat heeled, black boots instead of dress heels. Kevin was a lot taller than her, and the heels would've evened them out a bit, but comfort and safety were far more important on a winter night.

Her phone beeped, indicating a message had arrived.

Kevin: "Made reservations at a place out of town. See you soon."

Reservations being the operative phrase. At least she'd chosen a dressy outfit, so it wouldn't matter where they went.

Amanda: "Okay."

Amanda applied her makeup and then stepped back to observe her reflection in the mirror. Satisfied with her appearance, she headed downstairs, Cupcake close on her heels looking for her dinner now that she'd recovered from the park outing.

Kevin pulled into the driveway promptly at six-thirty. Amanda headed outside, locking up before she made her way to the car. It wasn't a date, and she didn't expect him to come to the front door for her. That would be awkward between friends.

He stepped out of the car and met her on the sidewalk. "Hi there. You look wonderful. Thanks for agreeing to come out with me." He leaned forward, his lips grazing the side of her cheek.

"Thanks for the invite. I'm always game for a free dinner," she teased. His lips had felt warm and tender against her cheek, reminding her once again of her grandpa's words. Maybe Kevin was interested in taking their friendship to the next level, and she was getting his message all wrong. Maybe he just wanted to take things slowly and see where the relationship would go before the twins were involved.

Her breath hitched at the possibilities. The question was, could she handle it? Part of her already knew the answer was yes. Kevin was different, and no matter how hard she tried to fight what was happening between them, every step of the way just seemed to bring them together and move her heart forward.

Kevin walked her around the car and opened the door to help her inside, before making his way back around the vehicle and sliding into the driver's seat. "It looks as if this place we're going is in Lancaster based on where you're headed."

"Good observation." He turned to smile at her but didn't elaborate.

"So, where *are* we going?" Amanda was more than curious.

"You'll see. It's a fabulous place I found recently. I'm sure you already know about it having lived here all your life, but I thought it rather quaint. A great place for us to be able to talk privately."

"That leaves quite a few possibilities." There were tons of restaurants in Lancaster, and it would be interesting to see what type of place appealed to Kevin. The conversation drifted to Grandpa, and Amanda filled him in. There was nothing to tell really, just a case of indigestion.

Kevin talked about the twins and the project they'd been assigned at school. They were acting like a normal couple out to dinner after a day at work, other than the fact his hand remained inches away but never strayed in her direction. Close enough for her to be aware, far enough for her to know he wasn't ready to make the leap. More reason to keep her mouth shut and not heed grandpa's advice. Open honesty might have worked for him and grandma, but times had changed. Things were more complicated than they were fifty years ago.

As they turned through the streets of the city, an uneasy feeling settled in the pit of her stomach. Minutes ticked by, and with each turn, her adrenaline level surged higher. She gripped the handle of the door tightly, memories of another time and place haunting her.

With all the restaurants to choose from in Lancaster, there was no way he'd manage to pick the one place she didn't want to go.

Wrong.

Kevin backed into one of the parking spots allocated to the Table Divine, an exclusive French restaurant noted for its fine food, excellent service, and quiet privacy.

Unfortunately, it was the same place her ex-boyfriend promised to take her for Valentine's Day two years ago. The same place she'd tried to meet up with him to apologize for not putting him first on Valentine's Day, only to discover he'd already had another date. She'd been a fool to chase after him, hoping to salvage their relationship.

"Have you ever been here? Is this okay?" Kevin turned to face her.

She looked away, not wanting him to guess the truth. Because that would require an explanation, something she didn't want to give. "I'm not sure. I've been here once, but never actually eaten here."

"You seem tense. Is this a bad choice? We can go somewhere else." Kevin had zeroed in on her tension and was sweet for offering, his consideration of her feelings making her even more aware of what a great guy he was.

"No. You picked this out, and it will be fine." At least, Amanda hoped it would be. For her, it was a chance to lay the past to rest. Maybe this is exactly what she needed to forget Greg and his treachery, to quit letting it control her life. But it could also be a sign that this whole thing with Kevin wasn't right.

"If you're sure," he said hesitantly. "Sit tight, and I'll get your door."

Kevin came around the front of the car and opened her door. She appreciated the simple gesture of respect. He took her hand as he helped her out, tucking it inside his own as they walked toward the restaurant. Holding the door open, he stepped back to let her pass through first. Kevin approached the maître d'.

"I have a reservation for two. Name's Kevin Thompson."

"Yes, Mr. Thompson. I've got you right here. Follow me, please."

Kevin kept his hand against the small of her back as they followed the man through the restaurant. Even through the material of her coat, she enjoyed the possessiveness of the gesture. Amanda was all for independence, but there was nothing wrong with wanting to be cherished.

The maître d' handed them their menus and wine list. "Your server will be right with you, and she'll explain the specials and get your drink order." The maître d' held Amanda's chair out, indicating for her to take a seat.

Kevin sat on the opposite side of the table facing her. "Thank you."

The man walked away, leaving the two of them alone. She glanced around. The place was more intimate than she'd expected. Low lighting, green privacy plants, and soft piano jazz playing in the background. The artwork focused on couples in all parts of the world. She felt the blood drain from her face as her gaze landed on the table where she discovered Greg and his new date.

"What's wrong, Amanda? And don't say nothing, I can see it in your eyes." Kevin leaned forward and took her hand in his—the warm strength comforting.

She tried to find the right words. Kevin deserved the truth.

"Did I do something wrong bringing you here? We can leave." Kevin was just too nice. Too perfect. There had to be a flaw somewhere.

"No, it's not you." Nothing could be further from the truth. "It's just something that happened two years ago." She looked away, not liking the feeling of being the subject of a microscopic investigation.

"Tell me what happened?" His voice was sincere and caring and concerned, and it was enough to melt Amanda's resistance.

She let out a deep sigh. "I was dating a guy, and I thought we were in love. My mother had just passed away, and things got hectic with the business. I guess I put more focus on the bakery than on him, and he didn't appreciate it. We had dinner reservations here on Valentine's Day. When he stopped by the bakery to pick me up, I couldn't leave. He broke off our date, and he broke off our relationship."

Kevin didn't interrupt. His thumb, however, caressed the back of her hand. The gesture was far more of a distraction than anything he could have said at that moment. Amanda tried to refocus.

"On Valentine's Day, this place is a prepaid meal by reservation only. I knew Greg wouldn't let the meal go to waste, that he'd show up anyway. After he left, I realized I wasn't being fair, and I closed the bakery as quickly as I could and headed this way to surprise him and see if I could salvage our relationship. Imagine my surprise when I arrived to find he'd already replaced me with another woman. It took him less than an hour to move on."

Kevin scowled. "Wow. The guy's clearly a complete jerk. You're better off without him."

"I'm sure his wife would agree. He married the girl." Looking back, she knew Kevin was right. She was better off without Greg. At the time, however, she hadn't seen it that way.

"I'm sorry. Is that why you're anti-Valentine's Day?" Kevin's compassion brought tears to her eyes.

"Maybe. Probably," Amanda admitted. "I realized, or rather decided, that love was for fools, and therefore Valentine's Day is for suckers."

Kevin smiled. "Is that where February Fool's Day originated?"

"Absolutely."

"We can go somewhere else. In fact, I think we *should* go somewhere else."

"Or maybe it's time for a new memory. Maybe it's time to put the past in the past and forget about it." She appreciated his support and understanding, but it was better this way.

Kevin nodded as the server approached. After placing their orders, Amanda leaned back to relax. It was just her and Kevin, and she wanted to enjoy the evening. It might be the only time it ever happened, and she wanted to make a memory because anything with Kevin in it would be worth remembering.

"Tell me about yourself. What kinds of things do you enjoy doing on your own?" Amanda was curious about Kevin outside of his parenting role. And it was easier than jumping into whatever he wanted to talk about and the reason for their dinner.

"It's been a long time since I've been able to think about what I want to do. I'm always in work or parent mode. I love spending time with them and taking them to school events or activities, watching them grow, although sometimes it feels as if it's happening too fast." Kevin sat back in his seat, his gaze never leaving her.

He was going to make her dig, but she was up to the challenge. "What did you do for fun before you had children?"

"Let's see. Before I met Victoria, I played on the softball team, hiked, went sailing, and hung out with friends. After I met her, everything changed." The grooves across his brow deepened as if the memories weren't the best.

"How so?"

"She caught my attention. Pretty girls, lots of friends, and all about having fun. At the time, I couldn't believe she would give me the time of day. I was young and too foolish to see or understand what someone like her needed. Victoria craved the limelight. First, a big wedding. Then the pregnancy. Everything she did was designed to keep her the center of attention."

"Not a good reason to get pregnant." Amanda shook her head, sympathizing with what he must have had to deal with.

"No, it wasn't. But we were young and made mistakes."

"I will say, I was surprised to find out you had children, even more so to realize they were almost teenagers. Did you have them when you were like twelve or something?" she teased.

"No. More like nineteen." Kevin shrugged.

"So you're really turning thirty? Wow, I never would have guessed."

"The kids keep me young. Victoria never enjoyed the responsibility that came with parenting. She doubled the amount of time she went to the gym trying to get back in shape while I worked all day and returned home to be a parent at night. I realized we were never on the same page. When she was home, we fought a lot.

Divorce wasn't something I wanted to go through; it was something I realized I had to do, knowing my relationship with Victoria had deteriorated to the point it was hurting the twins. I've been a single parent for way longer than I've been divorced. But enough of my sob story."

Amanda couldn't help but fall harder for the father who put his children above all else. "Thank you for sharing that. You're a great dad, and the love you have for the twins is obvious to everyone around you. More importantly, the girls know it. You should be proud of that. You've made sacrifices some people wouldn't choose to make."

Kevin nodded. "Thanks. It's not always easy, but in the end, it's worth it. I don't get many nights out like this. You know, the kind with adult-only conversation. Thank you for agreeing to come with me."

"Honestly, I was excited when you asked."

The startled look in Kevin's eyes was quickly replaced by a teasing light. "I know, free meal and all, right?"

"There is that," she joked.

"There is one thing I want to get out of the way, sort of the reason I asked you here in the first place. I wanted to say I'm sorry." Kevin rubbed the back of his neck and then reached for his glass of wine.

"Sorry for what?" They were moving into the conversation she didn't want to have judging by his tone.

"For the kiss the other day. I know I started to apologize once already, but we were interrupted before I could explain."

"Explanations aren't necessary. I think *sorry* pretty much covers it. And then I humiliated myself by telling you I wasn't sorry about it. Not exactly a subject I want to talk about now." She took a sip of her drink, hoping he'd assume the flush of her cheeks was from the wine.

"It's not what you think. I kissed you because I'm attracted to you—don't ever doubt that. But I have so much going on in my life with the girls that anything between us would be impossible. I keep telling you it's not fair to confuse them, but it's also not fair to confuse you. Or, for that matter, to confuse me. I can't have what other people have." He sat back and shook his head.

"Why not?" I know you told me you don't date, but you're an attractive man, and there's no reason not to. It doesn't make any sense."

"It would if you knew Victoria."

"I told you about Greg. Now it's your turn to fess up and tell me about her. What's she got to do with this now? You're divorced."

"Victoria and I have an agreement. She agreed to give me full custody with the condition that I don't date or have any relationships. As long as I stay focused on the girls, she lets me maintain full physical custody. I don't want a long, drawn-out court battle that ends up hurting the twins."

Amanda couldn't imagine anyone agreeing to such ludicrous terms. "But that's not fair to you."

"Fair is that I have my girls. Victoria's afraid someone will take her place in the twin's lives and that she'll lose her safety net of being able to come home if the modeling doesn't work out. But seeing as I have no desire for the girls to be traipsing all over Paris with their mother, this is for the best."

"Do you still love her?" Amanda hated to ask the question but couldn't stop herself. The idea he might still be in love with his ex would end any growing feelings she had for him. It would be the flaw she kept looking for, sure there was one. Emotionally unavailable would be a huge stop sign when it came to her feelings for Kevin.

"No. She *thinks* she has a safety net. There's a difference between thinking and having, but there's no sense forcing her to face the reality of our situation. I'm not looking to make things worse than they already are."

Amanda let out of sigh of relief, although the idea his ex-wife thought she could waltz back into his life at any time didn't sit well with her. "Victoria has no reason to be worried about anyone taking her place if she stays in their life. The title of mother belongs exclusively to her and it's not a competition. There's no possible way she's going to want them with her all the time if she's as into herself as you say. Would it be so bad if they visited her every now and then? A girl needs her mother. Even one that's a high-flying model centered on herself." Amanda was probably crossing unspoken lines with her questions and advice, but it was a topic she was passionate about, having lived through it with her own mother doing the exact same thing.

Kevin shook his head. "I'm not willing to risk that you're wrong." Honestly, all I wanted to do tonight was to explain why I kissed you, and why it can't mean anything. I needed to clear the air and I thought it should be done in person. You're an amazing woman, and if I did date, it would certainly be someone like you. Someone beautiful on the inside and outside. I just can't date, but I did want to warn you about the girls."

Warn. It was a strong word and one she didn't understand, given the context of the conversation. "What about the girls?"

"Their mother just started dating, and I think they're getting ideas about you and me. But they don't know about the agreement, and I don't want them to find out." This just kept getting better and better by the minute. He was out of his mind to agree to his ex-wife's terms.

"She gets to date, and you don't? That's a bit one-sided. And wrong."

"I know. I'll admit it was hard to digest when I found out the other day. But it doesn't change the fact that at any time she could slap me with a joint-custody suit, something I'm not prepared for."

"At some point, you need to talk to her. You can't go on this way. The problem with what your doing is that by closing yourself off to dating and a future with someone, you're not setting an example for the twins. Where will they get a role model to show them what a real relationship can be like?"

"I don't know. Friend's families maybe." He shrugged. She could feel him pulling away from her as if a brick wall had been erected.

"You have nothing to worry about with me. I'm not looking for a relationship either." At least she hadn't spilled the beans and told him the truth. His reminder was exactly what she needed to put everything back in perspective. She'd been a fool to think this was an official date. Or to have been hoping for it to be one at any rate. The last thing she wanted to do was open her heart to someone and allow them the opportunity to crush it.

"Amanda? What a surprise to see you here." She looked up, stunned to see Greg and the same petite blonde woman he'd been with two years ago, the woman he'd married.

Taken by surprise, Amanda had a hard time finding her voice as she jumped to her feet, knocking over a glass of water. She grabbed the glass and tried scooping up some of the ice just as Kevin took his napkin and dabbed at the water as it soaked into the tablecloth. The server ran over, prepared for a quick cleanup.

"I'm sorry," Amanda muttered, humiliated that Greg had seen it all happen. She wanted to crawl under a rock, or at the very least, the table.

"Don't worry about it, ma'am. It happens." The server was gone as quickly as she arrived, the mess under control.

Amanda turned back to face Greg and then glanced down to where Kevin sat watching her, a questioning gaze in his eyes.

"Hi, Greg. Yes, I enjoy this place. I come here frequently." *Stupid thing to say, considering it wasn't true.*

"Really? I've never seen you here before, and this is our favorite place. What a coincidence." He smiled and held out his hand to Kevin. "Hi. Name's Greg Miller, an old friend of Amanda's. This is my wife, Helena."

"And this is Kevin Thompson, my boyfriend. He's the one who insists on coming here all the time. He says it's romantic," she replied, the words coming out of her mouth before she could filter them. It was a stupid panicked reaction. Amanda shot Kevin a pleading glance, praying he wouldn't out her lie.

Chapter Fifteen

♥

KEVIN WAS GRATEFUL HE hadn't been eating or drinking when Amanda introduced him, or for sure, he would have choked. *Boyfriend*. Somehow, he managed to hold back the automatic denial, the pleading expression in her eyes and on her face enough to stop him. *Greg*. That was the name of her ex. The one who dumped her in this very restaurant for the woman standing next to him. *The wife.*

Things weren't working out the way he planned tonight. It was supposed to be a simple dinner between friends to clear the air. Instead, it was fast becoming a comical nightmare.

"Hi there. Nice to meet you." His words were not at all a reflection of his thoughts. An urge to deck the guy for what he put Amanda through washed over Kevin, but he squashed it. He'd play along with the charade for Amanda's sake. At least they weren't in Hallbrook, and no one would get wind of this. It was the one saving grace to the situation.

"I'm glad you found someone special." Greg smiled at Amanda awkwardly.

"Yes, she has." Kevin reached for her hand. "She's quite a woman, and I feel blessed to have her in my life." Might as well go in all the way and have fun. "Any man that ever let her go must've been a fool." He glanced directly at Greg, emphasizing the direct hit.

The man coughed, a red flush washing over his face and throat. Interestingly, Amanda wore the same color. Did she still have feelings for the jerk?

"Kevin, Greg *is* my ex." Amanda grinned, putting Kevin at ease. "But he's happily married, and everything worked out exactly as it should. Otherwise, I wouldn't have you in my life, darling." She was laying it on thick. The problem was, Kevin liked it. Way too much.

Greg seemed uncomfortable with the direction the conversation had taken and tugged at the knot of his tie. "Yes, they did. We are expecting a baby."

Helena remained quietly by his side, staring at Amanda. Her eyes grew wide as a dawning recognition hit the woman.

Kevin couldn't resist the urge to take another shot on Amanda's behalf. "Congratulations. We already have twins, and we're talking about expanding our family more." It wasn't a lie. He was talking about expanding the family by adding a dog. Let the guy stew on that a while.

Greg's shocked expression was more than satisfying. "Well, um, yes. It looks as though our table is ready."

"Enjoy your evening. I know we will." Kevin's enjoyment had intensified the minute he'd joined in the charade. He couldn't remember the last time he'd done something so crazy, but it had felt so right doing it.

Greg nodded. "Night." He walked away with his wife following close behind.

Kevin noticed the not-so-happy expression on the woman's face before she turned away, leading him to believe Greg's night wouldn't be enjoyable at all, given his wife's current state of mind.

Amanda sat back down at the table. "Thanks for doing that. I'm sorry." She had the good graces to seem apologetic.

"How did we get from just friends to a relationship?" He was curious why Amanda had made the announcement, but he wasn't upset. There was a level of satisfaction from putting the man in his place. He couldn't imagine what Amanda had seen in a guy who seemed far too self-absorbed.

"I'm sorry. I just panicked. Seeing him brought everything rushing back. I had just told you about what happened, and it came spewing out."

"Stop. It's fine. And it was more than a little enjoyable, truth be told," he said, laughing to help put her at ease.

Amanda shook her head. "I'm glad you think so. Personally, I was freaking out."

Kevin glanced over to the table where the pair had sat down. He reached for Amanda's hand, causing her to jump.

"What are you doing? They can't hear us." She glanced down at their entwined hands and then back at him.

"But they can see us. And your friend Greg is more than interested based on how many times he's already looked this way. This is one play I intend to finish. Didn't think much of the guy myself."

"Are you sure? It...um, this just seems weird. And, yes, I see that now. But hindsight being all that it is, wasn't letting me see how things really stood with him."

"Let me ask you something. When I joined in and took that first shot at Greg, you seemed flustered. Much like he was. Why was that? Do you still have feelings for him?"

"No. None. I promise."

"Then why the reaction?"

Amanda stayed silent for a few seconds. "Honestly, I admired that you stood up for me. I felt special. It was stupid, I know, considering we're friends, but the kiss..." She shrugged. "And then what you said..."

"So, the blush was because of feelings between us and nothing to do with him?"

"Yes. I'm sorry. We both have good reasons not to be in a relationship, but sometimes, I think about it. You're a great guy."

"I appreciate the honesty. Trust me, I feel the same, and I wish things could be different. But for tonight, let's have fun. Let's enjoy this one night and pretend we're in a play and that we're madly in love with each other on a hot date. All for Greg's benefit. He deserves it." Kevin was about to tell her he wanted it for himself as well. It wasn't often he would have an opportunity such as this one, but now that he had it, he was loathed to let it go.

"I don't know if we have to go quite that far." Amanda frowned.

"Loosen up and have some fun. No one knows we're here. This will be our secret."

Amanda looked around, her gaze stopping at Greg's table. She squeezed Kevin's hand and grinned. "You're on. I took an acting class in high school. I'm sure I can do this." Amanda slid her place setting closer to his, switching chairs to move closer, which in turn, put her back to Greg.

"Nice move." Kevin brushed a lock of hair back from her face and over her shoulder. Her hair was silky to the touch, but he resisted the urge to touch it a second time.

Amanda put her hand on his forearm and leaned in to whisper. "What are you going to have for dinner tonight?" Her eyes twinkled as she looked up at him and batted her eyelashes.

"Why don't we order an appetizer, something along the lines of oysters, I've heard they're an aphrodisiac. Maybe for later," Kevin teased. Two could play the acting game.

Amanda's flushed face and shocked expression made it worthwhile. A man could get used to watching the emotions play out on her face.

"I-I—," she stuttered, her mouth dropping open as if at a loss for what to say.

"I'll take that as a yes. And maybe we should order a bottle of champagne to celebrate, considering we're talking about expanding our family and all." He added, making sure she knew it was all about playacting and having fun.

Amanda nodded her head in agreement and grinned. "Not to mention, I have twins apparently. You went all-in with that one." With raised eyebrows and dimpled cheeks, she joined in the charade whole-heartedly.

"I couldn't resist. The guy irritated me."

The server arrived to take their order and then left, giving them a chance to talk about whatever came to mind. Likes. Dislikes. Life. The new bond between them had managed to remove any earlier awkwardness, and they laughed and teased as though they'd known each other for years.

The oysters arrived. Amanda took one glance and shook her head. "No way."

Kevin carefully pried one from the shell on a fork and held it out to her. Her lips remained tightly pursed. "Come on, just try. If you hate it, you can use a napkin and discreetly get rid of it. That's how I get the twins to try new things," he said, grinning.

Amanda made several moves to open her mouth, closing it just as quickly as she tried to get up the nerve.

"Open wide, and let it slide," he teased, bringing it closer to her mouth.

Amanda scrunched up her face and leaned forward, opening her mouth to let him feed her the oyster. She immediately grabbed the napkin, her eyes wide with disgust. Much to his surprise she swallowed, grabbing water to chase the oyster, her shoulders shaking in revulsion as she wiped her lips with the napkin.

"Raw is not my thing. Never again." She took another drink of water and ate a piece of bread.

"I'm proud of you for trying. I'll send the slippery suckers back and have them cooked."

"No. Don't do that on my behalf. You're more than welcome to eat them all."

"After watching you, you've got to be kidding. I'm not trying one."

"Trying? You've never had them before?" Amanda looked shocked, and not altogether happy about his admission.

"Nope, and I don't intend to now."

Amanda swatted his arm playfully. "You brat." She shook her head and leaned in closer, picking up one of the oysters with her fork. "Eat." She picked up a napkin and then held the oyster out to him. "Go ahead. Here's a napkin if you need it, wise guy." It was her turn to have fun at his expense.

He glanced at the slimy looking grayish ball. "No chance you're letting me out of this one, is there?"

"Nope. Open wide and let it slide," she tossed his words back at him.

Kevin opened his mouth and let her feed him, following his own directions and swallowing it whole. Amanda's reaction was spot on, but he forced himself not to grimace in disgust. "Now I know for sure they aren't my thing either. Happy?"

"Yes, turnabout was only fair. Shall we move on to dinner and our salads and skip the appetizer?"

"Good idea." Kevin signaled the server and had the oysters removed.

Between friendly banter and an occasional touch to emphasize the relationship was more than friends for the benefit of Greg and his wife, Kevin was finding it difficult to distinguish between fact and fiction. The fiction version was far more fun. The connection he felt with Amanda came naturally, unlike the younger version of himself who'd chased after the popular socialite in college, convincing himself it was love and not lust. He couldn't have been more wrong where Victoria was concerned, where as this, with Amanda, was feeling all too right.

Kevin paid the bill, and they got up to leave.

"Thank you. It was a lovely meal," Amanda said, reaching for his arms and smiling up at him.

Kevin leaned forward and kissed her on the cheek. "Just in case Greg's watching," he whispered in her ear.

"I see. Thanks for reminding me. Wouldn't want to start getting any fanciful notions that you'd fallen in love with me magically over dinner," she joked.

"It only happens in fairy tales, not real life." Kevin helped her with her coat.

Amanda smiled up at him and nodded. "I agree."

"Seems we agree on a lot of things," he teased, pausing just long enough to turn back to Greg, catching the man watching. He lifted his hand to wave farewell, letting his other hand fall to her waist as he led her toward the door.

Once they exited, Kevin dropped his arm, reality checking in. He was surprised to find he wanted to put it back where it belonged—on her.

"That was fun," Amanda said, her laughter like sweet music. "I have to say, I know it was stupid of me to introduce you as my boyfriend, but it worked out perfectly. You were amazing."

"Thanks. You were pretty amazing yourself. And it was a lot of fun. We make a good team." Amanda deserved the truth and more, but it was the more he couldn't give her.

Unless...

Unless there was a way for them to have the best of both worlds.

"I agree," Amanda smiled at him. Maybe she was thinking the same thing he was.

There were the kids to consider. And his ex-wife. And the bakery. But then, tonight had worked out. Why couldn't they have more nights like tonight?

He helped her into the car, slid into the driver's seat and then turned to face her. "I've been thinking, and maybe this is crazy, but I've got to ask you something."

She looked over at him, the light from the streetlamp illuminating the questioning gaze on her face.

He swallowed hard, trying to find the right words. "All kidding aside, tonight was fun. And I was wondering if maybe we could do it again? Like a friend date. A secret date, though. You already know why, but if there's a way around Victoria's limitations, I'm all for trying. I want to spend more time with you. Would that be so bad?" It sounded lame even to his own ears.

"A secret relationship?" Amanda shook her head, her smile disappearing.

He couldn't take back what he'd said. "I mean, not really a relationship. Just friends getting together secretly. So that we can spend time together. Can't men and women just be friends?" He sounded like a sixteen year old boy asking a girl out on their first date. No, make that a twelve year old.

"They can, but the secret part throws me for a loop. I like you a lot also, but I'm not sure about the secret part. It sounds...off," her voice trailed to a whisper, but he heard her loud and clear.

"I get it, I do. I'm sorry. Just forget it. It really was a stupid suggestion." Given her reaction, Kevin knew he'd bungled the brainless offer. Not many women would agree to a clandestine friendship, of all things. He let out a deep breath. It had been wishful thinking on his part, but not very well thought out.

"I understand why you're asking, don't worry. The whole secret thing just sounds wrong. I mean, it would be great to hang out sometime, maybe go to dinner and a movie. I have so much going on with my business, maybe a secret friendship is exactly what we both need since I'm not looking for a relationship either. It would keep everyone, including your ex-wife out of our business. But I just don't know if it's right for me. I'll think about it, I promise. I don't want to make any snap decisions and end up regretting them."

A maybe was better than a no. "Okay. You decide and let me know. Whatever you're comfortable with is fine by me." It made him realize how truly unique and special Amanda really was, and more importantly, made him more unsure of what he'd offered. She deserved better.

Kevin drove back to Hallbrook and pulled into her driveway. "Let me get your door." He slid out of the car, went around to the passenger side, helping her out. The ride home had been quiet, the awkwardness between them slipping back into place as reality intruded into the night.

He walked her to the front door. "Thank you for tonight."

"Thank you for dinner, and, of course, for letting me save face tonight."

"You're welcome. Amanda..." Kevin wanted to tell her to forget his offer but couldn't say the words. Not while he still had a chance to make it work.

"What is it?" She tilted her head slightly to one side and gazed up at him.

"Nothing." Only it wasn't nothing. The memory of another kiss assailed him. "This." He pulled her in his arms and kissed her, unable to resist the urge to hold her again. It might be the last chance he got if she didn't agree with his suggestion.

Her response encouraged him to continue, savoring every second. Kevin pulled back before he got too carried away, leaning his forehead against hers.

"Goodnight, *friend,*" he said softly, before letting her go.

"Goodnight, Kevin." Amanda's hand went to her lips as she slipped inside the house, Cupcake's bark welcoming her home.

At least she had someone to come home to. With the twins gone, his house was empty, which meant there'd be nothing to keep him from thinking about Amanda and the kiss and hoping against hope she'd say yes to his proposal. He wasn't ready to let her go.

Amanda was more confused than ever by Kevin's offer and then his kiss. Secret friends, ones who kissed goodnight, was probably not what Grandpa had in mind for her when he'd pushed her in Kevin's direction. Friends who kissed would be akin to hanging over the edge of a cliff when it came to emotional safety. Something she'd vowed not to do.

But who would it hurt if she agreed? Maybe, just maybe, she should say yes, this one time. Kevin was worthy of an exception to her rules, wasn't he?

Chapter Sixteen

A LITTLE OVER TWENTY-FOUR hours later, although who was counting, Kevin got word from Amanda. During that time, he'd warred with the right and wrong of his offer in the wake of her silence. He'd known in his gut she'd turn him down, so it had come as a surprise when her text said otherwise. And not only agreed to a secret friendship, but also suggested they try to meet up over the coming weekend if his schedule was open.

It wasn't until the girls asked to sleep over at a friend's house that he was able to confirm availability, and after a couple of quick texts back and forth, they'd managed to confirm their first official secret-friend date. By Wednesday, Kevin had to admit he was looking forward to Friday night, with an excitement he hadn't felt in a long time.

His phone rang just as the students began filing into the classroom. He moved to silence the call and recognized the number. *Victoria.* He'd been expecting her call ever since he overheard the twins telling their mother about Amanda, but now wasn't a good time for the discussion that would ensue.

"Hey, kids, take out your books and start to read about the experiment we're going to be doing on page 176. I have to take this call, and I'll be just outside the door, so no monkey business."

The kids got loud; their teasing banter directed at him. "Oh, Mr. Thompson's got a girlfriend. Trying to set up a hot date?" Tommy, the class clown asked.

"Just read and leave your imagination for art class." He shot them a stern look and shook his head. He stepped into the hallway and mashed the button to answer.

"What's up, Victoria? I'm in class." He could guess what she wanted, but he wasn't going to let on.

"You tell me. I talked to the girls last night, and from what I hear, you've got a new girlfriend. We had a deal," her icy tone confirming how he knew she'd react. It was exactly why he didn't want her to find out.

"I don't have a girlfriend, and I'm quite aware of our deal. Is there a better time we can have this conversation?" He lowered his voice as several students passed by, glancing at him, curiosity in their expressions. A teacher on the phone in the hallway during class was an anomaly.

"Absolutely. I'm flying into Mount Washington Regional Friday morning. I should be in Hallbrook not long after the girls go to school. That should give us plenty of time to talk before they get home. I'd love to see them again. I miss them."

She was coming here? This he hadn't expected. A phone call was surely more appropriate considering there wasn't anything to discuss. Or nothing anyone knew about. "Sure, you miss them. Is that in between your fittings, runway walks, and the new boyfriend?" He couldn't keep the derision out of his voice. "It was your choice to move halfway around the world."

"You don't understand. I'm done trying to convince you why it's so important to me. This is about you, not me and what I'm doing."

"So that's the real reason you're coming in town." Nothing had changed. Her priority had never been the girls.

"It's definitely a big portion of it, but whether you want to believe it or not, I do want to see the twins. When and where can we meet?"

"There's no reason for you to fly home. We can have this discussion later via the phone." He knew she wouldn't change her mind, but it was worth a shot.

"Like I said, I'm overdue to see the girls anyway. I have birthday presents to deliver." A Friday delivery being days late according to his calendar, but the girls would be over the moon. Who could compete with gifts from Paris?

"I have first period free. You'll have from 7:40, which is when I drop the girls at school, until 8:50. There's a place called Sally's in the middle of town on Main Street."

"It's a date. See you then."

"It's not a—" There was nothing about their meeting that spelled date, but Victoria had already hung up. The best thing he could do was have the conversation with his ex-wife and reassure her there was nothing to worry about, let her visit the girls, and then hope she left town as quickly as she'd arrived.

And now that Victoria knew, there was no choice but for him to break things off with Amanda. He couldn't risk having anyone find out they were secretly hanging out, and the twins telling their mother. But Kevin also knew he owed Amanda the courtesy of telling her in person. He'd been a fool to think he could date her secretly or otherwise and not pay the price.

The next two days were miserably long, but Friday morning arrived, Kevin looking forward to his meeting with Victoria about the same way he looked forward to a visit with the dentist. *Or worse. Definitely worse.*

He dropped the girls off at school like any other day, only this morning he headed for Sally's Diner. Minutes later, he entered, choosing a corner booth in the back, knowing the fewer people who saw him, the better. Less questions that way.

He kept an eye on the front door as several people arrived and left, the familiar jingle of the overhead bell alerting him each time the door opened. Never one for promptness, it was no surprise Victoria didn't appear until ten after eight. Or was it just that she always wanted everything to revolve around her.

Probably the latter.

Kevin stood as she approached the table and waited for her to take a seat. Unfortunately, she took the move as a warmer welcome than he'd intended and leaned forward to embrace him. It was like hugging a cold fish.

"You look nice, Kevin." Victoria tossed her blonde, silky hair over her shoulder in a practiced move.

"As do you." Playing cordial was critical when dealing with his ex. She was like a child, her emotions all over the place when things didn't go her way.

She slid into the booth across from him and glanced around. "Couldn't you have picked a better place to meet?" The corner of her upper lip curled in distaste.

"It's the only place in town open for breakfast."

"I passed a cute bakery that would have been nicer than this."

Kevin choked on his coffee. "Coffee went down the wrong pipe," he offered by way of explanation.

The last place he'd take her was to Amanda's bakery.

"This menu is somewhat lacking. No Eggs Benedict even. Guess I'll stick with coffee. It won't be like the Parisian blend I enjoy, but hopefully, it's passable enough." Her airs and graces wouldn't be appreciated by anyone, least of all him.

"Take it or leave it. I don't think Sally Little has been to Paris lately, so you're not likely to get anything fancy." He let the comeback rip without giving it much thought.

"Be nice, Kevin. Your condescending attitude doesn't become you." She shook her head, her scolding tone irritating him.

"You flew here from Paris. What is it you want to discuss that couldn't have been discussed on the phone? Time is ticking."

"Why, your new friend, of course. The girls told me all about her. How you took her with you for their birthday. Skating. Dinner. You've had her over to cook for you. Twice." Victoria's eyes had narrowed slightly as her gaze never left his face.

He forced himself not to react. "Sounds to me as though you interrogated the twins."

Victoria's expression darkened. "I didn't have to. They were extolling her virtues all on their own. She's made quite an impression on *my* daughters. But it seems to me, you and I made an agreement you'd be focused on the twins and not on chasing some woman."

"I'm not chasing some woman, as you call it. Amanda is a friend. She's a sweet person. One I might add, who the girls pulled a prank on. I felt obligated to help out." It was the truth, even if there was more to it than that.

"The girls seem attached to the woman you claim to be just helping out." Victoria had never worn jealously well and now was no exception. More to the point, it reminded him she was trying to control more than the outcome with the twins, she was trying to control him.

"I can't help who they become friends with. They were the ones who asked her to go with us that night, and that was because you weren't here. Leave me out of the equation."

"That doesn't change things. We had a deal." Victoria trailed her finger around the rim of the mug as she glanced up at him. "I just want to make sure that we are on the same page still. I know you'd prefer to stay out of the courts, and for the girls' sake, I agree. But that only works if we both do what we agreed to." Victoria reached for his hand, her rings and bracelet glistening in the overhead light.

Kevin struggled not to yank his arm away. Amanda's words flitted through his brain, giving him the courage to push the envelope. "So how is it that you get to date? The girls' words, not mine. Apparently, it's okay for you to have a new man in your life, but you don't want me to have a new woman."

"My relationship status is of no concern to you, and my ability to date was never part of our agreement. You're the one who has the girls full-time. It's your behavior they see, and that must be exemplary. You promised you'd stay focused on the twins, and you can't do that if you're dating someone."

Kevin shook his head. It was useless trying to make her understand. It's not as if he was planning on marrying anybody, for Pete's sake. It would just be great to be able to enjoy the companionship of a woman on occasion. *Amanda's company*. There were times that being a father and a teacher wasn't enough for Kevin, but those times weren't enough for him to risk losing the twins.

"You have nothing to worry about."

"See that it stays that way. It's either that, or I'll see you in court. I'm sure the judge will want the girls to be with their mother." Her threat stuck in the middle of his gut and twisted hard. He hated the control she had over him, her words driving him over the edge.

"You didn't fight to take them because you couldn't handle them and maintain your highfalutin career. It would be a mistake for you to go for custody, and you know it. And you have no right to dictate who I'm friends with, or who I date, for that matter. You lost that right when we divorced." Kevin couldn't stop once he started, erasing all the groundwork he'd laid over the past year trying to be agreeable in the hopes of keeping everything civil for the girl's sake.

"Try me." Victoria shot him an evil grin that all too clearly suggested she would follow through on her threat.

"I know what you're doing, and it won't work. You and I will never be together again. No matter what happens with your career, I'm not your landing zone." She was controlling so much of his life, but this was one area she couldn't control, and he was determined to make sure she knew it.

"But, darling, we have the girls to think about." Victoria's grin reminded him of a snake before it struck its prey. "What time do the girls get off school? I can't wait to surprise them." It was as though she'd flipped a switch.

"I'm sure they'll be thrilled." Problem was, they were the only ones who would be. As far as he was concerned, she couldn't leave town fast enough.

"When's your flight out of here?"

"Trying to get rid of me already?" She shook her head and smiled.

"Just trying to know what to tell the girls."

She let out a heavy sigh. "I have to catch a red-eye flight leaving at seven o'clock tonight. It'll be heck on my complexion, but I've got a show to do tomorrow night." Of course, it was all about her. Some things never changed.

Kevin breathed a sigh of relief. Victoria would have to be at the airport by five, and therefore, would be long gone before he was scheduled to pick up Amanda for their official first and last date.

"Diana, I really appreciate you working a few hours this morning since your off school. I'm going to head over to Sally's to grab some take-out breakfast. Can I bring you anything?" Amanda stopped by the register to grab her purse.

"I don't mind picking up the extra hours. And yes, to breakfast. I love the pancake, sausage, and hash-brown special. I don't know what Sally puts in those pancakes, but they sure do keep me coming back for more." Diana laughed, reaching into her pocket to pull out a ten, handing it to Amanda.

"They are delicious. She adds vanilla and orange juice to the batter. But I agree, they're better when she makes them. Trust me, I've tried. It must be her loving touch." Amanda grinned. "I'll be right back. The timer is set for the scones in the oven and they'll be done in about ten minutes. I can top them when I get back."

"Will do." Diana turned to see who had come into the bakery.

"Good morning, Brandon. I've got your order ready," Amanda greeted the young officer.

"Good morning, Amanda." He stomped his snowy boots on the welcome mat.

"I'm just heading out, but Diana can take care of you." Amanda turned back to Diana. "That's the order under the counter in the white bag. I've already totaled it up and deducted for the police department's discount."

"Gotcha." Diana waved the bag in the air to show she'd located it.

Amanda zipped up her coat, put on her cable knit hat, and wrapped her scarf around her neck to ward off the cold. She walked the short distance to Sally's and pushed open the front door, the bell jingling above her head, offering her a warm welcome.

She glanced around the diner, taking note of several familiar faces. Her gaze froze when it landed on Kevin and a strikingly beautiful woman sitting in the corner booth. The woman's hand lay across his arm as they leaned forward to speak to each other, the gesture all too familiar and lover-like.

Amanda shook her head, trying to fathom what she was seeing. It was like déjà vu. Her breath caught in her throat. She needed to leave. If she stayed, he was sure to spot her, and that was the last thing she wanted to happen. She'd been a fool to let her fancy take a whimsical turn and think he cared more than he did.

No wonder he wanted a secret date.

How about no date? Amanda turned and fled from Sally's, unwilling to let Kevin see her and try to come up with some lame explanation. In no time at all, she was back at the bakery, safe from prying eyes.

All except Diana's, that is. The young woman looked up at her and frowned, her gaze dropping to Amanda's empty hands.

"I thought you went for food?" Diana asked hesitantly, as if sensing something was wrong.

Except Amanda didn't want to talk about it. "There was a really long line, and I was worried you'd get more business than you can handle," she made up the first excuse that came to mind.

"That's fine. Your pastries are far better in my book anyway." Diana had the good graces not to call her out on the lie, but they both knew the bakery was never that busy anymore.

"Thanks. I'm sorry." Amanda shrugged and handed Diana her money back. "My treat next time."

"You're on." Diana smiled, making her way over to the case and picking out a pastry for breakfast.

Amanda spent the rest of the morning baking and prepping the next day's pastries. Each time she picked up the knife, she forced herself to focus on what she was doing, not wanting her anger at Kevin to cost her a finger. He wasn't worth it.

Each time she tossed the dough onto the counter, the flour sprayed up, dusting her blouse and face. Tears threatened to escape, but she brushed them away with her forearm before they could spill over. She forced herself to think of something positive. Like winning the contest. Today was the cutoff for the finalist's selection, and the judges would soon start the taste testing part of the contest.

Try as she might, her thoughts drifted back to Kevin and the gorgeous woman. She slammed the oven door closed, retreated to her office and closed the door. Amanda knew exactly what she needed to do. She pulled out her phone and called Kevin, timing it so that he should be leaving the high school and heading to pick up the girls. It would keep the conversation short. *Not sweet, but short.*

No answer. *Drat.* Amanda hung up the phone. A text was the next best thing.

Amanda: "I changed my mind about tonight. And with regards to your secret relationship suggestion, I've changed my mind and I'll pass.

A text breakup may not be the classiest thing to do, but perhaps this was the easiest. And considering the situation, it was more than acceptable. An incoming text notification alerted her to his quick response, something she hadn't expected.

Kevin: "I agree. About tonight and in the future. You deserve more than a secret status, something I can't give you. Sorry."

Darn right you can't give me what I need, because you're too busy entertaining other women. *Good riddance.*

Although deep down a part of her was hurt by the fact he hadn't even tried to change her mind, it was the right ending to a bad situation.

Chapter Seventeen

♥

WITH EACH DAY THAT passed, the announcement of the contest winner drew closer, and the ache in Amanda's stomach intensified. It was one thing to be positive and excited about the possibility of winning, quite another now that the anticipated moment was days away. So much was riding on the outcome.

Amanda loved the bakery and prayed she could save it, but the bank had been clear. There would be no more extensions for her to catch up her payments. And without the online advertising campaign, there was nothing she could do to make the amount of money necessary to stall foreclosure. And even if she could, it would only delay the closing, not prevent it. The prize of the ad campaign would be a proactive way to increase business by mail. After having done extensive research, she was confident she could make it work, but everything hinged on her winning.

Amanda set the timer on a batch of old-fashioned baked donuts. She sipped a cup of coffee, her thoughts drifting to Kevin and the girls. As much as she hated to admit it, she missed spending time with all of them, the night of the twin's birthday a reminder of what it felt like to have a family. It was only now she also admitted the reason she'd agreed to his insane proposal. She'd secretly been hoping it would grow into more. Her silly heart never stood a chance when it came to Kevin and she'd fallen for him even when she didn't want to. It was the only reason she would have agreed to the arrangement in the first place.

Unfortunately, Kevin didn't have the same problem. He was too busy playing games with people's hearts, all in the name of honoring the agreement with his wife. Amanda understood the love he had for the girls and the lengths he would go to keep them out of the fray with his ex, after all, it was one of the things she loved about him. *Correction. Liked.*

But that's where she drew the line. The last thing Amanda needed, was to become one the casualties in his strange arrangement with Victoria.

The door opened, the bell jingling to announce a customer. She looked up, surprised to see Lacy and Macy charging through the door, a couple of friends in tow, and a few adults trailing not far behind them.

"Hey, Miss Amanda. We came to see you. You promised to help us with Daddy's cake. He's got an after-school meeting, so this is the perfect time. We want to keep it a surprise. These are some of our new friends. They wanted to come and get some of your pastries." Macy beamed; her eyes lit with excitement.

Lacy made her way around the counter, followed by her sister.

"It's great to see you, girls. I was just thinking about you." Amanda leaned down to give each one of them a hug, her heart overflowing with joy to see them. She smiled at the children who'd come in with the twins, recognizing each one of them.

"Why don't you come over anymore?" Lacy asked the dreaded question.

"Remember, I told you from the start, your dad and I are just friends. Friends don't see each other all the time." She shrugged, willing them to understand. Especially since, as far as she was concerned, Kevin wasn't precisely the kind of guy she wanted for a friend anymore. Their values were completely different when it came to relationships, something she would never concede on *if* she ever found herself wanting to date again, which she didn't.

Most girls dreamed of walking down the church aisle for their special wedding day with a man she loved. Amanda wasn't any different, she'd just never been lucky enough to meet the kind of man who instilled that kind of devotion, and she was tired of trying and failing. Kevin had tripped her up a bit, but now that she knew his true colors, Amanda's heart armor was firmly back in place.

"I see. Are we friends?" Macy asked.

Amanda smiled. "Of course, I'll always be your friend."

"Then you can come and see us once in a while. And then you can come and see Dad once in a while. Then we would see you twice as often. Problem solved." The twins high fived each other, laughing at Macy's line of reasoning to get what they wanted.

Amanda reached out to hug both girls close again. Now that they were on the same team, she couldn't get enough of them, making her resent Kevin that much more. It wasn't fair that he had made her start to wish for things she'd shut out of her life. "I'll see what I can do. You're always welcome to visit me here." *That is if she could keep the place open.*

"These are our friends, Claire and Lori, and their moms." Lacy pointed to everyone by way of introduction.

"Yes, I know the girls and Mrs. Miller and Mrs. Jennings. They are regulars here at the bakery. It's nice to see you all again." Amanda smiled at the two women she'd gone to school with. Both happily married with children. Something Amanda had not managed to figure out how to do.

"Nice to see you, too. The twins begged us to bring them here so you could help them with this cake for their dad. It sounds as though no other cake in the world would do." They all laughed, but not the kids. They looked on as if the grownups had lost their minds.

"You know how kids can be once they get their minds set on something. I'd love to help them. Can

I get you some coffee, and chocolate for the girls? I've got freshly baked pastries you might enjoy while you wait, compliments of the house." Amanda moved behind the counter as she spoke, grabbing four mugs and plates.

"We are always more than willing to pay. Your treats are worth every penny. Take your time, we're in no hurry," Barbara said, stepping up to the register. "That bakery in Glen Haven has nothing on you. Are the contest results coming out soon? We're rooting for you to win."

"Oh, you heard about that. Yes, the results should be announced on Sunday."

"Who hasn't heard about it? The silent-chef auction and the Anything Chocolate contest have been the talk of the town. And then, of course," Janet stepped closer and leaned in, "there's the rumor about you and Kevin Thompson." Thankfully, the twins and their friends had moved off to check out the wide variety of desserts in the glass case.

"Whatever do you mean? Kevin and I are friends." Amanda shrugged, preferring not to discuss the only topic the town seemed to dwell on these days. It was amazing how fast the gossip had spread; too bad the retraction was slow or non-existent as far as she could tell. Country living at its finest.

"That's not what's on the rumor mill." Barbara grinned.

"Well, the rumor mill is wrong. People need to find something else to talk about. I can assure you, neither one of us is interested in dating." Why wouldn't people just accept the truth? The gossips of Hallbrook needed something other than her and Kevin to dwell on, and Amanda hoped whatever it was, it would happen sooner versus later.

Amanda rang up the order and made the change, handing it back to Barbara.

"That's not what Mr. and Mrs. Roberts are telling everyone. They saw you two over in Lancaster at the Table Divine holding hands and looking all cozy," Janet whispered.

Amanda flinched, trying to school her features quickly. Kevin would be upset if he knew they'd been caught out. He'd helped her that night and now she might have brought trouble in a heaping dose on his shoulders. "They must've misunderstood. We went to dinner as friends to discuss some things about the twins and the recipe mix-up." She was fighting a losing battle, but she had to try. *Only time would make this go away.*

"So, there's nothing to the fact that Mrs. Crabtree saw Kevin kissing you on your doorstep the same night." Janet quirked one eyebrow up, her grin ear to ear.

A lot of time. Amanda closed her eyes and took a deep breath. *This was a disaster.*

"I promise you, it's not what it seems." She shook her head. "There's nothing between us." No matter what she added, no one would believe her. Heck, she wouldn't believe herself against the eye-witness reports.

"Or at least nothing you're willing to tell. Yet." Janet ginned.

"Leave her alone, Janet." At least Barbara believed her. "Any fool with two eyes in their head could see the connection they had when they met at the auction. Give them time to figure it out."

Or not.

The women were talking as if she wasn't here. "Let me know if there's anything I can get you. I should get started on the cake with the twins." Amanda walked away, putting together a plate of scones and a variety of other pastries for the group to enjoy.

"Ready, girls?" she asked the twins as she delivered the plate to their table.

"Ready," they spoke in unison.

They followed her into the kitchen, and Amanda picked up the recipe and held it out to them "Read this, while I get out the ingredients. It'll give you an idea of what we are doing."

"This looks easy enough," Lacy said.

"I know we're making the chocolate cake because it's our Dad's favorite, but can we do something special for a topping, kind of like what you did for us?" Macy asked.

"Absolutely. What do you have in mind?" Amanda wanted this to be their special gift to Kevin, not hers.

"I don't know. What do you think we should do?" Lacy's expression was one of sweet innocence as she asked the question. They could be up to something, but maybe they really did want ideas. There could be no harm in helping.

"I'm not sure. Let me think. We know he's a geeky chemistry teacher, and he likes to be outdoors. He's got a great sense of humor." It was his heart that was the problem. *She wasn't sure he had one.* No, that wasn't true. He showed his love for the girls in everything he did. She was finding it hard to stay mad at him, even though he'd hurt her. "I've got it," she exclaimed.

"What?" both girls asked, their faces lit with excitement.

"In my decoration kit, I've got small, cake-sized men. One of you could use a marker and make the hair the same color as your dad's, and then you can draw some glasses on the man. Make it look like your father. I'll get something that resembles a beaker jar and we can put coffee in it, and then glue it to his hands. We can use some chocolate sticks and different colored frosting to make a campfire. It'll appear as if your dad is trying to cook a beaker of coffee over the fire." The image was irresistibly silly, causing her and the girls to laugh.

"That would be funny," Macy said.

"And totally something I can see him doing," Lacy added.

"Totally. Then that's exactly what we'll do."

The three of them finished mixing up the cake, getting more of the flour on themselves and the floor, than what made it into the cake. Amanda slid the pan in the oven and set the timer. The twins went to sit with their friends while it baked, leaving Amanda to clean up and finish fixing the Kevin geek doll.

"When did you say his birthday is again?" she called out to the girls.

"Tomorrow."

"Well, how about I finish this up, and you can stop by and pick it up tomorrow after school? Or I can drop it off at your house." Amanda preferred them to pick it up, eliminating any chance of her running into their father.

Macy joined her behind the counter. "I'm not sure if we can get here again. Maybe it would be better if you drop it by the house." Macy shifted and looked away as if uncomfortable, or up to something.

Amanda was betting on up to something. "Okay. Consider it done."

Macy nodded; her gaze once again fixated on Amanda. "Did you know our mom showed up for a visit?"

Victoria was here? In Hallbrook. Amanda tried to school her expression, but shock wasn't easy to hide. "I didn't. Did you have a pleasant visit?"

"She didn't stay long." Macy didn't seem overly happy considering she'd just seen their mother, leaving Amanda to wonder what was wrong.

It explained who the woman was Amanda had seen Kevin with, but she wasn't sure the knowledge didn't make it worse. After all, most divorced couples wouldn't be sitting arm in arm having an intimate lunch, even if it was Sally's Diner. Were they reconciling? Was that the reason for Kevin's sudden change of heart? *It made sense.*

"We think she was in town more to see Dad," Macy added, lowering her voice so the others couldn't hear.

"I'm sure she loved seeing you." Who wouldn't love spending time with the girls? They were fun, energetic, and full of laughter. Once you got to know them, she smiled inwardly, remembering the rocky beginning.

"Well, we only saw her for like an hour. She gave us our birthday presents and then told us she had to rush back to Paris for another show today. She's got a boyfriend, you know?"

Amanda did know, but she couldn't tell the girls, or they'd wonder how she'd found out. And all trails would lead back to Kevin. Macy was referring to a current situation, so perhaps Kevin and their mother hadn't reconciled, or not that they were telling the girls.

"I bet her gifts were lovely. And a boyfriend? How do you feel about that? Not long ago, I know you wanted them to get back together." It was a few weeks ago, but who was counting?

"She gave us these new coats. Fresh from a designer in Paris. We do love them, but we were hoping for more time with her. We used to hope our parents would get back together, but we realized they're happier without each other. And that's okay, but we think it stinks we're affected by the split. I mean, like, our mom not being here or spending time with us."

"I'm sorry, honey. Sometimes things don't work out that way. People get together and later find out that maybe being together is not the best thing. That it was a mistake. I think it takes a brave person to admit they made a mistake and move on. That's what your parents are trying to do." Kevin probably wouldn't appreciate her interference, but she wouldn't sidestep the issue.

"Does that mean that Lacy and I are mistakes?"

"Oh, no, honey. I'm sure neither one of your parents think that. I know how much your dad loves you, and I'm sure your mom does, too. What's not to love? I imagine it's difficult for her being so far away. But for some people, careers are important, and unfortunately, hers keeps her in Paris."

"What are you two talking about?" Lacy asked as she approached.

"Just stuff," Macy shrugged off the conversation.

Amanda's phone rang. She glanced at the caller id and answered when she saw that it was her grandfather calling.

"Amanda, dear. I don't feel good. My chest hurts. And there's numbness in my arm. It's different from last time." Grandpa sounded as though he'd run a marathon mile, his labored breathing a sure sign something was wrong.

"I'm calling an ambulance. Don't do anything. Are you sitting down?" Amanda's head was spinning with worry, making it hard to think coherently.

"Yes." The fact he wasn't arguing was another bad sign.

"Okay. Stay put, and I'll be there in a few minutes." Fear washed down her spine, but Amanda shoved it aside. Now wasn't the time to give in to her fears. She had to be strong for his sake.

"I love you, Amanda. Just want you to know that." Her grandfather's words tripped her up, knowing they revealed the depth of his worry that he might not survive.

"And I love you, too. But don't you be checking out on me. I'm not ready for that. I'll be right there." Amanda hated to hang up, but she needed to dial 9-1-1.

"9-1-1 operator. How may I help you?"

"My grandfather is Joe Maddox. He lives at 110 Beech Drive in Hallbrook. I think he's having a heart attack. Can you send an ambulance?" Her heart raced, adrenaline surging through every pore of her body, filling her with the fear of losing the only family she had left. Nothing could happen to him. *Nothing.*

"And your name, ma'am?" the woman asked, her tone level.

Amanda tried to draw strength from her. "Amanda Tillman."

"Try to stay calm. We will dispatch somebody immediately. Is there someone there with him now?"

"No, but I'm on my way," Amanda assured the woman.

"They will transport him to Lancaster General if necessary." The woman continued to remain calm and Amanda fought to do the same. She would be useless to Grandpa if she lost it.

"Thank you. I'll meet the paramedics at the house."

"What is it, Miss Amanda," Lacy asked, her eyes wide with concern.

"Sorry, everyone. I need to close the bakery. I think my grandfather is having a heart attack. I need to get to the house to meet the paramedics." She spoke loud enough to get Barbara and Janet's attention, knowing they would understand.

"Go. Go. Give me the keys, and I'll lock up the place. I can drop them off at Jennifer's house tonight," Barbara insisted.

Small-town living at its best, something Amanda would do well to remember when she found herself on the gossip end of the bargain and felt like complaining. "Thank you, ladies. That would be a great help." The girls hugged her goodbye and Amanda raced out the door, more than willing to let the others close the bakery.

Amanda headed for his house, brushing back the tears in her eyes. "Please, dear Lord, Let Grandpa be okay. I pray for your healing touch, and for you to guide me and give me the strength to help him in any way necessary. Amen." Her own fear of not being where she needed to be pressed hard on her heart as she spoke the words out loud, hoping to find a sense of peace in them.

It was like a repeat of another time...when she'd failed her mother.

Chapter Eighteen

♥

KEVIN DROVE UP TO the front of the elementary school and waited for the girls. He'd managed to get through the day without anyone knowing it was his birthday. One of the perks of being new in town.

The girls were a different story entirely. They'd fixed him breakfast, forcing him to remain in bed, leaving him to worry if they would burn the house down. Their track record in the kitchen was less than stellar. But to their credit, it had been passable. Oatmeal, toast and jam, and coffee. Well, the coffee he could have done without. Maybe it was time to invest in one of those easy K-cup coffee machines.

"Happy birthday, Daddy," Lacy said, giving him a hug from the back seat as she slid in the car.

"Happy birthday, Daddy," Macy echoed, following suit.

"What's with the extra birthday wishes?" You already gave me a special gift this morning."

"I know, but it's your birthday all day long. We need to do something special tonight. Only..." Lacy started but let out a deep sigh without continuing, looking lost deep in thought.

"Only what? Is there a problem?" he asked, hoping they hadn't gotten in trouble at school again.

"Well, you see, it's kind of like this. There's a problem with your cake."

"Is that all? Don't worry about it. I don't need a cake." Amanda was supposed to help them out, but Kevin was pretty sure it would never happen, not after the way things had ended between them.

"But that's just it. We had a cake. Or almost had a cake. Amanda helped us, but things didn't work out." Macy shrugged. "Poor Amanda."

This was the first he'd heard of it. "You saw her? When?" He glanced back at the girls in the rearview mirror as he drove to the house.

"Yes. We were at the bakery yesterday afternoon," Lacy spoke up.

Poor Amanda. Something was wrong, and he hated he couldn't be there for her and didn't even know about whatever was going on. "How is she?"

"Not good. Her grandpa had a heart attack, and she closed the shop. They called the ambulance and were taking him to the hospital. That's why we don't have your cake finished."

"It's okay about the cake. I promise. I appreciate the effort you went to. Amanda's close to her grandfather and I bet she's quite upset. I hope he's doing okay." On the way home, he took a detour and drove past the bakery just to see what was happening. The place was closed, just as the girls had mentioned.

He wasn't sure what it meant in terms of her grandfather, but as Amanda's friend, he needed to be there for her. Everything that had transpired between them couldn't change the fact that he cared about her. In fact, there was a good chance he was half in love with her.

And yet, because of some ridiculous promise to Victoria, Kevin was shutting Amanda out of his life and the girls' life. The question became, however, was it the only reason? Or had it been easier to agree with Victoria, conveniently using her as a reason to avoid relationships and protect himself from getting hurt again? And yet it was happening anyway—with Amanda. For the first time since the divorce, he realized it was time to reclaim his life from Victoria and the hold she had over him. He wanted a chance at a future with Amanda if she'd ever forgive him, but first, he'd have to talk to Victoria and change the rules of their arrangement.

Kevin loved his girls, but given time to find out, he was pretty sure he was in love with Amanda too. And she needed his help as she faced losing the two most important things in her life. Amanda was the most giving person he knew, and now it was time for people to give back.

Kevin might not be able to control her grandfather's future, but he would do everything in his power to make sure she didn't lose the bakery when her life was already in shambles. And that meant come morning, the Sweeter Side of Life had to open for business come morning.

"Hey, girls. Would you mind if I dropped you at Lori's house for a bit? I'd like to run over to the hospital to check on Amanda and her grandfather and see if there's anything I can do to help. I've always told you friends help friends."

"Definitely, Dad. You should go." He glanced into the rearview mirror just in time to see the two girls high five each other, grins on their faces. Maybe he wasn't the only one missing Amanda.

"Perfect. I'll let you know when I'm on my way back, and we can go out to dinner." He called Barbara Jennings to make sure it was okay for the twins to come by and hang out with Lori. After dropping them off, he headed for the hospital, thinking about Amanda and the situation. He had a couple of ideas, but they would take help. Lots of help.

Amanda stood close to Grandpa's bed, holding his hand. "Guess you can't blame my cooking now." She grinned, trying to make him smile when the worry that choked her own throat barely let her speak. It'd been a close call. *Too close.*

His half-hearted smile made her feel better, although he was still pale. The doctor's report that he was stable gave her the extra reassurance she needed. They didn't know why his heart rhythms had gone crazy, but it did alert them to fact he needed surgery to get a pacemaker put in. *God was definitely watching over them.*

Until the surgery, they'd keep a close eye on him in ICU, and Amanda would be by his side through the whole ordeal.

"You don't have to stay. Doc said I'd be fine."

"I heard him, same as you did. I'm not here because I have to be. I'm here because I want to be. Don't even bother trying to get rid of me."

"Amanda, honey." He covered her hand with his frail one. "Your mother was sick, and it was her time. God called her home, and I think she preferred things to happen the way they did. She was worried about you. You didn't do anything wrong when you left to shower and change clothes, for heaven's sake. You need to let it go, and you need to go home. I'll be fine, and I'm in good hands. These doctors are taking good care of me."

"Maybe, maybe not. But I'm sticking by your side like glue until you're in the clear. So, quit trying to get rid of me," she teased. Nothing could change the past, but she darn well could make sure it didn't happen again.

Luckily, she had Jennifer to step in and help. Jennifer had agreed to stay at the house and take care of Cupcake, and to check in on the bakery over the next few days. More as a formality, since Amanda didn't expect someone to try and break in and steal stale donuts. With the bakery closed to business, she'd never make the next payment to the bank, but it couldn't be helped. She had to trust that whatever happened to the bakery, was also in God's hands.

Amanda held out her phone to Grandpa. "Do you want to play solitaire on here? I can talk to the nurses and see about getting us a checkerboard. What about reading material? I can have Jennifer bring some things when she drops off a bag for me later tonight."

He took the phone from her and glanced at it. "Nope. Screen's too small. Checkers would be fun. So would a milkshake." He chuckled. "Strawberry."

"Of course. But I'll have to see what the doc says first."

"Party pooper."

"Name-calling doesn't become you, and it won't change a thing." She grinned. Taking her phone back, she called Jennifer. "Hey, there. How's Cupcake?"

"She's fine, of course. She loves me. Always has. How's your grandfather?"

"Ornery. When you come this way with my bag, can you bring the checkerboard? Oh, and a deck of cards."

"No problem. I know where you keep everything."

Amanda turned and walked away from the bed. "He also wants a strawberry milkshake."

"Is that doctor approved?"

"No, but you get it, and I'll double-check. Worst-case scenario, I'll drink it."

"Sounds good. Consider it done."

"Thanks, Jennifer. You're a lifesaver, and I can't thank you enough for keeping an eye on Cupcake and the bakery."

"That's what friends are for."

New friends and old friends.

Amanda had plenty of both and was grateful for all that she had in her life. An image of the twins making a mess as they mixed their father's birthday cake came to mind, making her smile. Those two went into the sweet friend category for sure.

It suddenly dawned on her that today was Kevin's birthday, and she hadn't finished the cake like she'd promised the girls. "One other thing. When you check on the bakery, can you finish an order and deliver it? Please. It's special and due today."

"I think they'll understand why you can't get it done considering the circumstances, whoever it is."

"No, they won't. Trust me. They're eleven."

"As in the twins?" Jennifer asked.

"Yes. It's Kevin's birthday cake. Here's what I need you to do." Amanda described the topping they'd planned, telling Jennifer how to finish it. She gave her Kevin's address after exacting the promise to deliver the special dessert for the twins.

After they hung up, Amanda was tempted to text Kevin a happy birthday wish but slid the phone back in her pocket where it belonged. She might know who the woman at Sally's was, but it didn't change Kevin's attitude toward relationships. It was safer if she kept her distance and the wall around her heart.

"Everything okay?" Grandpa asked, his gaze landing on her.

"Right as rain. Better if all this equipment hooked up to you would quit beeping and whirring." She tried to make light of the noise she hated. She'd had more than her share of time listening to the sounds while she sat with her mother in the hospital, waiting for the inevitable end. She hated this place and the memories that came with it.

"Comes with the territory. You could always spring me from this joint. You know I hate hospitals."

"I do know, but you aren't going anywhere until the doc clears you. Jennifer should be here around seven, and then we can play checkers or cards."

"You love playing cards, so you have a fighting chance of beating me."

"You love checkers, so you'll win. Guess that makes us even." She winked.

The door opened behind them, and Amanda turned to talk to the doctor. Except it wasn't him.

Kevin. The last person she expected to see here.

"Hey, there. I just came to check on you and see how your grandfather is doing." Handsome as ever, she couldn't help the rush of pleasure at seeing him. It was like this every time he walked into a room, as though her heart recognized him.

"You don't have to whisper, young man. I'm not dying." Grandpa smiled at Kevin, letting him know he was teasing.

"Sorry, sir. I wasn't sure," Kevin laughed as he moved closer to the bed, not at all affronted by her grandfather's remark.

Her grandfather chuckled. "I like this one, Amanda. Definitely a keeper."

"Stop. We're just friends." Or at least they had been until she'd shut him out, something he hadn't exactly tried to stop from happening. "Grandpa, this is Kevin. The guy I told you that helped me with the recipe. Kevin, this is Joe Maddox, my grandpa."

Kevin nodded. "Good to meet you, sir. You look well, all things considered. Did you get good news?" This time, he asked her grandfather directly.

"According to this one—" her grandfather pointed at her, "—I did. But I don't think cutting a man open for anything means you can check the good box."

"I hear you on that. Hospitals aren't my favorite place, either." Kevin frowned, as if the place reminded him of something he preferred to forget.

"He's getting a pacemaker put in," Amanda said, clasping her grandfather's hand in her own. "It'll be a lifesaver, and that's what takes top priority, not his qualms about the procedure."

"They tell me I'll feel ten years younger. I reckon that's a good thing if I can flirt with the nurses." Grandpa shot her a wink, knowing his comment would rile her.

"Grandpa. Stop." She looked over at Kevin. "He's teasing."

"I'm not getting in the middle of this one. I just stopped in to see if either of you needed anything. Oh, and this is for you," Kevin handed her a brown paper bag. It's a sub from O'Malley's. I figured hospital food isn't exactly good for meals while you're playing guardian angel."

She wasn't surprised at his generosity or kindness. It was one of the things she really liked about him. *A lot*. "Thank you. That's thoughtful of you. Oh, and happy birthday." Talking to him in person was far better than the text she thought of sending earlier.

"Thanks. When I head back to town, I've got to pick up the twins and take them to dinner."

"Give the girls a hug for me and tell them not to worry about my grandfather." She'd seen them yesterday, but a lot had happened since then. Their youthful exuberance was always a pick-me-up.

"I heard what you did to help the girls with a cake for me, and don't worry about it not working out. Maybe next year." He gazed at her, the slight smile on his face for her alone.

"Next year?" She had to ask, the comment linking the two of them together going forward.

"Sure thing. I'm not going anywhere, are you?"

She shook her head. "Not that I know of."

"Then next year, I get a redo." His grin was soft and warm, making her toes curl with appreciation. "I look forward to more of your creations. A man could get hooked on them if he's not careful. You have a way of making a person come back for more."

Are we still talking about cake? "Well, actually, it won't be a redo." She turned the table on him, loving the confused expression on his face. "Jennifer's delivering your cake as we speak."

"You're kidding?" Kevin shook his head in wonder.

"Nope. Since you're not at home, I'll text her to leave it on the front porch."

"You're one amazing woman, Amanda. I don't know how you keep it all together, but you do." His gaze held tenderness and caring and something else. She wanted to ask, but not with her grandpa watching. He already had far too many opinions about Kevin.

"Now that's something we can both agree on, young man. Just remember to make your admiration count." Grandpa wasn't shy about jumping in the conversation. His gaze went back and forth between her and Kevin, a sly smile on his face as if he held the key to a secret.

"Grandpa. Stop. I mean it."

"Or what? You'll call the nurse? Make sure it's the blonde." The man was in ICU and still he joked. *Men.*

"You're incorrigible. I'm sorry, Kevin." Amanda shrugged, trying to move past the awkwardness her grandfather's comments created.

"I'm not." Kevin chuckled and turned to leave, only stopping at the door to turned back. "Hey, what's happening with the bakery?"

Amanda frowned, his question reminding her of a whole other problem, one she'd tried to forget in the short term. She glanced at her grandfather, unsure of how to answer. She hadn't told him the truth about everything and now wasn't the time for him to find out she was losing the bakery. "It's temporarily closed. Just while I'm staying with Grand-pa."

"I saw that. How long do you expect to be here?"

"Five or six days, depending on how things go, and if this guy—" she pointed at Grandpa, "—co-operates."

"I keep telling her to leave, but she doesn't listen to me. She's a strong-willed woman just like her mother and grandmother were."

"Why? Missing your pastry fix?" Amanda asked Kevin, trying to alleviate the new tension in the room.

"Something like that. Let me know if you need anything. I mean it." He flashed her a smile and was gone before she could answer.

Chapter Nineteen

♥

ALL THROUGH HIS BIRTHDAY dinner, Kevin found it hard to focus. It wasn't that he wasn't interested in the girls' conversations about school, but he was trying to figure out a way to help Amanda.

The lines of tension on her face had deepened when he'd asked about the bakery. He knew from previous conversations that things were tight enough that the bank was threatening foreclosure. Being closed for a week would make it worse. And the contest results wouldn't be announced until Sunday. Winning would tide her over until she could reorganize, but first, they had to get to Sunday.

Eventually, he came up with a plan of action, one he was almost positive would work, but only if her best friend and the people in town chipped in to help. By the time he and the girls arrived home, he was more than ready to get down to business and call Jennifer.

"Look, Dad. There's a package on the doorstep. It must be a present for you. I wonder who it's from?" Lacy picked up the box.

He'd forgotten about the cake. "I know what it is, and so should you," he teased.

"Why would we know?" Macy asked, her brow scrunched up as she tried to figure it out.

"Because it's a birthday present from you." He grinned. "It's my cake."

"Seriously? Amanda finished the cake?" Macy's face lit up, followed closely by her sister's matching look of surprise.

"So it would seem with a little help from her friend. I'd say it's time for dessert, and then I need to make a few calls. I think I know a way we can help Amanda while she's busy at the hospital with her grandfather."

"Yay! Count me in. She's super cool!" Lacy said, real affection in every word uttered.

"Me, too. She's the best friend ever," Macy joined in, not to be outdone.

They headed straight for the kitchen and took out plates, napkins, and forks before sitting down. Kevin peeled off the tape to open the box, curious what the three of them had put together. He wasn't disappointed. The geeky science professor heating a beaker over a campfire was hilarious. The man even looked like him.

"We helped. Do you like it?" Lacy asked.

"I love it." He nodded. "Best cake ever."

The girls high fived each other and then broke into their own rendition of "Happy Birthday." It was music to his ears even if they were off-key, the love far more important in his book.

They each polished off their piece of cake, but he'd noticed they seemed to be slowing down despite the sugar rush. When Lacy yawned, it reminded him morning would arrive all too soon. "You both have school in the morning and should probably get your showers, figure out tomorrow's clothes and then get to bed. Thanks for a wonderful birthday full of surprises."

The twins hugged him goodnight. "Night, Dad," they said in unison before leaving the room. Kevin took out his phone. He had a lot to do tonight, but first, he wanted to send Amanda a text.

Kevin: "Thank you. Love the geeky scientist. Is that how you see me?"

He didn't have to wait long for an answer.

Amanda: "A baker never gives away her secrets."

Kevin shook his head, chuckling. A non-answer if he ever saw one, but at least she wasn't telling him to get lost. And she had every right to do so after the way he'd treated her.

He dialed Jennifer's number, ready to see if his plan would work. Jennifer was a huge part of it and would require her assistance in a big way.

"Hello?" she answered on the first ring.

"Hey. This is Kevin Thompson. Remember me? From the festival?" She would more easily remember him as the guy who blew off her friend in a not-so-subtle way, but he wasn't about to bring that up.

"How could I not remember you? You were the guy who got hoodwinked into a large donation at the auction and won a meal from Amanda," she teased. It was great that Jennifer had a sense of humor, even if it was at his expense. More importantly, it sounded like she didn't hold any grudges against him.

"There was that. Listen, I wanted to catch you when you weren't with Amanda, and she told me you're going over to the hospital sometime tonight."

"Actually, I just left. She mentioned you stopped by. It was thoughtful of you. Thanks."

"No need to thank me. It was the right thing to do. Amanda's a special lady." He'd been six times a fool not to realize just how special.

"So, you didn't go for Joe Maddox?" Her question zeroed in on the heart of the matter.

"No. Other than to offer him my get-well wishes. I've never met the man before."

"*Hmmm.* Interesting."

"Why is that?" Kevin knew Jennifer was smart enough to add up two and two, the question was, did she get the right four for an answer? As in two adults, two children, and a future. It was definitely the answer he had been toying with more and more, never able to completely get Amanda out of his head and almost certain he knew why.

"Nothing. What's up?" Non-committal and a change of subject. Her opinion of the matter would remain unknown, but it wouldn't change his.

"I've been thinking about Amanda, the bakery, and the financial issues she's having. Being closed isn't helping her one bit."

"Amanda told you about her finances? She's normally a rather private person," Jennifer commented, surprise lacing her voice.

"We've talked about a lot of things. I know she's banking on winning the contest, but we both know there's no guarantee." There were liable to be hundreds, even thousands, of entries from around the state. He'd read the rules over and over. There was no limit to how many times a person could submit.

"So, what are you thinking?"

"What if we open the bakery in the morning?"

"And how do you propose we do that?" At least she hadn't come right out and nixed the idea. She was interested, he could tell.

"Between you and me and Diana, and maybe some of the townspeople Amanda's close to, we could pitch in and catch different shifts. Some cooking, some serving. We just need to see who's available and willing. That's where you come in. You know who would help and can call in some favors. If the bank sees the store closed two days in a row, they won't threaten foreclosure, they'll start the process."

Jennifer let out a deep sigh. "You have a good point. Give me a minute to think this through." The silence ebbed on, all except the ticking of the clock on the wall. "I think it's doable."

Kevin exhaled the breath he'd been holding. "I can go first thing in the mornings and get things started and stay through my first period class. After school, the girls and I can come back. They'll be more than willing to help, and I'm sure they could learn to operate the register. Do you think you can get the rest of the hours covered? If you make the pastries the night before, I'm sure I can manage to cook them if you leave me specific directions for temperature and time."

"Wow. You must really like Amanda."

"I do." More than like, but Jennifer was not the first person who would be hearing it from him.

"So why doesn't she know that?" Jennifer's directness caught him off guard.

"It's complicated."

"So uncomplicate it," Jennifer remarked, stating the obvious.

"I'm working on it." Part of which meant confronting Victoria with the truth and hoping they could come to some new arrangement. Amanda's insights made him realize it was important to concede on some visitation issues, but he also realized it was time for him to quit hiding behind the custody arrangement as a way to protect his own heart. And Amanda was worth taking a chance.

"Okay, then. You work on that, and I'll work on a schedule. I've already got the keys. I'll stop by there tonight and see what I can do for morning pastries and donuts. I'll cover the late mornings and see who we can get to cover from noon to three. This weekend, we can all chip in."

"Sounds like a plan. And, Jennifer, thanks." Friends were important, and Jennifer was one of the best. She was always there for Amanda when she needed her. Unlike him. But that was about to change.

"No. Thank you. Amanda's my best friend, and she's one of the nicest people I know. I think it will be awesome if the community helps when she needs it the most. We both know she won't ask, so it's up to us. Oh, and Kevin, don't mention it to her. I have a feeling she'll shut us down in a heartbeat. She doesn't like to impose."

"I'll make sure everyone keeps it a secret." He trusted Jennifer's judgment on the matter, although he wasn't sure Amanda would be any happier when she found out what they were doing. But hopefully, intent counted for more than a violation of privacy and usurping one's authority without asking.

"Perfect."

They hung up, and Kevin sat there, satisfied with the call. The problem was, the measures were short-term fixes to a bigger problem. Sunday, the contest winners would be announced. But what if Amanda didn't win?

Kevin lay in bed that night, tossing out possible ideas when one finally hit him. Mark Mitchell, part-owner of the Carlisle Food Corporation, a college buddy and good friend, might be exactly what, or who, Amanda needed in the eleventh hour to save her bakery. Kevin wasn't above using his connections and quickly typed out an email to Mark.

Amanda might not appreciate him sending her recipe to someone, but Kevin trusted his friend to keep it confidential and hoped he'd at least consider the proposal to add Amanda's cake to their product line. It might not be the direction she was looking to go, but at least it was doing something more than putting all the hope in the Anything Chocolate contest.

Not that he didn't think she'd win. This was just a backup plan—and a long shot at that.

Kevin shoved a couple of trays of pastry products into the oven, following the directions Jennifer left for him each night. He and the girls arrived bright and early each morning, the twins all too ready to help. Of course, there were perks, like free pastries. They were quick to jump in and set up the tables, refresh the condiments, and even learned how to make a mean pot of coffee, something that would come in handy at home. He laughed to himself, remembering the last time they'd made him a cup of mud. It wasn't that long ago. In fact, it was only four days since the undrinkable birthday brew he'd been forced to drink.

The only problem they ran into was what to do with the daily deposit. And there was plenty of it.

Once people in town got wind of what was going on, they showed up in droves to either help with cooking or help with the eating and spending loads of money in the process. Without access to Amanda's bank accounts, he'd been forced to lock up the money in the shop.

Today, they were here for the long haul. Kevin regretted not being able to visit Amanda, but he was needed here at the bakery. There was so much to be done. Not to mention, he wasn't sure the girls could keep a secret or that Amanda wouldn't guess he was up to something.

Kevin made his way to the office. He wasn't comfortable going through her desk to find the information he needed, but he wanted to make the deposit. There had to be some bank account information somewhere. He started with the mail, hoping for a bank statement that would clue him in.

He spotted an envelope marked urgent from the bank in the pile he'd been stacking up from the daily postal deliveries. Kevin shouldn't open it, but there was no way he couldn't. Having pretty much taken over the business with Jennifer until Amanda could return, he felt obligated to follow through on all aspects.

Kevin slid the envelope open. Shock radiated in waves as he realized what he was holding. This wasn't a foreclosure warning; it was a foreclose notice. *A final foreclosure notice.*

Based on the money they were looking for to catch up her account and avoid foreclosure proceedings, Kevin didn't have near enough in the deposits. And that was only the mortgage. There were other bills that needed to be paid, including her suppliers.

Amanda had drawn a great big heart around tomorrow's date on her desk calendar, an AC written inside it. She had banked everything on this final chance at saving the bakery.

The bell over the door jingled. Kevin walked out of the office to see one of the early morning regulars walk in. "Good morning, Mrs. Jenkins. Nice to see you again."

"Wouldn't miss it. Been getting my coffee here in the morning for nigh on twenty years. It's my way to start the day before I head to the library." The older woman unwound the scarf from around her neck and let it hang loose. Her hat was one of those fancy toques with feathers and jewels on one side, reminding him of royalty.

But from what he could gather, Mrs. Jenkins *was* the queen of the library, not a country. "That's a great way to start the day. The usual?"

"Of course. I'm glad you and Jennifer have stepped in to help Amanda. She must be relieved." Mrs. Jenkins stepped up to the counter and placed a twenty there.

"Well, actually, we haven't told her." He shrugged.

"Probably a good idea. You just let me know if there's anything I can do."

"Thanks." He handed her the change and then slid a donut and a cup of coffee her way.

The bell jingled over the door, and Jennifer walked in, passing Mrs. Jenkins and exchanging a few pleasantries before the older woman left.

"Good morning," Jennifer called out as she removed her jacket and hung it on the coat rack.

"Hey there. You're awfully chipper for a Saturday morning." He smiled, wishing he had her kind of energy. But keeping up with the twins, his job, and the bakery was draining.

"That's because I got a text from Amanda. They're moving her grandfather from ICU to a regular room tomorrow. Things are looking up."

"That's great news for sure. Did Amanda say anything about the shop?" He worried with each day that passed, she would find out and be furious with him.

"No. She still thinks it's closed. I've been dropping by the hospital with food and clothes. No one else that has stopped in to see Joe has said anything, either."

Kevin breathed a sigh of relief. "That's good."

"Stop worrying. If she's mad, it will be at us both. We just need to stick together as a team." Jennifer smiled. "I was thinking I could get some work done from here on my computer this afternoon if you want some relief. Maybe you could take the girls out to do something fun for a change."

"Sounds like a great idea. We can get lunch and go to the park. I'll even stop in and get Cupcake if you give me Amanda's house key. The kids will love it."

"That would be great. Thanks for thinking of the dog." Jennifer moved behind the counter and tied on an apron.

"No problem."

Jennifer removed a key from her chain and tossed it in his direction. "Here."

Kevin just wished he could fix all of Amanda's problems this easily. The contest winner would be announced tomorrow, but his friend Mark Mitchell hadn't answered him. For all he knew, his friend was on vacation or out of the country. Either way, it would seem the back-up option wasn't an option any longer, and even if something came of him reaching out to Mark, it would be too late to help Amanda.

The contest was her only hope.

Kevin said a prayer, hoping things would turn out right.

Chapter Twenty

♥

AMANDA WATCHED AS HER grandfather slept peacefully. Lots of people had stopped by to check on Grandpa the past few days, going out of their way to drive to Lancaster and visit. It was times like these that brought their close-knit community even closer. Cards and flowers filled Grandpa's room, and although he acted as though it was all an unnecessary fuss, she caught the way he gazed around the room each time he woke up, a slight smile on his lips as he spotted the loving generosity.

His eyelids fluttered open. "Are you still here?" Don't you have a home to go to?" Grandpa smiled, his voice cracking.

"Not that easy to get rid of me. But after the medical team gets you settled in the new room today, I'll head out and check on things. That way, the nurses can come and flirt with you without your grand-daughter standing guard to run interference."

"That works. I figure if I flirt now, it'll make it easier to ask them out when I get out of this place," he teased.

"Well, it won't be long now. The doctor is pleased with your progress."

"How come your young man ain't been back? I liked him."

"You know he's not *my* man. Don't go feeding the rumor mill."

"He's obviously interested, or he wouldn't have shown up here." Her grandfather's gaze followed her as she crossed the room, trying to appear un-affected by his words.

She had been disappointed he hadn't returned, but it didn't do any good to dwell on it. Even worse, would be to let her grandfather know it bothered her. "It's not that easy. We're friends, that's it."

"In this town, there's usually a spark to feed the fire when it comes to the rumors. Is there some-thing you haven't told me that makes them think one thing and you another?" His gaze intensified.

It was obvious he'd heard things and she wouldn't lie. Perhaps gloss over a few things, but not lie. "All we did was go to dinner. As friends. And everyone's making a big deal of it."

"Why is that?" he persisted.

"Well, there were a few hiccups along the way that night. No big deal, really."

"Such as?" Grandpa was like a bulldog, not backing down and determined to know everything.

"Such as Greg showed up, and I introduced Kevin as my boyfriend. And then he was sweet enough to help a friend in need of saving face, but then someone from Hallbrook saw us acting our parts and decided we were an item."

"Sounds to me as though you might be just that—an item, that is. Kevin went along, you say? How far did it go?"

"I'm old enough not to have to play twenty questions or explain myself."

"How far did it go?" he pressed, ignoring her comment. "Reckon I need to know if I should call the young fellow out for taking indecent liberties with my granddaughter."

"Oh, for heaven's sake, he kissed me. Satisfied?" She shook her head, disgusted that she'd given in and told him, but tired of the direction of the conversation and wanting it over.

"Yup." He grinned.

"You already heard the rumor, didn't you? You never intended to do a thing to Kevin, you old coot."

"You need to take time out and see what's between you, 'cause it sounds to me like a whole lot more than a rumor mill. I call them facts. Maybe it's time you face them."

"I don't have time for a relationship, and neither does he. We've talked about it. Happy?"

"Not really. Maybe you both need to make time. I saw the way he looked at you. I may have had a bad ticker, but my eyesight is pretty darn good. You need more than the bakery, Amanda. You need love and family and fun. I'm telling you he cares more than he's letting on."

"And what is it you're suggesting I do about it?" Amanda let out a heavy sigh, tired of fighting the inevitable. Whatever he wanted to say, would be said, and there was no changing the subject or making it go away until he was done.

"Tell him how you feel. You can pretend it doesn't exist, but it won't make it go away. If I'd let fear get in the way, I would never have asked your grandmother to marry me. She could have had her pick of anyone in town, but I was the one brave enough to ask her out, and she said yes. One thing led to another, and then we got married. But it all started with bravery. Don't ever let fear stop you from anything, especially love." His eyes glistened with tears as he talked about love and her grandmother. The two of them had shared something rare and beautiful.

"I'll think about it. I just don't know." It was the best she could offer.

"Go home, Amanda. Take care of business. And go set the record straight with Kevin."

She grinned. "You're stuck with me, but nice try." Amanda kissed him on the forehead. "Take a nap, and I'll go see what I can get for lunch at the cafeteria."

Amanda made her way down the hall and took the elevator to the main floor, heading for the café to grab an iced tea and a sandwich. She watched as several families arrived and others left. One young girl smiled up at her mother, hugging her tightly as they waited to be seen. The mother wrapped the little girl in a blanket and kissed her forehead.

It reminded Amanda of a time when she'd wanted a family. The time when she'd believed in love and happily-ever-after. The time before Greg. Her grandpa was right. Was she really going to let one man rob her of happiness in the future and a family? That was giving him far too much power over her life.

And, yes, her father had walked away also, but the one thing that stood out was that every time things went sour, the men in her life had moved on to find love and happiness. *Greg and her father had that in common.*

It was the women who continued to let the relationship failure destroy their lives. Her mother had never recovered, and Amanda had closed herself off to the possibility of love, afraid to be hurt again.

Maybe it was simply a matter of two people who weren't a match, making a mistake. Just like Kevin and his ex-wife.

Amanda didn't want to be the kind of person who ran away anymore. All these years, she'd thought fools fall in love, but now she realized the real fools were the ones who ran away from a chance at love. The one thing she knew for certain was that Kevin made her feel safe and special, and he could always make her laugh. With him, she was comfortable. With him, she was sure she'd fallen in love. Her attempts to fight against the possibility of love hadn't been able to stop the real thing from happening. Now, it only remained for her to discover if it was one-sided or mutual.

But she wouldn't live with the regret of not telling him. Whatever he was facing with Victoria or in his own heart, he'd have to deal with it himself and make his own choice. But his decision wouldn't be because he didn't know the truth.

Amanda returned to her grandfather's room after they'd gotten him settled in the new wing. As he slept, she sat in the recliner by the window, watching him sleep. There were a lot fewer machines and wires, and the room was far less intimidating than ICU. She pulled out her phone and checked to make sure she hadn't missed a call for the umpteenth time. It was set to vibrate to get around the hospital policy of no cell phones, her intent to make a beeline for the waiting area if a call came in. This wasn't the time to ignore or block strange numbers. It was Sunday—the day they would announce the winner of the Anything Chocolate contest.

What she didn't know, was whether they would call or email, but with each passing hour, her nervousness increased, to the point she couldn't sit still. She stopped in front of the window and tapped on the icon for her email account, scanning through the inbox subject lines and senders. Her gaze landed on one from the Mega Online Media Corporation—the contest people.

A rush of excitement filled her. This was it. Everything in her future hinged on this email. She clicked on it and waited for it to open, her heart in her throat.

Congratulations Bethany Wagoner of Scofield, New Hampshire.

Amanda couldn't breathe, the words ringing in her head as she stared down at Bethany Wagoner's name. Sitting in the recliner, Amanda rocked back and forth, trying to dispel the agitation and disappointment overwhelming her. *It was over. She'd lost.* There was nothing she could do to save the bakery now. Her eyes filled with tears and trickled down her face. She brushed them away with the sleeve of her shirt, not wanting Grandpa to catch her in a moment of weakness. He had enough trouble without her adding to it.

She stared out the window, a sense of emptiness overtaking her. Amanda took a deep breath and glanced back down at the list. The letter went on to congratulate everyone who'd made it to the finals and to those who'd placed. Her gaze slid down the page. There at the number two spot, she saw her name. Amanda Tillman. Winner of five-hundred dollars. It was a blessing, but not one that would save the bakery. She scrolled to the bottom of the page, curious to see if they'd posted the winning dessert. Sure enough, there was a picture and the name. *Bethany's Magnificent Chocolate Torte.*

Amanda shook her head, second-guessing her decision not to send the torte recipe. The dessert looked delicious, but it also looked complicated to make, which made it less than desirable for every-day women in their homes. Amanda's recipe had been more practical, but it hadn't been enough to win.

"Why the sad face?"

She glanced up to find Grandpa watching her wide-eyed and alert. "Nothing for you to worry about. I've got everything under control." There was no way she would tell him now. She didn't want to take a chance on giving him another heart attack. He'd find out soon enough that she'd lost everything.

"You're not a good liar. But I can tell by the firm set of your shoulders there will be no getting it out of you today. And it's time for you to go home. I'm in my new room, so you are all out of excuses for why you can't leave."

"Don't I know it. And, yes, that's what I planned on doing. I just wanted to wait until you woke up before I left. I'll be back this evening, Grandpa. Try not to flirt too much with the nurses while I'm gone." She faked a laugh, dropped a kiss on his forehead, and gave him a hug before she left. If she stayed much longer, he'd see right through her.

Amanda drove home first, deciding the bakery could wait, especially considering it wouldn't be hers much longer. More importantly, she needed to hug and hold her sweet baby because doggy licks were always good for soothing the soul.

Chapter Twenty-One

♥

"CUPPY, I'M HOME," AMANDA called out as soon as she opened the front door. The dog raced toward her, tail wagging in high speed as she bounced up and down in excitement. Amanda patted the dog's head and back, hugging her tightly. "I'm sorry I've been away." She dropped to one knee to get a better hug and scratch behind the dog's ears. "Grandpa's doing better, but I've lost the bakery. Maybe now I'll have more time to spend with you. At least until I find a new job. I've got to go take care of some things at the shop, but then I'll be back."

Cupcake lapped her tongue, catching Amanda on the cheek. "I promise I won't be gone long this time." She stood, one hand on the door.

The dog whined. Amanda's heart ached for Cupcake. She didn't want to leave her again, no more than Cupcake wanted to be left.

To heck with it. The bakery was closing anyway. There wasn't anything worse that the health department could do to her beyond what the bank intended to do. "Come on, girl. Let's go." The dog could roam freely in the building for all she cared.

Cupcake jumped in the back seat of the car, trying to get comfortable and watch out the window as they made their way across town. When Amanda turned down Main Street, she glanced ahead, trying to locate a parking spot. She was surprised to see the street lined with cars on both sides. A car pulled out ahead of her, and she moved into place, preparing to back in and parallel park her vehicle.

She opened the back door and let the dog jump out. "Cuppy, heel." Quick to command, the dog stayed by Amanda's side as she made her way down the sidewalk toward the bakery. Amanda drew close, surprised to see people going in and out of the place. Was something wrong? The place wasn't supposed to be open.

Amanda picked up her pace and then stopped in front of the bakery. The sign indicated the place was open, which didn't make any sense. She pulled open the door, grabbing hold of Cupcake's collar, wishing now she'd thought to grab her leash. Once inside, she couldn't believe what she saw. There were at least six customers eating pastries and drinking coffee.

Everyone looked up as she walked in, and suddenly the place was buzzing with activity. People approached, giving her hugs. "It's nice to see you again," Mrs. Elliot said, stepping back to let the others greet her.

"How's your grandfather?" Mrs. Higgins asked, the sincerity in her voice beyond that of the town gossip looking for news.

"How are you?" Tanner gave her a bear hug.

"Grandpa is fine. I'm fine. What's going on? The bakery isn't supposed to be open."

They all smiled and stepped back, clearing a path for her to see the front counter.

The twins were behind the register ringing up a customer. Kevin was behind the counter rolling out dough, looking as if he had more flour on him than on the counter. She took a step forward, pulling Cupcake with her.

One of the twins looked up and spotted her. "Miss Amanda!" Lacy called out, racing around the counter toward her.

"And Cupcake," Macy exclaimed, following her sister.

Within seconds, Amanda was bombarded with hugs from the girls. Cupcake broke free in the excitement, and the twins turned their attention to her, squealing with delight to have Cupcake playing with them.

Amanda glanced back at Kevin, his gaze steady on her. Walking toward him slowly, everything else around her faded. "Hi," she murmured, her voice dropping a notch. "What's going on?"

Kevin grinned one of those good-old-boy smiles that always made her catch her breath when he turned it on her.

"Welcome back." He came around from behind the counter. "How's your grandfather? I heard he was moving to a regular room today."

"He's doing great. They will keep him for observation for a few more days, but then he should be coming home. How did you hear he was moved?"

"Jennifer filled me in. I couldn't visit with everything here and at school and with the girls, but she kept me informed."

"Everything?"

"This." He waved his hand around the bakery. "It's just something Jennifer and I worked out together." He grinned, clearly pleased with his efforts.

"Jennifer? She knew about this and didn't tell me?" Amanda was trying to comprehend what she was hearing but it wasn't adding up. She saw Jennifer everyday and yet her best friend hadn't said a thing.

"Because we both knew you'd tell us not to do it. Better to do it our way and not have you worried. You had enough to think about." Kevin didn't seem so sure of himself now.

"What exactly are you doing?"

"Running your business. You were occupied with your grandfather, and I know how much the place means to you. I wanted to help you keep it open, so Jennifer and I have been going back and forth, coordinating our schedules. Some of the people in town have helped, too. Even Sally's been doing some of the baking."

"I can't believe this." Amanda didn't know what to say. Words would never properly show her appreciation for everyone's well-meaning efforts. "Thank you so much. How do I every repay everyone for their kindness?"

"You don't, except of course, by just being yourself. The kind, compassionate, helpful person you've always been when it comes to others. Trust me, it's been an eye-opener for me, too, seeing how people come together to help a neighbor. The twins and I feel like a part of the community. Any doubts I had about moving here were lifted over the last couple of days. The girls absolutely love it here now."

"I still can't believe you did this." She shook her head and looked around the bakery.

"Oh, there is one thing I couldn't do. I've got all the money from the sales in your office. Locked up, of course. I don't know your account information, so I haven't made any deposits." His expression darkened.

"What is it?"

"Nothing. It's nice to have you back."

"Spill it, Kevin."

He glanced around, pulling her off to the side. He clearly didn't want anyone to overhear what he had to say. "It's just that a lot of bills are backing up. *One in particular.*"

"Did the bank threaten foreclosure again?" she asked, trying to calm the impending sense of disaster as she waited for the bad news.

"It's more than that. You got a letter and the bank started the proceedings. I'm sorry. We were determined to keep the place opened until you heard from the contest people."

"Well, I heard...and I didn't win. I got second place, which means all of this that you did was for nothing. I'm so sorry." Amanda fought back the tears threatening to fall. With all everyone had done to keep the place running, her imminent failure was like a knife to the gut, intensifying the pain of losing the bakery.

"I'm sorry. I wish there was something I could do to help." Kevin hugged her, Amanda reveling in the feeling of his strength, desperate to lean on him more than he knew. It was like coming home out of a dark storm to safety. She tried to pull herself together, not wanting everyone else to see her break down.

Right now, she needed to suck it up and say thanks to the people who'd tried to help her. She made her way around the room, stopping to talk to each person. Amanda still couldn't believe Kevin, Jennifer, and the girls had put all this together to help her save the business. She smiled, watching Macy handle the customers like a pro. Lacy was busy keeping Cupcake out of trouble, and away from the people at the tables, something Cupcake didn't mind at all judging by the looks of things. The two of them were curled up in the corner at the back of the bakery, Lacy rubbing the dog's belly on her tickle spot.

The four of them worked side by side until it was time to close the bakery. Kevin could see why Amanda loved the place so much. And the people loved her, but then what wasn't there to love? Her kindness knew no bounds. She talked to others, concealing her inner turmoil as she dealt with the disappointment of losing the contest and, therefore, the bakery.

She was far more focused on showing her gratitude toward everyone for their help. Amanda made him feel as if he was already home whenever she was around. He watched her as she crossed the room to talk with more customers who had come in.

Poise and grace and a big heart. She'd be an amazing role model for any child, and more than ever, he wanted that for the twins. *Family.* The word had a pleasant ring to it.

Working together like this, as a team, confirmed the knowledge he wanted her in his life. He'd done everything this past week with Jennifer and so many other people in town who cared about Amanda, because he cared about her as a friend, but there was so much more to it. And for the first time, he was willing to put a name to it.

Love.

It was something he wouldn't walk away from. Not by a long shot. It was love that had made him trust Amanda's insights, and that had given him the confidence to face Victoria. It was love that drove him to go to extreme measures to make things better for Amanda. It was love that made him feel her hurts and disappointments as if they were his own and made him want to bring joy into her life.

It was as though she were his soulmate, their time together precious and filled with joy.

Amanda turned the sign to closed on the front door as the last customer left. She moved slowly; the weight of the action significant. He knew she was closing the place for the last time. People would find out the truth soon enough.

He was glad he hadn't told her about submitting the recipe to his friend. He wasn't sure she could handle the double rejection in her attempts to save her mother's business.

She shook her head, her eyes misted over with tears. "I still can't believe you kept this place running."

"I wanted to show you how much I cared about you. I was a fool to think I could ignore what is happening between us." He took her hands and drew her near, glancing over at the girls to confirm they were still occupied with Cupcake. "I know I've asked some things of you that shouldn't have been asked. You're a light in my life, and I was wrong to try and hide the light behind a curtain. I was a fool. I'm not good with words but trying to help you...that I could do."

A soft ray of dawning hope lit her eyes, but just as quickly, it was gone. "I'm just sorry it was for nothing."

"It's not for nothing if I still have you by my side. What do you say? Will you give me a second chance? We can weather this storm of yours together." He reached up to cup her face gently.

"I'd like that; honestly I would. But I really counted on winning the contest, and now that it hasn't happened, I don't know what my future holds. Other than vast amounts of debt. I can't expect you to take that on with me. And what about Victoria?" She shook her head, the weight of the world on her shoulders and in her expression.

"Your future holds Cupcake, and me, and the twins, if you'll let us be a part of your life. And as to Victoria, she and I talked. Thanks to you, we're in a good place. I wish there was something I could do to save the bakery, but us being together is more important. That can't change, not if you feel the same way as I do, and I'm hoping you do." Kevin was putting his heart on the line, but Amanda was worth it.

"I'm okay with together." She nodded, a shy smile lighting her face—a welcome change, one that gave him hope this might all work out in the end. "I'd like that. I was prepared to visit you and make sure you knew why I canceled our date and to let you know how much I care about you, too. I wasn't walking away without letting you know the truth."

Kevin grinned, breathing a sigh of relief. Amanda cared, maybe even loved him. "I don't care why you canceled as long as you're here now and letting me make amends for my stupidity."

"Apparently, you're not the only one afflicted by that particular condition. Which is what I need to tell you since we're clearing the air." She shrugged.

He furrowed his brow in confusion. "What do you mean?" Not that anything she said would change his mind about her, but he would listen.

"I saw you with Victoria at Sally's. I didn't know it was her, and I thought you were seeing someone else. You two looked pretty cozy, and I got jealous. I'm sorry. I should have talked to you about it."

Kevin zeroed in on the one word that made his heart race. Jealousy was another indicator of deep feelings. "Jealous? There's no reason to be. Victoria has always assumed I'd be there for her if things didn't work out with her career. It's why she's tried hard to control my personal life. But here's the thing, I let her because I wasn't interested in start-ing a new relationship with anyone. She gave me the easy excuse to hide behind. Until you."

"So, what's actually changed between the two of you?" Amanda gazed up at him in earnest, wanting to hear the answer.

"I told you I talked to her. It was long overdue and needed after I began to realize how much I cared about you. It's hard to deny that special feeling I get when you walk in a room, or how alive it makes me feel. I told her the truth about you and my hopes to get to know you better and to have you in my life. We reopened the custody discussion, and I conceded a few visitation issues you made me see differently. From there, we were finally able to reach another agreement."

"What issues?" Amanda asked, not following him.

"The part where you told me the girls need their mother and how important it is for them to spend time with her. I've agreed to let them visit Paris whenever Victoria has downtime that coordinates with their availably from school." It had been a hard decision, but he'd come to the realization Amanda was right. It had also been the turning point for Victoria and him in their conversation. She'd come to realize he was serious about moving on, and she'd been thrilled when he'd finally agreed to let the girls go to Paris. It had been a big step for them both in the right direction.

"I'm so proud of you. Don't worry, Victoria will take care of the twins. The girls love her, and I trust their judgement. So should you." Her soft smile made him believe every word. It was always this way with her.

"I do, thanks to you. What changed your mind about me?" He couldn't help his curiosity, but it was also a need for reassurance that they were on the same page moving forward. Putting his heart on the line again had left him a little insecure apparently.

The corners of her eyes crinkled as she grinned. "Grandpa. I talked to him, and he made me face my feelings and trust what I knew. He knew what I was too blind to see or acknowledge. He's been singing your praises ever since the two of you met, and even some before that. Grandpa made me realize I was a fool for not giving us a chance or telling you how I feel. He told me regret comes from the road not traveled."

"Tell me now—how much you care, that is." He stepped closer, wanting, no needing, to hear the words.

"I care this much," she said, her smile warm and radiant. Amanda opened her arms as wide as they could go.

"And I care more than that." He shook his head, not wanting to be outdone. Not to mention, he loved to tease her.

"How would you know if it's more or less?" she asked, placing her hands on her hips as she questioned his comment.

"Because I care this much." He spread his arms wide, knowing his arms were longer than hers.

Amanda laughed. "That's not fair."

"I love you." Kevin pulled her close, wrapping his arms around her.

"I love you, too. It will be difficult to close the bakery, but knowing you and the girls are in my life will make it bearable. Thank you."

He leaned in, lowering his mouth toward hers, kissing her with every ounce of emotion he'd been feeling. It was a moment he wanted to remember forever.

"When did the bakery become a make-out ally?" Macy teased. She'd come to stand next to them.

Kevin stepped back, embarrassed to be caught necking by his daughters.

"Does this mean you're finally going to admit you like each other?" Lacy asked.

"I think so." Kevin winked.

The twins turned each other, exchanging a big high five. "Yay!"

"I guess it means you two girls are okay with me dating your dad?" Amanda asked. It was a fair question given the history.

"We've been trying to tell you that for almost two weeks. *Geez.* Adults can sometimes be thickhead-ed." Macy shook her head, hands on her hips.

Kevin and Amanda laughed as he moved to stand behind her, pulling her back against his chest and wrapped his arms around her.

"I think when it came to the twin trouble you two were busy causing, I was better off playing it safe," Amanda teased.

"Us? We weren't *that* bad." Macy grinned.

"Let's just agree to disagree on that one. But I'm glad you changed your mind about me." Amanda leaned down, pulling the twins into a group hug.

"And we're glad you changed your mind about our dad." Macy laughed.

Chapter Twenty-Two

♥

A TAP ON THE glass of the front door of the bakery caught their attention, and Amanda moved to open it. It was after hours and the guy looked like a city banker, the combination of the two thoughts settling like a rock in her stomach, growing heavier with each step she took.

Once upon a time, she'd tried to keep the business afloat by refinancing locally, but they'd turned her down flat, citing her risk factors after inheriting the business and the debt. She'd been left dealing with a guy who didn't care one iota about her business or the memories that came with the place. The only thing he cared about was the money.

She opened the door only a crack, preferring not to let the man inside. "Can I help you? The bakery's closed." It was hard enough to come to terms with losing the place, without having the others around to witness the exchange. The man would have to come back tomorrow when she would be alone.

"My name is Mark Mitchell. I'm hoping to catch up with a woman by the name of Amanda Tillman." His dark brown eyes never left her face, the man knowing full well who she was, and daring her to deny it.

"You've found her." Amanda swallowed hard, biting back the urge to tell him to get lost. She wanted to ignore his outstretched hand but couldn't make herself be mean.

"Wonderful. I normally would have called first, but I thought a surprise visit might be a nice touch and give me a chance to catch up with Kevin. Is he around?"

"Kevin?" she repeated, dumbfounded when the city slicker dropped his name. She glanced back at Kevin, only to find him coming toward her. Amanda pushed open the door, glaring at the two men, determined to find out what was going on.

"Mark? Is that you?" The two men shook hands as though they were old friends.

"Great to see you again. Are you missing the city yet and ready to come back?"

Amanda frowned, not liking the implication of the bank man and Kevin being such good friends.

"Not a bit. I, um, have other interests keeping me occupied these days." Kevin took her hand and held it firmly, unwilling to let her go when she tried to pull away.

Mark grinned. "I see. Lucky guy."

"I'm surprised to see you here. I never heard back from you and thought maybe you weren't interested or were too busy. Come on in." Kevin ushered the man inside, taking over the situation much to Amanda's dismay.

Mark removed his coat and hung it on the coatrack. "Nothing could be further from the truth. In fact, that's why I'm here." He laid his briefcase on the closest table and popped open the locks.

"Can someone please tell me what's going on?" Amanda looked back and forth between the men, totally confused.

The bank man looked at Kevin, one eyebrow shooting upward in a look of surprise. "You didn't tell her about this?" Mark took a folder out of the briefcase and waved it in the air.

Kevin shrugged. "I didn't see the point at the time. It was just a feeler."

"That sort of presents a problem." Mark shook his head and looked directly at her, his expression questioning and concerned.

Amanda stepped closer, her gaze zeroing in on the folder Mark held. Sweeter Side of Life was written across the front. She glared at Kevin. "What's going on? Did you go behind my back and talk a friend of yours about buying my business?" He'd stepped over the line on this one, and it hurt. More than she wanted to admit. Talk about misplaced trust.

Mark coughed. "Buy your business? Hardly. My company wants to buy your recipe," he explained as if the comment should shed light on the entire conversation.

"My recipe for what? I don't understand." She drilled the man with a hard stare, wanting answers, but angry enough with Kevin she didn't want them from him. He'd have plenty of explaining to do later.

"Amanda's Depression Cake." Mark and Kevin spoke at the same time.

"What in the world is Amanda's Depression Cake?" she asked disdainfully, close to throwing both men out of the bakery. Kevin's betrayal was too much on the heels of her grandfather's surgery and hospital stay.

Kevin stepped closer. "I can explain. Mark is a friend of mine from the city. I sent him a copy of your chocolate cake recipe to see if they would be interested in it for their company. Mark owns a food corporation and is always on the hunt for the next big thing to add to their production line."

Amanda wasn't sure what to think...or feel, for that matter. Talk about being blindsided. "Why didn't you tell me?"

"Because you were tied up at the hospital with your grandfather and had enough to worry about. Plus, I thought if you won the contest, you might not need to sell it. I was just trying to find a backup option." Kevin let out a deep breath. "I'm sorry. I should have told you, but honestly, I didn't think anything would come of it, but I felt compelled to help."

"Backup option?" She knew the answer before he said it as she tried to wrap her brain around the implications.

Kevin took her hand and tugged her close. "To save the bakery."

She couldn't believe it. Kevin may have gone behind her back, but it was with the purest of hearts and best of intentions. No wonder she was crazy about him.

Amanda glanced at Mark. "Just how much does someone pay to buy a recipe? She tamped down all seeds of hope that tried to sprout, unwilling to let herself get excited, only to have her hopes dashed. A few hundred dollars, or even a few thousand, wouldn't change her situation.

Mark named a sum of money that made her eyes go wide. Hope sprouted like it had wings and there was no way to call it back. "Are you serious? Why would anyone pay that much money for one recipe?"

"Yes, I'm serious." Mark laughed. "As to why, you'd be selling us all rights to the recipe. We mass-market produce the dessert and sell it all over the country. We tested it out, and it scored perfectly for what we need. It can be reproduced in large quantities, can be frozen, and tastes great. Plus, we love the marketing aspect of a Depression Cake. Very nostalgic, and it should appeal to a large segment of our buyers." Mark handed her the folder. "The terms are all here."

"Wow. You've really thought this out. I still find it hard to believe you're serious about the offer. I don't know what to think." She looked down at the folder in her hand.

Mark smiled and shrugged. "Just say yes. I'm came here personally to meet you, present the offer, and get you to sign. Plus, it was a great excuse to get out of the office and see this crazy guy again." He nodded toward Kevin.

"You can trust Mark. We go back a long way, and he's one of the good corporate guys." Kevin's reassurance made her feel better. After all, he was the one who'd set this up for her in the first place.

Amanda's brain raced with the possibilities. It was a short-term fix to save the bakery. The money would run out eventually, and she'd be right back where she was today. It still didn't give her the marketing edge she needed to make the Sweeter Side of Life viable long-term.

"Okay, but on one condition." She hoped she wasn't ruining her chance for the blessing dropped in her lap, but she had to try to fix things. Permanently. "You give me exclusive rights to buy and sell the cake from the bakery in addition to what you offer to markets across the nation. The name recognition and online sales could be the boost I need to put the bakery on the map and save the Sweeter Side of Life."

Mark's brow lines deepened as he considered her suggestion. Seconds felt like minutes when he didn't answer.

Kevin took her hand and smiled but didn't say a word. She appreciated that he hadn't stepped in to take control of her decision. And she loved the idea he'd gone to all this trouble to help her. It was her business, and although he'd initiated the deal, this was entirely her decision.

"Okay," Mark nodded. "I need to run it by the board, but I don't see it as a problem. The confidentiality agreement prevents you from ever disclosing the ingredients, and I think I can sell the idea to the board based on increased name recognition. People will like the real-life connection." He held out his hand.

Amanda shook on the deal. "Thank you. I accept." She hugged Kevin in her excitement, and then turned to hug Mark. The two men were friends and there was no reason to stand on formalities.

The Sweeter Side of Life would stay open. *A true miracle. Thank you, God.*

"My pleasure." Mark grinned.

"Does this mean you saved the bakery, Dad?" Lacy approached them and slid her hand into her father's.

"No, honey. I didn't. You girls and Amanda saved it. It was her recipe and your help with the recipe." He pulled the twins in to hug them, love shining in his eyes. It was a proud-parent moment for sure.

"I'd say that makes it all of us because you're the one who sent it to Mark," Amanda interjected.

"Fair enough. We all did."

"We make a great team," Amanda added, joining in on the hug.

"Would you like to join us for dinner tonight to celebrate?" Kevin asked his friend.

Mark nodded. "That sounds fun. It'll be great to catch up."

"How about meeting up at seven at O'Malley's Charm? It's an Irish pub and restaurant just down the street."

"Sounds great." Mark snapped his briefcase closed and headed for the front door. "See you all then."

Amanda locked the door behind Mark, then turned back to the others, letting out a squeal of delight. "We did it." She was so glad she hadn't pushed Kevin away. Everything in her world was perfectly right because she'd opened herself up to new possibilities.

"*Woof. Woof.*" Cupcake sat down next to her, nudging her hand and thumping her tail on the ground furiously.

The twins jumped up and down, joining in the excitement of the moment. Grandpa was right, she would have been a fool to miss out on all this, no matter what the future held.

Epilogue

ONE YEAR LATER...

Amanda twirled in front of the mirror, her heart light with love.

It was hard to believe they'd been together for a year, and so much had happened. She'd paid off the bakery loan with the money from the sale of the recipe. Grandpa was healthy and becoming more active in the community. The girls had visited their mother in Paris and had a blast, and Kevin had survived the ordeal. Mostly because Amanda had been able to talk him through it and keep him occupied.

She'd even met Victoria, and, against all the odds, they'd become friends, both realizing that the more people who loved the girls, the stronger and more confident the twins would be. Nothing would take away the love the girls felt for their mother, and Amanda wasn't looking to replace her. The fashion industry was competitive, but Victoria's daughter's affection would never be a competition.

Amanda had chosen a warm outfit but hadn't been able to resist the temptation to dress up. The red sweater dress and white pearls were perfect for Valentine's Day. February Fool's Day had ceased to exist, and in its place, her appreciation and understanding of the day set aside to honor love and hope had blossomed. Kevin was taking her to O'Malley's Charm for dinner. Low key but special because it would be with him.

A knock sounded on the door. *Kevin.*

She raced for the door and opened it, eager to see him. Even after a year, every day with him felt special.

"Happy Valentine's Day." Kevin handed her a bouquet of roses and kissed her.

"Thank you. They are beautiful." She lifted them closer to face to inhale the fragrant scent emanating from the blossoms.

"Like you." He grinned.

"Let me put these in water, and then I'm ready."

"A woman always on time. One of the many things I love about you."

Amanda grinned. "That's because I'm eager to see you. I'm looking forward to spending the night alone. It's always hectic this time of year. You wouldn't believe the online business for the Twin Delight Depression cake." The company had agreed to combine both names, and the girls, of course, had been ecstatic.

"Oh, I do believe it." He grinned. "Mark reminds me all the time what a shrewd business move it was when you added it to the deal." Kevin pulled her close for a kiss.

For the compliment, she gave him two. "Thank you, kind sir. It *was* a spectacular idea. I just can't believe he went for it, and the board approved it." Amanda grinned. She put the bouquet in a vase and filled it halfway with water.

"They knew a good deal when they had it. Trust me, their sales are making them more than happy. Shall we go?" Kevin took her by the arm and led her to the car. Much to her surprise, the twins were there. She shot Kevin a questioning look but didn't say a thing. Maybe he was dropping them off somewhere.

She smiled at the twins. "Hi, girls. This is a pleasant surprise. Happy Valentine's Day."

"Happy Valentine's Day," Lacy said. It was great to see her standing on her own two feet lately and not always a shadow to her sister.

"Happy Valentine's Day," Macy chimed in. The girls had dressed alike, yet different. Same coat. Same hat. Different colors. It was a suggestion Amanda had made to help them express their uniqueness as well as the special bond they shared.

"I hope you don't mind we are tagging along." Macy scrunched her face. "Our friend's parents had something come up, and we couldn't go to their house like we planned."

"Don't you worry about it. Valentine's Day is about love, and you know I love you both." She *had* been looking forward to a night alone with Kevin, but this would work. O'Malley's had become their family date night place each week, a time when they all slowed down from busy activities to share time as a family unit. This would be the same kind of special night.

Kevin drove carefully toward the restaurant. The roads were slick with the recent snowfall that had yet to completely melt and dry.

"Did you both have a nice day at school?" Amanda asked.

"Yup. We had parties today. And I got lots of Valentines." Macy's smile revealed how pleased the silly cards had made her feel. She wasn't always as tough as she wanted to portray.

"She got one from Randy. He's a boy that likes her," Lacy said, her face all scrunched up in distaste.

Macy jabbed her sister. "Does not."

"Does, too. Mary Ellen is his sister, and she told me that he talks about Macy at home, and that he has a crush on her."

"Whatever. Mind your own business," Macy huffed.

Amanda laughed. The two might fuss with each other, but the bond was undeniable.

"Don't even start thinking about boys and dating. You've got years before I'll consider the possibility," Kevin said firmly, shaking his head.

"Oh, Daddy. One day, you're going to have to face the fact we're practically teenagers." Macy sat back, folding her arms across her chest.

"Don't remind me," he retorted.

They arrived at the restaurant, but parking appeared to be at a premium. Everyone not out on a Valentine's date or with other special plans had apparently shown up to attend the Heart-to-Heart festival at the Masonic Lodge.

"With so many people at the festival, we shouldn't have a wait at the restaurant. If we can just find a place to park." Amanda scanned the street, looking for an opening.

"Good point, and lucky for us since I didn't make reservations," Kevin said, looking guilty.

"Oh, I thought you were going to." She frowned. It wasn't like Kevin to forget things.

"I was busy, but like you said, it'll be fine. I'm positive." He parked the car, and they walked toward the restaurant, Amanda drawing her coat tightly against the cold evening air.

"Hey, look, there's Jennifer. And she's with Lori. Dad, can we please go say hi?" Macy asked.

"Just a few minutes. Please?" Lacy added, her you-can't-say-no smile wide across her face as she reached up to grab her father's arm.

"I thought she was staying home with Will tonight. That's why she offered to watch Cupcake." Amanda wasn't worried about the dog being left alone, just confused that Jennifer had changed her plans without telling her.

"I guess a few minutes won't hurt. Okay?" Kevin looked at Amanda for confirmation.

"Sure. I can talk to Jennifer and see what's going on." They headed for the Masonic Lodge, waving at Jennifer as they drew near. The girls took off running to meet up with their friend.

"I can't believe you're standing outside in the cold, Jennifer. I thought you guys were staying home tonight?"

"Hey, there. We are, but I needed to drop by and talk to someone for a minute. I was waiting out here for them to show, but it's so cold I think I'll go inside with you and wait. Will's inside talking to some friends anyway."

The room was packed with even more people than last year.

"I'll be right back; I see Tanner and want to say hello to him and his wife," Kevin said, dropping a kiss on her cheek and walking away.

Amanda gazed after him, thankful for each new day they shared together. It had been a happy year filled with more love than she could possibly believe.

"Good turnout this year," Amanda said, gazing around the room, the place a sea of familiar faces.

Jennifer reached for her coat. "We have you to thank for that."

"I didn't do anything. I'll keep my coat, thanks. We're headed for O'Malley's for dinner, but the twins just wanted to talk to their friend for a few minutes."

Jennifer laughed. "I think everyone's decided this is the hottest spot to meet the love of their life. You have to stay for a few minutes and say hi. Just because you have a boyfriend doesn't mean you can't be sociable."

"Okay. You win." Amanda grinned and handed Jennifer her coat. "There's no sign of Kevin or the girls at the moment. A few minutes won't hurt. Oh, look, even Grandpa's here. And it looks like he brought a date." Amanda waved and crossed the room to his side. "Hi, Grandpa, who's your friend?" Amanda looked at the woman next to him with interest.

"This is Tricia Tate. She's a nurse at Lancaster General," Grandpa introduced his lady friend.

"Now that I can believe. It's nice to meet you." Amanda knew he went to Lancaster for regular checkups, but the old coot hadn't mentioned a word to her about seeing anyone.

"Nice to meet you, too." The older woman smiled as she held out a hand.

Someone tapped the microphone. "Good evening, everyone. It's time to kick this party off with a bang." Everyone cheered with way more enthusiasm than she could remember in the past.

She spotted Kevin across the room, walking towards her. People parted, making a wide path for him to reach her. The light in his eyes shone brightly with love, a look she would never grow tired of seeing.

When Kevin reached her side, he dropped down on one knee.

Her eyes filled with tears. There was only one reason a man went down on one knee in a situation such as this. But instead of reaching into his pocket for a ring, he lifted two fingers to his mouth and gave a shrill whistle.

Cupcake ran up to him with a box tied around her neck, the twins right behind her. Kevin opened the box, took out the ring, and then took her hand in his. Her heart raced, tears streaming down her face as she processed what was happening. It might all be blurry, but she wanted to remember this moment for the rest of her life.

"Amanda Tillman, I love you with all of my heart. I met you here last year and thought it fitting to bring you here to honor that moment and to start the next part of our lives. Together. Will you do me the honor of becoming my wife?"

"And our stepmother?" the girls added, moving in to stand one on each side of their father. *Her family.*

Life was still busy, but with the right guy, it made all the difference, and there was no doubt in her mind that Kevin was the right guy. "Yes, I will. I love you, too." Kevin slid the ring on her finger, the diamond dancing in the light.

"Yay," the girls shouted in unison, hugging Cupcake.

"You hear that girl; we're all going be family." Macy rubbed the dog's ears, much to her delight.

Everyone in the room clapped and shouted their congratulations.

Kevin stood and pulled her into his arms, dropping a kiss on her lips. "My heart, forever." He touched his chest with the palm of his hand before drawing her onto the dance floor. "Shall we?"

"Anytime, anywhere, for the rest of our forever lives." The music faded. Amanda's eyes, ears, and heart were focused on the man who had broken through her defenses, showing her that real love conquered all.

Forever sounded pretty amazing.

What to read next...

Love & Hope
Book 5 of the Holidays in Hallbrook series – A Sweet Mother's Day Romance.
Sometimes chaos is all you need to shake things up and then see where life lands...

If you enjoyed this sweet and charming romance, be sure to check out the
ALSO BY ELSIE DAVIS section on the next page for more clean and wholesome romance.

BONUS READ

Want to keep in touch with new releases and what's happening in the world of Elsie Davis?
Sign up for the monthly newsletter at Elsie Davis HEA (Happily-Ever-After) and enjoy DIGGING THE DRIVER (A Celebrity Corgi Romance) as a FREE BOOK!

The greatest compliment you could give an author is to leave a review in order to help other readers discover the same great stories you enjoyed. Amazon/Bookbub/Goodreads are all great places. Many thanks!!!
Another great way to keep in touch - *Follow Elsie Davis on FaceBook*

Also By Elsie Davis

Sweet, Clean and Wholesome Stories...with a Happily-Ever-After Guarantee!

Holidays in Hallbrook
(Sweet Romance Series for Holidays Throughout the Year)
Welcome to Hallbrook, New Hampshire. A small-town filled with the unexpected, lots of love, and of course, a beloved dog to ramp up the excitement.
Love & Order (Labor Day)
Love & Family (Thanksgiving)
Love & Peace (Christmas)
Love & Chocolate (Valentine's Day)
Love & Hope (Mother's Day)
Love & Liberty (Independence Day)
Love & Honor (Veteran's Day)

Love & Joy (Easter)
Love & Adventure (Father's Day)

Great Smoky Mountain Getaways
(Christian Inspirational – Women's Fiction Ro-
mances)
Juliet's Journey to Love
Poppy's Path to Love
Rachel's Road to Love

Crossroads Creek Cowboys
(Christian Inspirational Romances)
The Heart of a Cowboy
The Help of a Cowboy
The Return of a Cowboy
Coming Soon – The Care of a Cowboy

Crestfield Inn Romances
If you like special kinds of soulmates, a splash of
the supernatural, and wholesome relationships,
you'll adore this sweet bit of fun filled with romance and mystery.

Turning Back Time
Turning Up Roses
Turning Down Pie

Celebrity Corgi Romance
(Standalone Sweet Romance)
If you like light mystery mixed in with your happily-ever-after, you'll enjoy this second-chance romance and the race to save an adorable Corgi.
Digging the Driver

Gold Coast Retrievers
(Sweet Romance)
Special Golden Retrievers help their humans solve mysteries, save lives, and even find love...
Defending Dakota

Trinity River
(Sweet Western Romance)
Ranchers and farmers depend on the Trinity River for water, but when a secret conglomerate starts buying up property by fair means or foul,

it's time for the landowners of Tumble County to fight back—Texas style. But what they don't count on, is finding love in the process.
Back in the Rancher's Arms
Small Town, Big Secrets

Coming Soon! (2023-2024)

Sundancer's Legacy – 9 Book series

Sundancer's Star
Sundancer's Joy
Sundancer's Heart
Sundancer's Majesty
Sundancer's Miracle
Sundancer's Glory
Sundancer's Kiss
Sundancer's Moon
Sundancer's Splendor

About The Author

Elsie Davis is a *USA Today and International Bestselling Author* of over 25 sweet, clean, and wholesome romances, and a member of the ACFW. She discovered the world of Happily-Ever-After romance at the age of twelve when she began avidly reading Barbara Cartland, the Queen of Romance, and has been hooked ever since. After building her dream log home on top of a small mountain, she turned her attention to do what she loves most, writing. Elsie writes sweet Contemporary Romance and Contemporary Christian Romance from her heart...hoping to share a little love in a big world.

When she's not writing, she can be found birding, kayaking, camping, fishing, playing disc golf, and taking nature walks—hoping to spot wildlife. Basically, she loves all things outdoors, EXCEPT cold weather. She and her husband are avid Caribbean cruisers, but Elsie's favorite vacation was their cruise to Alaska. (In spite of the cold!) Indoors, she enjoys a toasty fire, and of course, a great romance with a guaranteed Happily-Ever-After.

https://www.elsiedavishea.com